ADVANCE PRAISE FOR *ROCKAWAY BLUE*

"A powerful tale of loss and redemption, *Rockaway Blue* delivers the real New York that I grew up in and hold close to my heart, the one that had no choice but to pick up the pieces and carry on in the aftermath of 9/11. A great read."

—Bobby Moresco, Academy-Award-Winning
Screenwriter for *Crash*

"When Larry Kirwan sets out on an artistic mission, there is no stopping halfway. So when Larry Kirwan sits down and writes a novel about New York, terrorism, the workings of the NYPD, and the inner life of Irish America, you can be sure not only is it well researched but filled with drama, tragedy, mystery, and, of course, being Irish, laughter. As is often the case, it takes a non–New Yorker to write about the city he loves. Larry Kirwan's *Rockaway Blue* is a must-read for New Yorkers and all those fascinated by the life of this amazing city."

—Malachy McCourt, author of *A Monk Swimming*

"Larry Kirwan has written a ballsy post-9/11 novel like only a New Yorker could. In *Rockaway Blue,* Kirwan punches through the romanticized courage of that awful September day and finds instead a gritty, unapologetic voice of truth. This is a rare glimpse into beachy blue-collar Rockaway and what the New York Irish really suffered in the making of their heroes."

—Jeanine Cummins, author of *American Dirt*

"Kirwan, a natural raconteur, tells a tale of fathers and sons with one foot on the sands of Rockaway Beach and the other on Ground Zero covered in the dust of the fallen Twin Towers. The plot moves with surprising intrigue and an ear for both the language and the attitude of New York's famed Irish Riviera. *Rockaway Blue* is involving, thoughtful, and totally entertaining."

—Dan Aquilante, former writer for the *New York Post*

ROCKAWAY BLUE

ROCKAWAY BLUE

A Novel

LARRY KIRWAN

THREE HILLS
an imprint of
Cornell University Press
Ithaca and London

First published 2021 by Cornell University Press

Printed in the United States of America

Library of Congress Cataloging-in-Publication Data

Names: Kirwan, Larry, author.
Title: Rockaway blue : a novel / Larry Kirwan.
Description: Ithaca [New York] : Three Hills, an imprint
   of Cornell University Press, 2021.
Identifiers: LCCN 2020035892 (print) | LCCN 2020035893 (ebook) |
   ISBN 9781501754227 (hardcover) | ISBN 9781501754234 (pdf) |
   ISBN 9781501754241 (epub)
Subjects: LCSH: September 11 Terrorist Attacks, 2001—Fiction. |
   Police—New York (State)—New York—Fiction. | Irish
   Americans—New Jersey—Rockaway—Fiction. |
   Rockaway (N.J.)—Fiction. | New York (N.Y.)—Fiction.
Classification: LCC PS3611.I79 R628 2021 (print) |
   LCC PS3611.I79 (ebook) | DDC 813/.6—dc23
LC record available at https://lccn.loc.gov/2020035892
LC ebook record available at https://lccn.loc.gov/2020035893

But a raving autumn shears
Blossom from the summer's wreath

—William Butler Yeats

To certain people there comes a day
When they must say the great Yes or the great No

—C. P. Cavafy

ONE

That first deep draught of salt sea air always cleared his head. Sometimes he even trekked down to the water's edge and played chicken with the surf and spray despite Maggie's insistence that the salt corroded his black leather shoes and that he was mad as a hatter not to wear sneakers like everyone else. Jimmy had never cared for sneakers—felt they took the dignity away from a man and, of late, there was little else holding him together.

More often than not he just leaned over the railing on the Rockaway boardwalk and gazed out at the breakers. He didn't need to be that close to the ocean anymore. It was bone deep inside him. Even halfway round the world when he was crawling on his gut up near the DMZ, sucking in the tang of jungle decay and the reek of Willie Pete, he could sink his face in memories of Rockaway surf and know that whatever happened to anyone else Jimmy Murphy was going to make it home alive.

And in the bad old days of the 70s when still a rookie cop, he often stood on the selfsame boardwalk spot and watched the sun rise up out of the Atlantic, and in those jittery dawns he could feel the first gentle rays burn away all the residual bullshit of the insomniac city. The echoes of artillery in his head were a lot stronger back then and he'd wait impatiently for the first purple clouds to come floating over the crimson horizon for they invariably soothed the jangling in his brain.

He never tired of his boardwalk ritual. It always grounded him— put things in perspective. He sometimes wondered how other New Yorkers dealt with the chaos of urban living. They had their rivers, their parks, and their religions, he supposed. But he had the ocean's vastness hardly more than a stone's throw from his kitchen. That set him and the peninsula apart. Sure, Rockaway might be tethered to the unfashionable south side of Queens but it thumbed its nose at the rest of the world and went its own unhurried way.

It's not that the people were different—take them off the peninsula and they passed for regular stressed-out New Yorkers, but plant them within shouting distance of the boardwalk and they instinctively displayed a quiet sense of themselves. Be they Irish, Italian, African, Jewish, Russian, or whatever else had recently blown in, once they put roots down in Rockaway's sandy soil it didn't matter—they belonged. But the peninsula was narrow—in more ways than one—newbies soon got the message loud and clear: either fit in or stroll on somewhere less demanding.

From time to time Jimmy chafed against the resultant insularity but it was the only home he'd ever known, and no matter where he dallied he always returned to his concrete strip of heaven that perched warily by the side of the unpredictable Atlantic.

"Next parish Ireland, Jimmy."

He hadn't heard Artie creep up behind him, but he did catch the note of triumph. The old man had pulled a number on Detective Sergeant James Murphy, thirty-year veteran of the NYPD. How about that?

"Yeah, Artie, just beyond the horizon." Jimmy acknowledged the small victory even as he studied the grizzled face. Had Artie lost another tooth? Hard to tell, but he had definitely gained a Red Sox cap, not the wisest thing to be wearing on Rockaway Beach.

"That's what the old people used to say." Artie nodded wisely.

"When they first came over, right?"

Always the same exchange while the old man screwed up his eyes and stared out into the sun, trawling for those elusive forty shades of green three thousand miles away.

You'll never make it over there now, Artie. But you wouldn't like it anyway, no shillelaghs, no leprechauns, they barely even notice Saint Paddy's Day except to make fun of Yanks looking for green beer. All a mirage, something we constructed out of the moon dust and memories of homesick old Irish immigrants.

"How's Maggie?"

"She's fine, Artie, just fine, babe."

For the first year or two that question had set him on edge, even coming from a harmless old beach bum. But on this May Day 2004, almost three years later, things weren't near as bad.

That was the problem with Rockaway, everyone knew your business: great when the kids were young, you always figured someone would keep an eye out for them. Brian didn't need a whole lot of looking after; but it came in handy enough with Kevin who was easily led.

When things went wrong and there was a need for a bit of space, that's when Rockaway was at its worst and made him long to be on the train trundling across Jamaica Bay and the hell off the incestuous peninsula. Everyone remembered everything, even when they weren't sure what they were remembering in the first place. Take Artie: kicked by a horse when he was a kid, turned him simple; at least that was the book on him, but was it true or just made for a better story than the cold, indifferent fact that he was born that way?

Maggie was a whole different kettle of fish: caused a sensation, bawling her head off on the boardwalk when everyone else was taking their lumps and sucking it up after the big bang. Mrs. Maggie Murphy, the English teacher at Stella Maris, always the together one, well dressed, just the right hint of makeup, who would have expected it?

Winnie Cleary, the beach gossip and general pain in the ass, lost her only son, Tommy the fireman, and she took it in stride, sorrowful but dignified, like the statue of Our Lady of Lourdes in the side altar at St. Rose of Lima.

The whole beach felt bad for the Murphys—they were good people, always there for everyone else, so his wife was cut some slack. And yet the question "How's Maggie?" still set Jimmy on edge and flung him right back to that September morning.

He'd found a working phone some blocks from the North Plaza and called Maggie to say Kevin was safe—someone had seen him up around Canal Street evacuating residents with his Fire crew.

"I know, he called and told me he was okay, but where's Brian, where's Brian?" Maggie had kept repeating as the line crackled cutting in and out.

"Call Rose, she'll know."

"He didn't come home last night. She has no idea where he is."

Though Jimmy's anger rose at another of his son's unexplained absences, he rattled off some crap about Brian going to DC on Giuliani business before hanging up.

It was the same story no matter where he inquired. "Cops and Fire missing big-time. Got to wait 'til the dust settles."

Back near the North Plaza he ran into Noah Jensen from Midtown North who said he was pretty sure Brian was off duty. But Jimmy knew he had to be nearby. Brian was always at the center of things. Why would this be any different?

"What makes you think he's down here?" Jensen coughed through the smoke and dust billowing up from the remains of the South Tower. "Even if he is on duty chances are he's uptown kissing Giuliani's ass."

Jimmy threw Jensen a fuck-you look, but the ground had begun to shake, and they both ran when they heard the same monstrous groan the South Tower had given.

Jensen sprinted ahead but when he turned to look back, Jimmy could see his eyes almost bulge from their sockets. Jimmy spun around just as the huge antenna sank into the collapsing roof 110 stories up; then the North Tower trembled before it tumbled methodically down sending a wind howling across the plaza and through the canyons of lower Manhattan. Jimmy surrendered to it and ran through clouds of dust but the gathering gray hurricane sent him staggering over a sidewalk curb. He picked himself up and stumbled on again, his arms outstretched in the viscous semidarkness until he hit a window frame. He slid to a halt, his forehead grazing against glass, and could go no further.

He had no idea where he was but he had gained some kind of shelter, for the force of the wind lessened. He covered his nose and mouth, and held on for dear life to what seemed like a doorframe. The overwhelming din of spars clattering, steel bending, and concrete collapsing rose in a crescendo, then faded very slowly until a dense eerie silence blanketed everything, like the morning after a blizzard. He stayed in the doorway scared out of his wits to move or even turn around. Finally when the smoke and choking filth had thinned somewhat he warily inched out into a big, dusty ploughed-up graveyard.

Where once two gleaming towers preened, boasting of their strength and permanence, now only a couple of gaping walls stood, the glass from their cathedral-like windows pulverized and floating about in the poisonous powdery grime.

Men were already clawing at twisted steel beams, slabs of rock, and mountains of rubble, and everywhere a smell like kerosene from the thousands of gallons of jet fuel. Coated in fine white dust, his throat dryer than it had ever been, he raised a yell that sounded more like a whisper: "Anyone seen Lieutenant Brian Murphy?"

No one paid any attention—they were all looking for their own people. Finally he ran into a Port Authority sergeant that Brian used to hang with when they were kids at Regis. Said he'd seen him escort a group of people out of the Tower only minutes ago, that he was okay and that Jimmy should haul ass out of there, the street was about to collapse.

But Jimmy kept searching and asking, clambering over huge slabs of concrete and metal spars, and it was all bedlam, with everyone else searching and asking too. Then he saw young Shay Kennedy from Long Beach. He had lost his Fire helmet and was sitting on the side of a battered office desk, the tears coursing like rivulets down his grimy face.

"Father Mychal's gone," Shay whispered. "Our chaplain's dead."

"Have you seen Brian?"

Shay looked away and Jimmy felt he was hiding something. He repeated the question but the young fireman had closed his swollen eyes and was no longer listening.

Jimmy hurried off, colliding with other searchers, slipping on twisted girders and stray pieces of shattered office furniture. Clouds of smoke and dust were ebbing and flowing amidst a steady confetti-like hail of paper illuminated by ghostly fires, and it was hard to see for minutes on end; occasionally the wind would shift and it would clear for a few seconds. Then with the sun burning through the haze he saw the Port Authority sergeant again, raced after him, and asked how he knew Brian was okay.

The sergeant said he'd seen him with Richie Sullivan inside the North Tower, and they had plenty of time to get out.

"What does that prove? Where's Sullivan?"

"Where do you think?" He lifted an imaginary drink to his mouth.

"Fucking asshole!"

The sergeant grabbed Jimmy by his dusty lapels. "What are you cursing at me for? I'm just telling you what I know."

But Jimmy had meant Sullivan. And he knew exactly where he'd be—in one of two nearby Irish pubs. The first was closed but Jimmy glimpsed his own reflection in the darkened window and it scared the hell out of him—grime and dust head to toe, eyes blazing like some maniac.

He found Sullivan in Kelly's of Cedar Street. The bartender was locking up, dumping envelopes stuffed with cash in a backpack. Sullivan was already half-gone from the shock and a pint glass of whiskey. Jimmy shook the large disheveled frame of his old partner as the white dust arose in plumes around them. It took a while but through all the crying and slobbering he made out that Brian had led seven people out of the North Tower, raced back in for more, and then the whole show came tumbling down on top of him. And Jimmy was screaming that the son of a bitch was lying and he'd better come clean. But Sullivan just kept bawling that he'd been with Brian since eight fifteen that morning and knew exactly what happened; finally Jimmy threw him over a table and bolted out the door.

He ran back to the North Plaza, but they'd cordoned it off and wouldn't let him through though he was roaring at them that he was a detective sergeant and had to find his son before it was too late, but they were afraid of the foundation collapsing.

Eventually his training took over and he walked and ran and hitch-hiked back uptown, pulled rank, and got a lift out to Rockaway. He barged through his front door on 120th Street nearly taking it off the hinges, but all was silent within.

Maggie already knew; no one had told her. She just knew. She was up in their bedroom. The blinds were drawn against the clear blue September day, and in the shadowy hush she was sitting on the side of the bed staring at the wall, her fists clenched, slim body taut. She didn't say anything, not a word, nor did he speak to her. The room was so quiet. It was like the birds would never sing again. The tears and the acres of emptiness would come later. But at that moment, he prayed to God he'd never hear quiet like that again.

Jimmy looked around. Artie was already shuffling down the board-walk. Never noticed the old bastard slipping away; maybe he was losing it. Two years off the job. Should never have left. But he did it for Maggie. She wanted him home. Couldn't handle not knowing where he was. Never bothered her all the years before the attack when she wouldn't hear from him from crack of dawn until the dead of night. Now he always carried a cell just so she could reassure herself with the sound of his voice.

That September day changed everything, nothing ever would or could be the same. And with that he surrendered to the urge, turned around, and gazed down the boardwalk toward Breezy Point and beyond. He couldn't see Manhattan but he knew exactly where it was, and he could feel himself being ineluctably reeled back to the yawning pit down on Liberty Street.

It had stopped smoldering and even the sweet sickly smell that no one dared identify had long since dissipated, but there was no denying the pit's gaping intensity or the hold it had on the city. So many questions, so few answers, and he had to be careful around Maggie.

She always knew when he'd been dwelling on Brian. She didn't have to be psychic—Brian was always there, with them, between them, around them, unseen by them. All well and good, he was their son, but the mere mention of his name could still set off depth charges that at times threatened to overwhelm them.

It was so typical of Brian. Even as a kid he had the whole enigma factor down to a science. It wasn't that they weren't close as a family. It's just that Brian had a way of keeping everyone at arm's length when he felt like it—particularly his old man. There were times when Jimmy had wanted to take his son and shake him, and he wished to God he had because by the time the kid was fourteen it was already too late.

Later on, after Brian graduated Georgetown and against all odds followed Jimmy into the NYPD, they finally had something in common again, whether it was a case they were both involved in, random shop gossip, or just bitching about some boss or other. Though more often than not just as they were making contact, he'd feel his son slipping away again and want to scream "For the love of Christ, man, let me in! We are flesh and blood and there's so many things I want to talk to you about, so many things I want to ask you."

He didn't blame Brian. Jimmy had never confided in his own old man either. Had Gerald Murphy, the revered Rockaway fire chief, been that unapproachable and reserved, or had Jimmy kept him at arm's length too?

And yet there were words of Brian's that stuck out like crags on a cliff face that Jimmy clung to, sentences that still rattled around in his head, clues to what his son may have been thinking. Like the night at Rocky Sullivan's on Lexington when Jimmy had one too many and tried to tear down the walls between them. But the Bushmills got in the way and he just kept going round in circles, trying to explain how he didn't really mind that Brian had leapfrogged ahead of him to become a lieutenant, and that it was only a coincidence that the bartender had teased him about it. When out of nowhere Brian stopped him cold with "That's the difference between you and me, Dad, there are no coincidences in my life."

He hadn't said it boastfully or unkindly, in fact he'd put his arm around his father like he used to when he was a gangly teenager, and God knows Brian did plan everything whereas Jimmy pretty much took life as it came.

Still the words had stung and Jimmy lashed out, "Watch your mouth."

"I'm not the one with the mouth, Dad."

In the end one of the owners, a cop himself, leaned in between them and asked them to tone it down. They were upsetting the clientele.

They'd made up as they usually did. More shots were bought and Jimmy woke up with a sore head in the morning, but the statement was never taken back or apologized for. Even now Jimmy could hear it echoing over the crash of the waves. There were no coincidences in Lieutenant Brian Murphy's life. He was down in the North Tower for a reason and no matter how much Jimmy tried to ignore it, that cold hard fact would not leave him be.

Though his family had been ripped damn near apart by what had happened, in some ways they'd come to terms with the consequences. Maggie might be floating around like an opiated angel wary of reengaging with a world that had betrayed her; still of late she had emerged from her isolation. While the once happy-go-lucky Kevin now occasionally cracked a joke about his Fire buddies, and it could only be a matter of time before he dusted off his guitar and started gigging again. Rose was the problem, or rather her son, Liam. Rockaway Rosie had her good days and bad down in the dream house Brian had built in Breezy Point, but Liam still couldn't bear to hear a mention of his father's name.

Rose rarely got in touch but that morning on the phone with Jimmy there had been a new note of desperation in her voice. She had casually asked Liam if he'd like to join the other heroes' sons and daughters at the commemoration in September.

The kid had crumpled to the floor at the very thought. He was too scared to go, he'd whispered, his dad had warned him. Warned him about what? He had never mentioned anything like that before. But he refused to say.

"I can't take any more, Jimmy," Rose had said. "We're all screwed up, and God knows if we'll ever be any different, but my son should be able to grow out of this and have a decent life. We've got to find out the truth about Brian once and for all—no matter what it does to us."

Jimmy turned for home in the hot May morning, the beach still cluttered with seaweed from yesterday's storm. The ocean hadn't helped—the waves had failed to work their magic. Nothing had changed; he couldn't take back what he had said to his son, and the same old question continued to ricochet around his skull: "What in the name of God were you doing down there thirty minutes before the attack, Brian?"

TWO

The guard waved Kevin on without checking and why wouldn't he? Brother of Lieutenant Brian Murphy. He used to stop the kid years back just to break his balls and let him know that what he could get away with in rough-and-ready Rockaway wasn't going to be in the cards in gated Breezy Point. Most people in Breezy didn't care one way or the other; they'd sprung from the same seed as their Rockaway brethren—except for a few of the blow-ins around 220th Street. That's where Brian had built his big house but, being a son of Jimmy Murphy, he was Rockaway royalty and welcomed the length and breadth of the peninsula.

Kevin opened the window wide and gunned down State Road. The wind off Jamaica Bay rippled through his hair. He knew the Riviera like the back of his hand; Maureen Byrne from Reid Avenue had seen to that, they'd dated right through high school. After she left for BC it was never the same. He idly wondered if she was still shacking up with that jerk up in Boston as he sped past Kennedy's parking lot, the scene of their final breakup.

Brian's house on 220th looked a little less than immaculate as Kevin pulled up outside; its many windows were stained by the ghost of the salt spray carried on the ever-present Atlantic breeze, while the whole place could have done with a fresh coat of paint. Dandelions sprouted through the narrow strip of once manicured lawn, and a child's base-ball bat and glove lay abandoned on the pathway. Still, the sprinkler worked well enough, for the mutinous grass was a deep green and the rose bushes, though spindly, were about to bloom in the crazy early May heat.

It had to be roses for Brian, and nothing but the best. He'd read in some magazine that they were the gems of any garden, and that was that—roses it was and the more the merrier. It never occurred to him that the local half-wild *Rosa rugosa* was more suited to a windy tip of barrier island jutting out into Jamaica Bay. No, Brian demanded expensive yellow hybrids that had to struggle to find a toehold in the thin sandy soil.

Kevin picked up his nephew's bat and glove, and hummed along with the song leaking from the house.

She said "don't you ever leave me
Oh, for God's sake, don't let me down"

Brian had loved that song back in the day but then there was a cop in the band that recorded it. Kevin could take it or leave it, and had never bothered figuring out the chords.

Liam's glove was damp and mildewy. Must have been lying there for days, sprayed every dawn and dusk. That would have driven Brian nuts. Everything had to be spic-and-span, he couldn't stand other people's clutter; kind of odd, since he often left an emotional mess in his trail. And yet, people forgave him anything because he had a big heart and always made it up to them. His wake was spiked with girls that he'd dumped but had continued to look out for—red-eyed as they recounted interventions with boyfriends, or a favorable word put in for them down at the precinct, but never a mention about the broken-hearted phone messages he hadn't returned after their dismissal.

Rose jumped up in alarm when the doorbell rang. She'd dozed off while listening to some CDs on shuffle. A pleading vocal emerged from the wildness of a saxophone:

So I made her all kinds of promises
How I'd always be around . . .

Weird to wake up to one of their "special" songs! It used to blast from all the jukeboxes down the beach when they were first dating. That saxophone always took her someplace else. Brian knew the player, used to bring her into Manhattan to see the band.

She clicked the remote and the CD paused awkwardly mid-bar. The silence was jarring, broken only by the distant cry of a seagull from beyond the screened window. Who would drop by without calling first?

It was hot and she looked a mess. She buttoned her shirt and shook out her hair, dug into her purse for lipstick but it wasn't there.

"Screw it," she muttered before opening the door.

She hadn't laid eyes on Kevin for months and now here he was, large as life, carrying a toolbox and sweating up a storm on her doorstep.

"Making house calls?"

"Mom said you were having trouble with the bathroom door."

"It's usually your father who comes."

"He got called in to Dolan's."

He avoided her eyes, just shifted his weight from one foot to the other, unsure of himself. She waited, forcing him to make eye contact. Then she stepped aside, but only slightly so he had to brush up against her. He hurried down the hall and into the kitchen.

He took care to arc backwards as she passed him on her way to the sink where she wiped a drop of sweat from her throat. She watched him take her measure in the mirror.

"What's the matter? Never seen a woman sweat before?" She wheeled around but he looked away and placed his toolbox on the kitchen table. "I like to sweat. Makes me feel like I'm alive."

It didn't take much to know that this was the last place on earth he wanted to be. He hadn't bothered dressing for her—that was for sure: tank top, cutoffs, flip-flops. But he'd been working out again—all muscle and lean tension.

"You want a cup of coffee?"

"I guess."

"You're as bad as the kid. *Is your homework done? I guess. Do you want Frosted Flakes? I guess. Is your mom going out of her head? I guess.*"

He glanced around the room—anywhere but at her. She followed his eyes. The sink full of dishes, the table hadn't been cleared, the once gleaming kitchen set had well and truly lost its sheen—besides she didn't look so hot herself. But it turned out all he was looking for was a clean glass. He took a Guinness pint tumbler from one of Brian's collections. She turned her back and listened to him run the tap and fumble around in the small medicine cabinet.

"The Advil is on the sink right in front of you," she said. "How come you're so hung over?"

"Stayed out late."

"Down The Inn?"

"Yeah. Pete was asking for you."

"Oh yeah?"

"Wanted to know why you don't come down no more."

When she turned around he was popping three Advil and taking a deep slug of water; he began to cough when a pill caught in his throat. She grabbed the pint glass from him and refilled it. He took another long drink then wiped his mouth.

"You want to know why I don't go down The Inn?"

"Seeing you put it like that, not particularly."

"Because you don't ask me." She stepped closer to him. He looked so like Brian sometimes, same full lips and forehead, and a head of wavy light-brown hair. His watery-blue eyes were different though. Brian had that glint of mica in his deep-blues that caused both men and women to give him a second look.

"Listen, I told you before, I'm just down there with Eddie Sweeney and the guys."

"So why can't I be one of the guys?"

"Because you're not."

"So what am I then?" She had to pinch herself to stop smiling when he almost tripped over Liam's old stool in an effort to move away.

"Jesus Christ, you're Rose! Who the hell do you think you are?"

But she wasn't Rose anymore. She was Brian Murphy's widow. And widows of heroes don't go out floozying on their own. No, they go to so many early-bird specials with their in-laws and relatives they might as well be down in Lauderdale. Or they go to support groups with the wives of other heroes and sit around drinking tea and talking about their kids, and telling each other how well they're doing until one of them cracks and begins to cry, and before they know it every last one of them is in tears.

"What did you come over here for, Kevin?"

"I come to fix your bathroom door."

"Oh, fuck my bathroom door!"

She rarely used to swear and her eyes welled up. She wanted to rest her head on his shoulder but that would only frighten him more.

To give her time to dry her stray tears Kevin stepped away from the kitchen area and looked longingly at the piano that he'd sworn he'd learn to play. Back before the attack he'd even arranged to drop by regularly for an hour's practice. Another promise down the drain! But then he noticed the largest picture on the Steinway had been turned to the wall—the one taken the day Brian made lieutenant. It had been a big occasion and both had dressed formally. Not a whole lot more than three years ago, but Rose looked older in the glossy studio setting, her hair recently colored and piled high.

It was still hard for Kevin to look directly at his brother. Though he dominated photos, they rarely captured the real Brian. When he posed you got the full show, the all-American guy to die for. But you never saw the compassion or the tenderness that set him apart.

"They say crying is good for you," Kevin said.

"They should try it 24/7, see how *they* feel."

"I suppose."

"You suppose? You cried for Brian, didn't you?"

"I don't know," he said. The days right after had been a blur. Wakes, funerals, heartbreaks, all lit by camera flashes, the whole world glaring in.

"What do you mean, you don't know? Jesus, your own brother?"

She lit a cigarette and offered him one but he ignored her. She exhaled gently and watched the smoke ease out like it used to for Marilyn or Ava Gardner in the old movies Brian loved.

"You want a drink?" she asked but sensed his disapproval. "Listen, I can't stay down the friggin' Inn all night, I got a kid to look after."

"Where is he?"

"Who?"

"Liam—who do you think?

"He's on a play date. Had to get him out of here before he started to look like the furniture."

She took two Bud Lights from the fridge, opened them, and strode into the sitting area—no walls for Brian, just a big open space like a SoHo loft, he had declared at the first party he had thrown in their dream house. And in the center of it all the Steinway that neither of them played—who cared, Liam would learn, and anyway Brian said it was a steal. The cold foam spilled over the tops of the bottles and dropped on the deep pile fawn carpet. She no longer cared, just pulled two crystal glasses from the sideboard and filled them.

He sat on the far side of the couch facing the black marble fireplace. Rose studied him as he shivered from the first taste. It was nice to have a beer with a man again even if he was five feet away and backing up. How complicated it all was now. That's why she didn't go down The Inn anymore. The minute she walked in the door the place turned into a morgue. Took her a couple of drinks before she could forget people were staring at her. Then when she finally relaxed and started to have a good time, it was like everyone was afraid she was going to whip off her shirt and do the grind with Carlos, the tattooed bar-back.

Round about the third drink when she was feeling no pain, Pete would start hinting that maybe he should call car service, right about the time some loser who couldn't stand Brian when he was alive would be slobbering on her shoulder and feeling her up, until she wanted to take Pete's baseball bat and smash every glass in the place. But just in time, she'd remember that she was Rose Murphy, wife of a martyred defender of the homeland, and she'd say, *Yes, Peter, I have a slight headache and I do believe I'll be heading home and thank you all very much for such a lovely evening.*

And before she knew it she'd be in the car, and the Haitian man with the great big sorry eyes would be making like she wasn't sobbing her brains out in the backseat. And when she got to her in-laws' to pick up her son she'd dry her eyes and blow her nose and totter in on her heels and tell Maggie that *Yes, I had a wonderful time with my friends but I'm a little tired, and I just want to go to bed and yes tomorrow is another day and God never shuts one door but he opens another, and yes I agree Liam is playing too many video games, and says nothing but "I guess."*

It always ended up the same, but Kevin didn't want to hear it anyway, and if he tried to put any more distance between them he'd bore a hole through the other side of the couch. And so she drained the last of her Bud and said, "Let's fix this damned door."

He went back into the kitchen for his toolbox and followed her over to the bathroom where she was already pulling at the handle, twisting it one way then the other.

"Feels like it's stuck for good this time," she griped. "Story of my life."

The whining nature of her remark angered him. That wasn't the Rose he remembered—why did everything have to be so different? He took a grip of the handle and tugged hard but the door shifted only slightly. He was furious and sweating and cursed under his breath. He'd never been good at fixing things around the house, but that door was going to open even if he had to take his Halligan hook to it. He backed off suddenly and she stepped out of his way. She'd seen his temper before, though he'd kept it under wraps when Brian was alive. He threw open his toolbox, pulled out a ten-inch metal file.

"What's that supposed to do?" she asked.

"It's going to open that damned door, I just need you to pull on the handle."

"What are you going to do, file the lock off?"

"They taught me how to punch through doors at the Academy— not fix 'em."

"Hey, if your mother could see us now." She laughed as she grasped the door handle.

"Shut the fuck up about my mother!"

For a moment she felt scared and edged away from him.

"For Christ's sake hold still and just pull on the damned thing. Ready?"

The door began to open; he worked the file in the narrow space between the jamb and the door, and pushed until the wood creaked under the pressure.

"We got it!" he shouted as the door opened more but just then the handle came loose in her hands. She screamed as she fell backwards and hit her head on a table leg. When she lay there with her eyes closed he panicked.

"Rose, are you okay? For God's sake, Rose!"

He helped her to her feet and pushed back her hair from her face. She was stunned and clung to him.

"Are you okay?" He whispered as he gently examined her head with his damp fingers, the care written all over his eyes.

His emotion was so naked she could barely look at him. Leaning forward she laid her head on his shoulder. She felt dizzy and began to sway slightly; he pulled her close to prevent her from falling. She could feel his heart pumping; it had been a long time since she'd been so near to a man. His longing felt so natural she clung even closer to him and he held her tight.

And for a few moments she was in Brian's arms again and had just awakened from a terrible nightmare. And as the pain, the loss, and the loneliness evaporated she thought, 'Oh my God, Brian's alive, our family is back together, Liam will have a father again.' But as the dizziness decreased she realized this was not Brian's body, but still she luxuriated in the familiarity of all the nights dancing with Kevin and learning to tango together. As if in answer, he held her even tighter. Then he suddenly stepped away and muttered, "I gotta go."

"No, wait." She reached out to him but he swept past her toward the front door. It slammed behind him. She didn't move but she could see him through the kitchen window stride across the lawn, open the unlocked car door, and peel out without even a wave good-bye.

THREE

Jimmy turned the key in his hall door. He held it open for a moment then closed it firmly behind him. He always did that at night. Maggie would have been listening for him; now she could sleep. They'd never spoken about this long-standing routine—it was just understood, for like many a cop's wife she wrestled with anxiety.

He hung his coat on the hall stand next to the landline that rarely rang anymore, then stepped into the kitchen and once again studied the new picture of the Sacred Heart that hung on the wall. Jesus stared back balefully but with little intention of spilling any secrets. Jimmy's mother used to have a similar picture that she lit a votive candle beneath; this modern update glowed relentlessly courtesy of its electric light. A bit of a waste during the day but it bathed the room in a comforting red in the lonely early morning.

Still it wasn't bright enough for reading so he switched on the overhead light and brought his book over to the plain wooden table that Maggie had bought along with four matching chairs up in Chatham shortly before they were married. She'd never liked clutter: every piece of furniture had a function and an anointed place in their small white clapboard house on 120th Street within sight of the ocean. The only other distinguishing piece in the kitchen was an oval wall mirror in a simple brown frame that added depth to the room.

All was quiet at four in the morning—a good time for a quick read—but he was really giving Maggie time to drift off. He had begun to read seriously again when the house still throbbed with grief. On his nights off before their world turned upside down he used to read the *Daily News* while listening to the scratch of her fountain pen as she graded papers; in the winter he'd often nod off by the fire waiting for her to finish, while in the summer he'd drink beer on their honeysuckle-draped front porch and watch the neighborhood parade by after she had turned to her standbys, Barbara Pym and Edith Wharton.

Such a different world in the rearview mirror—he could barely recall their small worries and domestic tiffs, only long stretches of uneven contentment. Strange how something that had taken so many years to build had so effortlessly fallen apart.

At first he'd consoled her, reasoned with her, or just allowed the flood of despair to wash over him; then with time her tears dried up, as tears eventually do. But with that came a dimming of the spirit and a reluctance to deal with a traitorous world that had taken away her son. Still, even with long hours of silence, it took him a while before he got into the swing of reading again. It became easier when he quit the job; with no bureaucracy to bang his head against, his whole system slowed down and he rediscovered the patience to once more wrestle with the considered written word.

The problem was, he didn't know what to read and he could find little to spark his interest. Over a whole winter he beat himself up for his stodgy taste but eventually he retreated to his old brigade: Greene, Fitzgerald, Hemingway, each with his own quandaries. Greene, one big moral dilemma after another, made him think too much, while Fitzgerald's snobbishness now bothered him. Some of Hemingway no longer rang true either; but *For Whom the Bell Tolls* still hit the mark, and he couldn't get enough of Robert Jordan.

The guy was in Spain fighting for principle. No one in Nam was into that kind of kick—at least that Jimmy knew. The draft had collared them all. There was the occasional psycho who'd gone over for the mayhem, but Jordan had joined the Lincoln Brigade for an idea.

Brian had a bit of Jordan in him. He ran into the North Tower and led people out. He'd been the same in high school when he was running back on the football field: all drive and drama—suck it up and fight to the last second for another yard. He was little different as a cop—gave 120 percent and was always in the thick of things but, unlike with Jordan, everything he did was connected to some far-reaching detailed plan. Move up the ranks as quickly as possible then get out while he was ahead and run for office.

That was the difference between them. Guys like Jimmy who'd gone toe-to-toe with tunnel-dwelling Viet Cong didn't follow leaders and most definitely did not watch their parking meters. They knew the slippery slope upstairs was paved in bullshit—it was the job itself that was important, collaring bad guys so that the system ran smoothly and regular people could get on with their lives.

Jimmy took his clothes off in the bathroom. He bent over and studied himself in the sink mirror. At just over five foot ten he was some inches shorter than both his sons but he'd never lost his lean appearance despite a slight new flabbiness around the midriff. His once thick brown hair had thinned and he wore it short to camouflage the sparseness. The touch of gray that The Dead sang about, however, was no longer confined to his hair, it tinted his very skin. His pale-blue eyes were watchful. Still, his jaw was firm despite the shots it had taken in thirty years of conflict with some of New York City's toughest. Truth be told, he didn't feel so great about himself anymore. The job had given him definition, something to get up and fight for every morning. Now he felt like he was just marking time, waiting, but for what?

He turned out the light and closed the door quietly. With the blinds drawn it was pitch-dark in their room but he knew exactly how many steps until he touched the bed frame. She had turned down the cover for him and he slipped silently into bed beside his wife. Maggie lay motionless, her breathing easy, but she could just as well be wide-awake. After the first year of public pain she erected a wall around herself and wore a mask for the world. He shouldn't have let that happen, for he too was often banished beyond the battlements. He blamed himself, although he wasn't sure what he could have done better; he just knew he wasn't man enough to fill up all the empty space that the day in September had left behind.

And so with time they drifted apart, lying side by side, but never touching until it became too painful to even try. She was the same person but something had changed and he had little idea what it could be, except he felt there was a pane of glass separating them. He was often on the verge of saying, "I'm here too, Maggie. I have the same hurts, the same loss. Hold on to me before I drift away."

But it had gone beyond that. They were two separate universes now.

She loved him, he knew that, and he'd loved her too, right from their high school days. They'd broken up when he'd been drafted. He'd wanted to sow some wild oats, but when he wrote to her from Nam to say he'd been a fool, she said she'd never even considered anyone else and would wait for him. Then all he wanted was to get home safely and be with her forever.

He did his best to put the past behind him the day he crossed the Marine Parkway Bridge on his return to Rockaway and never told her how he'd lived over there, what he'd done to stay alive; he was just so relieved she'd taken him back. And in the first years she comforted him when he could still hear the sounds of battle. Why couldn't she hold him when they lost Brian? He held her every night though he knew she was just a ghost in his arms and that something had fled when those towers came tumbling down.

It got even worse after he quit the job. He didn't want to—he took pride in his work though he'd never rise any higher. They said he was a loose cannon, but when they needed something done well, quietly, and in a hurry, he was the go-to guy. He just couldn't bring himself to kiss ass. His own son had raced past him up the ladder. The youngest lieutenant on the force, Brian didn't have to kiss anything, he was always heading in the right direction. Knew from the gut how to talk to the people that needed talking to.

Things Jimmy wanted to say rarely came out the right way. That was definitely his problem with Tony DeVito, or rather Captain Anthony DeVito. They'd grown up together in Rockaway—hung out in the East Village, saw the Allman Brothers at the Fillmore. It was hard to imagine now that straight-ass Tony DeVito would have got down on his knees and licked Duane's boots back in their beer-swilling, flannel-shirted days.

DeVito was the first one Jimmy went to for the real word on Brian. Balding and stocky, his shirtsleeves rolled up, but still exuding Calabrian passion, he took Jimmy in a bear hug and cried on his shoulder. Said Brian was a credit to Maggie and him, and the Department. That he was their brightest star and couldn't be replaced. He sent out for coffee and they talked about the old days and how they should spend more time together, and how he and Maggie had to come to his and Rita's place up in Westchester, how close the two couples used to be, and maybe there'd be one silver lining in this disaster, and blah, blah, blah, until Jimmy finally had to cut to the chase. "Tell me the real story, Tony. What was Brian doing down the Towers at eight fifteen on a Tuesday morning?"

DeVito had stood up, made his way over to the window, stared out at West 54th Street, and spoken in his best brass manner. "I can't get into it, Jimmy. Brian was operating on a whole different level. That's as much as I can say. He's an American hero—saved seven lives; he didn't have to go back in. But he did. I have to leave it at that."

And before Jimmy knew it he was back on the street outside Midtown North trying to make sense of the whole thing. But there was no sense, just like there wasn't in Nam. Still, he let it sit for over a year because he didn't want to lay any more pain on Maggie, but it nagged away at him. When he couldn't take any more he called DeVito who said, "Sure, come back in, Jimmy. We're always here for you, man."

And they were. This time DeVito had squeezed himself into a size-too-small Joe Bank's suit and was sitting cheek by jowl with an inspector, along with a guy from Internal Affairs running a recorder.

Jimmy asked for the truth—what was Brian really doing down there half an hour before the attack—but they gave him the same old hero bullshit. And when he cut loose and let them know what he was thinking, there was a big silence before they got back on the party line. "Listen, Jimmy, you're right, Brian was pursuing a confidential line of inquiry. But it's further up the ladder than us, we got no choice but to leave it at that."

Jimmy paused on the staircase on his way down. He could tell Maggie hadn't heard his descent. She was bent over, noisily rearranging some pots in the kitchen while Kevin sipped his coffee at the table. Though he was still foggy from a poor night's sleep, he didn't want the thought to evaporate again. What had Brian meant with that weird question about DeVito?

It had come out of the blue one morning they were bantering about baseball stats, Brian studying his *Times*, Jimmy poring over the *News*. It had been three years ago, sometime around the start of baseball season when all hopes still ran high. Brian had dropped by for a quick visit as he occasionally did on his way to Manhattan. Must have been a weekend since Maggie was there. He had waited until his mother had stepped out into her back garden.

"Did DeVito ever put a tail on you?" Brian had said matter-of-factly.

"Why the hell would Tony DeVito put a tail on me?"

"I don't know, maybe Internal Affairs wanted to know something?"

"Internal Affairs is capable of finding out anything they want without DeVito's help. You think he's put a tail on you?"

"I just got this feeling."

"You want me to talk to him?"

"No, forget about it. He already thinks I'm a bit pushy—just my imagination."

At that moment Maggie had breezed back in with a handful of lobelia and was commenting on their blueness, whereupon Brian raised the *Times* in front of his face to abruptly cut off the discussion.

It was probably nothing and Jimmy hadn't given it a thought until after his second unsatisfying visit to DeVito. But since then the suspicion had surfaced on a regular basis. His "no coincidence" son didn't believe in "just my imagination" unless The Temptations were singing it.

"What are you doing standing there like a statue on the stairs, Jimmy Murphy?" Maggie called up to him.

"I was just thinking about something."

"Well think about it down here. I made fresh coffee and I don't want you complaining about it being cold."

Jimmy stepped forward onto the loudest of the creaky steps. He usually managed to avoid it.

"I found the waffle iron," Maggie said with some satisfaction.

"I didn't know it was missing."

"You don't remember our conversation yesterday?"

Jimmy shrugged and winked at Kevin who handed him some pages of the *News* as he sat down. Kevin nodded his understanding, glad that for once his father was the subject of his mother's attention.

"What time did you get home last night?"

"Late! That A train is going from bad to worse."

"You should take the car."

"And deal with midtown traffic? Spend half my paycheck on parking?"

"How was it anyway?" Maggie persisted while cleaning the waffle iron.

"Oh, wonderful." He didn't look up from the *News*.

"Dolan was there again?"

"No, our illustrious owner and his fumes of Old Spice was once more a no-show."

Jimmy didn't know why Dolan bothered him so much. He'd had worse bosses in the Department. Somehow or other, though, he'd shared something with them; at the least they'd all passed through the Academy. Dolan was an asshole plain and simple, a little guy with a big Dublin attitude and an almost unintelligible gurrier accent. Liked to throw his weight around when he was drinking which was often. He was a cop buff, loved to talk tough, drop names, and never messed with Jimmy. But how long would that last?

What was the big deal last night anyway? A bunch of kids with IDs so fake he almost felt insulted, until the one with the buzz cut said he was shipping to Iraq in a week. What a country! Go half-way around the world to get your head blown off with the marines but can't score a legal drink in your own burg. What a job for a detective sergeant!

"It was your decision to retire," Maggie murmured as if reciting a mantra.

"No, it was *our* decision, Maggie."

Kevin shifted uneasily. He knew where this was going unless the old man headed it off at the pass.

"Oh well, it could be a lot worse. I see many men your age walking around doing nothing," Maggie said distractedly as she peered at the waffle iron.

"My age?" Jimmy sputtered on his coffee. "What the hell's that supposed to mean?"

"Nothing in particular. It's just that a lot of men in their fifties take the money and go fishing."

"The best way I know to ruin a nice look at the ocean."

Maybe that's what he should have done. Brought his six-pack down to the water's edge like the rest of them, swapped the same old stories and hauled in seaweed with oversized fishing rods. Instead he was chief of security for one of the biggest restaurants in midtown—or a glorified chucker-out for a trumped-up, overpriced saloon.

Maggie rinsed off some plates then ran the dishwasher. Jimmy looked up from the paper and watched her go about her business. He had never lost his attraction to his wife and her ways. Even when she was a teenager people had been drawn to her, for she had a certain bearing allied to a feeling that she knew exactly what she was doing and you wouldn't be led astray if you chose to follow her.

She had one flaw, a small birthmark on her left cheek, but even that only served to heighten her beauty. She had never mentioned it nor tried to cover it, although he never doubted that it bothered her for she took pride in her looks.

For a long time after the attack she hadn't been concerned with her appearance, especially after she quit teaching. But lately she had begun rifling through her wardrobe again. He recognized the shirt she was wearing, dark and slim-fitting with a print of red roses, he'd given it to her for her birthday back God knows when. It looked good on her and still matched her chestnut brown hair even though that was now well streaked with gray. It wasn't like her to wear such a shirt in the kitchen; she had probably attended early mass and hadn't bothered to take it off.

He did miss the soft look in her gray eyes, now often clouded over with anxiety, and wondered if he was responsible in any way. Was there something he could have done? Brought her away on a cruise, perhaps? The one short trip they'd taken to Clearwater right before the first anniversary of the attack had been a disaster. She hadn't slept a wink. They came home after two days—she couldn't bear to be so far away from Brian. He understood her pain and loss, but there was an intensity to it that wore on him and he longed for a return to some kind of normality, whatever that might be.

He sighed and turned his attention to Kevin. "So, how was Rose?"

"Rose?"

"No, the Queen of Sheba! You did look after her yesterday?"

Kevin looked sharply at him before muttering, "Yeah, sure I did."

"You fixed her up, like?"

"Eh . . ."

"What are you squirming about? You either fixed her bathroom door or you didn't."

"Sure I did. What are you so uptight about?"

"Me, uptight? Maggie, do I seem in the least bit uptight?"

"This dishwasher has never been the same since we got it serviced." Maggie laid a restraining hand on the bouncing machine.

"For all the good that did!" Jimmy shook his head at this sore point. "Damned thing is going to take off through the ceiling someday."

"Well, I couldn't stand the way it used to shudder, but we paid good money to have it serviced and now it's even worse," she said. "Anyway, you should have gone over to Rose's yourself; Kevin was never good at that kind of thing . . . though I'm sure you did your best, love."

"Yeah." Kevin looked away.

"I'd have gone if I could," Jimmy said. "It's just that Dolan wanted me to cover that early party."

"She wouldn't be waiting for the best part of a week if our Brian was alive," Maggie interrupted him.

Jimmy and Kevin studied the *News* while she methodically folded her apron. A seagull squealed out in the garden, the shrillness between a laugh and a cry. They were expecting her to retreat up to her room so the casual nature of her question surprised them. "Did she mention Liam's birthday, Kevin?"

"I don't . . . I don't think we ever got around to that," Kevin stuttered.

"That's odd. She was full of it yesterday on the phone. Are you sure?"

"No, I . . . she was . . . you know, had her mind on other things."

With a sudden kick the dishwasher began thumping again; Maggie studied it from a distance, her arms folded protectively across her chest.

Jimmy took a sip of coffee and leaned back in his chair. "You know, Rose would be a lot better off if she got a job."

"And what about Liam? Supposing she got held up at work? Anyway, she won't want for money as long as we're here."

"She doesn't need our money, Maggie. She's got her pension, and the rest of the settlement's coming when that damned lawyer gets up off his ass. But she's a young woman—she needs to get back out in the world instead of sitting in that big empty house on her own."

"That will happen in due course. Now, Kevin, you drop over the gift for Liam today."

"Me? I got an appointment."

"With whom?"

"With whoever!"

"Whomever."

"Jesus Christ, Mom, you're not in the classroom anymore."

"Nor are you down at the fire station."

"Why can't you go yourself?" Kevin demanded.

"I promised Father Clancy I'd help him dress the altar. She can talk to you about music or girls or whatever. It always seems strained when I bring up something like that."

"No kidding?" Jimmy imitated her. *"Now, Rose, can you give me your considered opinion of Fifty Cent or whomever?"*

"Laugh all you like. Grammar is important. Oh, Kevin, she sounded so happy this morning when I told her you'd be dropping by."

"Jesus Christ, Mom, will you stop meddling!"

"It's not meddling, it's looking out for our own."

"I'll do it, okay?" Jimmy dug in his pocket for his cell. "Go on, kid, don't be late for your *appointment*. It wouldn't be down The Inn, would it?"

Kevin tossed the sports section into the middle of the table. Jimmy had to stretch to prevent the milk jug from keeling over.

"What time will you be home?" Maggie called after Kevin as he barged out of the room, slamming the front door behind him.

"You know he is thirty years of age."

But she had already turned her attention back to the dishwasher. Jimmy studied his cell then hit a number.

"Hey, how you doing, Siobhán? . . . Yeah, I'm fine. Listen do me a solid, tell Marcella I'm running a couple of hours late, okay? I got to drop off a birthday gift for my grandson. . . . Yeah, that's right, just got the one. Now make sure you tell Marcella when she comes in. Okay? Later."

Maggie had been staring at him but he hadn't noticed until he slid the cell back in his pocket. It was almost a relief to see a quizzical look in her eyes, even if it contained a hint of pique; there was no doubt about it, she had been changing. He looked away, unused to the attention—or the scrutiny.

"Coffee still hot?" He held out his cup.

"Funny name for an Irish girl—Marcella," Maggie said as she filled it.

"Yeah, Marcella Fitzgerald."

"What county is she from?"

"I don't know." He yawned. "Mayo or somewhere."

"You don't know where she's from, and you spend half the night out drinking with her?"

"She's just one of a crowd. I'm pretty sure it's Mayo. I'll ask her today, if I remember."

The dishwasher gave a final loud thump and settled into a quieter spin. "You've become very friendly with her, that's for sure. Marcella this, Marcella that!"

"Jesus, Maggie, she's the goddamn day manager."

"Who works nights too?"

"Yeah, she's a real go-getter, never turns down a shift. Where's the gift? I'll drop it over now."

"It's in the living room. Make sure you keep Rose company for a while. "

"Yeah, we're overdue for a heart-to-heart about Britney."

"You'll find something to talk about. You always do."

FOUR

It was good to sit behind the wheel of the old yellow Caddy again after the long winter. Too cumbersome to take into midtown, but on a nice short run down to Breezy with the sun sparkling on the water it was hard to beat. Sit tall in the plush leather and watch the sandy peninsula wax green with weeds, reeds, and grasses courtesy of the late April rains.

First thing he bought when he got home from Nam, that big old badass convertible, borrowed the bucks from one of the wise guys down the boardwalk—his old man went ballistic.

"What do you want to be showing off for and taking money from those people—and you a decorated vet?"

"Because I'm over twenty-one, Dad, and *you* wouldn't give me the loan."

Fathers and sons, it never changed! His old man might know what it was like to run into a burning building with all of Rockaway cheering you on, but he'd never crawled out of one with the VC and the NVA lobbing grenades at you. Jimmy had survived Nam by the skin of his teeth. Other kids hadn't. It was important that he own something substantial—something to celebrate over—something to squire Maggie around in. She'd just got out of Fordham. She was beautiful and smart, her eyes glinting with merriment, and he was alive and kicking—despite the dreams that did his head in some nights.

They went everywhere in the Caddy that magic summer of 1969, the radio blasting. Her favorite song was "Hey Jude"; Jimmy's was "Bad Moon Rising." Brought him right back to Quang Nam province, crazy Asian moon hovering right over the jungle. Fogerty's voice was urgent, straight from the heart. It somehow gave Jimmy hope that he could fit back in and resume a normal Rockaway life.

They got engaged that September when she started student teaching in Manhattan. Got married in a hurry when they found out Brian was on the way. Jesus, her father freaked! If Da Nang was bad, it had nothing on the night Jimmy came over to break the news, all duded up in his suit, Maggie holding on to his hand. Her old lady nearly took a bread knife to him.

After six months of humping bricks on a construction site, the Police Academy began to look good. He hadn't really wanted to join but took to the job like a fish to water. Gave purpose to his life and there was always Maggie and beautiful baby Brian to come home to. Kev arrived three years later—thought they were never going to have a second. A quiet kid, polar opposite of his brother—just lay there and stared up at them. Couldn't keep Brian in the crib or the stroller—kid was devouring books almost from the get-go. You had to wonder where he got his brains—Maggie, no doubt, reciting him her beloved Yeats, and reading him stories way ahead of his age.

But she loved Jimmy and Kev too. Everyone got his share. It's just that Kev wasn't into books—more than content to trail around behind his precocious big brother. She worked all the angles to get him interested but Kev never really shone at anything. Though he was decent at sports, Brian was a hard act to follow and people weren't shy about letting his little brother know. It was as hard on Maggie as it was on the kid.

Jimmy wasn't always around either; the habits and actions of bad guys rarely took a family's needs into account. There were whole years he couldn't put his finger on. Pictures of himself in family albums when he could tell his mind was elsewhere—back in Manhattan on the job.

But he never screwed around. Never needed to. So why did he lie last night? He didn't take the A train, got a ride home with Marcella. They were drinking with the bartenders and when he was leaving she offered him a lift. No big deal, she had moved to Long Beach out on the Island for the surfing, bought an old Honda, could drop him off as long as he told her how to get back to the highway, no point in taking the train.

He liked her—she was quiet, deliberate, even a bit on the old-fashioned side. There was no harm in taking a lift. Or was there?

"Hey, Marty, how you doin'?" He had slowed down at the Breezy Point security check. Would have been fine to drive on through—they knew him well enough—he and Marty McCann had gone to school together.

"Another day above ground, Jimmy. You know how it is."

"Yeah, you can sing that, man."

And he could. Marty was lucky to be looking down at the daisies rather than the other way around. Best swimmer on the beach back in high school, girls all crazy about him, worked behind the bar for his father in Irish Town—drinks, dames, and blow every night until he got caught with his hand in the register, hit the skids all through the 80s like Rockaway itself. Needle up his arm more often than not, but he'd been on the straight and narrow for years, big gut hanging out over his belt, skinny junkie days a universe behind. The Association knew what it was doing when they hired old eagle-eye Marty—talk about someone who could suss out skells and ne'er-do-wells—but in the end it was the same old game, keep multicultural Far Rockaway as far from white-bread Breezy as possible.

"Going down to see Rose?"

"Yeah. Bit early for The Blarney."

"Remember a time you couldn't keep us out—happy hour 24/7!"

"Not today or yesterday, Marty."

"You ain't kidding, Jimmy. Mornings I wake up now pain in my leg lets me know I'm alive. Anyways, I look out for Rosie and the little guy. Keep an eye on the house when she's out."

"I know you do, man.

"She should get out more often. Know what I mean?"

"Come in its own time. Later, okay." Jimmy waved and drove on. Last thing he needed was a heart-to-heart with Marty McCann about his daughter-in-law.

Guy was right though. Sitting in that big mausoleum with Brian's pictures and medals—nothing changed since the last morning he left except the dust gathering. Grieving might be tough, but it was often harder to leave the loss behind.

Rose never knew what hit her, and she had the kid to deal with, spitting image of his dad, same build, mouth, hair, and those blue eyes with the flash of mica. It was like staring at Brian back when he made his first communion. And that memory ripped the heart out of Jimmy because there was no going back and none of them, as yet, had found a way forward.

If Brian had been whacked by a drug dealer or something else in the line of duty Rose would be mending a lot faster. But this 9/11 thing never let up. The wives of martyrs and heroes were like guardians of some sacred patriotic flame. People damn near bowed in their presence. It was a wonder they weren't required to get dolled up like Lady Liberty, a torch in one hand, the Stars and Stripes in the other, and sent off to Fallujah to whip some sense into those ungrateful Arabs.

Rosie wasn't built for this kind of psychotic patriotic jamboree. Just a Rockaway bungalow girl, she barely fit in at Breezy. It had never occurred to him that Brian would marry her. Sure, she was the belle of the beach, but Brian was already moving with a different crowd in a league of his own making.

Maggie was devastated. Never in a month of Sundays could Rockaway Rosie have lived up to her expectations for her eldest son. Jesus, what would she have settled for—some uptown girl, a cross between Grace Kelly and Jackie Kennedy maybe?

Rosie had never cracked a book beyond Jackie Collins. To add fat to the fire, Maggie tried to make the girl feel at home by dumbing herself down. But women spot that kind of thing a mile away. Rosie was smart, just not in a bookish way, and she had a big heart, full to the brim with loving for Brian. He loved her too. It's just that he could be confusing—give his passionate best one day, act all cool and collected the next; while Rosie had only one setting, pedal to the metal, Rockaway love at full throttle.

Had she ever really known Brian? Maybe at first in the wine and roses days, but Brian was always a work in progress with interests and ambitions that reached way beyond the peninsula. There was a lot of strain between them in those last years. Jimmy steered clear of it, and for the most part kept Maggie away too, but it was hard to ignore the friction. So many times he wanted to say something to his son but they just never had that kind of relationship. Anytime Jimmy touched on the subject Brian would just spin him on a dime and before he knew it they were arguing Mets and Yankees or Giuliani's ego.

Everything went into high gear after Brian made lieutenant—weekdays with the mayor, weekends in DC, taking calls out on the deck, brooding, distant, a weight on his shoulders, whatever they were laying on him.

He had that look Jimmy knew only too well—two and two were adding up to something way beyond four and he couldn't for the life of him tell why. What had Brian stumbled on that just didn't make sense?

When they were both detectives they used to bullshit and share a few laughs. That all ended after the promotion. The brass had Brian doing different stuff—"national security," DeVito said. But they were hiding something. Jimmy could smell a cover-up. Only one problem: What else might surface if he got to the bottom of it all?

Even in Rose's happiest moments Maggie could cast a dark shadow. It wasn't that she actively disliked her mother-in-law, it was just that the older woman's sense of superiority pricked deep beneath her skin. For days on end she'd pay Maggie no mind, then out of the blue her shadow would descend and there'd be no banishing it. Today it was clothes. Maggie had always shopped at the best stores. Everything matched in her wardrobe and every new purchase had a function and place.

With the 9/11 commemoration looming at the end of summer Maggie would soon show up again on 220th Street, inspecting Rose's wardrobe and insisting on another Manhattan trip where they'd traipse up and down Fifth Avenue looking for "just the right outfit."

She did have good taste: there was no denying that. It was just her "little things matter" attitude.

Rose often felt like saying, "No they don't! Who cares about little things anyway?" Having a home and a family was all Rose ever wanted, although as usual Brian had gone overboard with the big spread in Breezy; still, it was a nice house to receive guests and Rose insisted that Maggie visit her just as often as Rose made her required pilgrimages to the Murphys' house in Rockaway.

With Brian's death Rose had pressed pause on their relationship. She no longer felt the obligation to socialize, just drop Liam off for a visit every month or six weeks. But even that became a chore, so much so that she often felt like packing up and moving south to her mother's apartment and losing herself in the anonymity of Fort Lauderdale.

She had been surprised when Maggie had called earlier that morning to say that Kevin would be dropping by with a gift for Liam's birthday. She hadn't expected another visit so soon after he bolted away like a frightened puppy. Maybe she had leaned into him a little too closely but she was feeling dizzy after hitting her head, and anyway he'd often held her tight when they showed off their tango moves down The Inn or at Connolly's. Whatever, he needn't have panicked; she'd barely even know how to make out with a guy it had been so long—almost three years now!

She and Kevin had been friends even before she began dating Brian. And God knows they'd spent enough time together all the nights Brian was off schmoozing with big shots; that's when she and Kev would talk about everything, big sister to little brother. She'd always known, but what harm was there in a young guy's crush? Nothing was ever going to happen. Then the world came tumbling down and he never even wanted to be near her anymore; that hurt, but there was so much pain on the peninsula, who knew what was what?

Once she'd sealed off Maggie from her thoughts it had been fun to dress up for Kevin, especially after all the tears and screaming with Liam the last week. Kev liked short skirts. She remembered that. Used to talk about her great legs when she wore the denim one. She'd found it at the bottom of a drawer and matched it with last year's sandal-heels. He'd always complimented her bright-red lipstick, so she'd taken time getting it just right.

The doorbell rang. Rose hurried down the hall but slowed the last few steps. No point in panting or breaking into a sweat. Really frighten him off!

She hummed a snatch of the Cyndi song about girls having fun as she checked herself in the hall mirror. Not bad for someone who hadn't given a damn in years. And a widow at that. She smiled before throwing open the door.

"Jimmy!" She almost fainted at the sight of her father-in-law wrestling with a big box on her doorstep.

He noticed her surprise, but juggled the kid's gift in front of his face to hide his own at her appearance. "Goddamned box! It's so big, I nearly dropped it."

"Jimmy?"

"In the flesh!" He did a little two-step to give her time to gather herself and purposefully wobbled the box again.

"Jesus! Let me help you!"

"No, no, it's okay. You'll get your good clothes messed up."

"No, it's fine, really. I was just trying on some things."

"They look nice."

"Yeah, figured I'd wear them down the store."

"Hey, it's good to dress up every now and again."

"Yeah. Tired of people seeing me wear the same old . . ."

". . . Same old. Can I come in? Got Liam's birthday gift here."

"Sure, of course, what was I thinking?"

He followed her through a haze of perfume. Chanel No. 5—used to give it to Maggie for Christmas—pretty glitzy for a stroll down the store! And what gives with the skirt and heels?

"Put it down here. Get you a cup of coffee or something?"

"Nah, drinking it all day in Dolan's. Can't sleep at night."

"Tell me about it."

"Still having trouble?"

"You know . . ."

"You don't take the pills anymore?"

"They make me dopey all day, afraid I'm going to nod out on Liam."

"Wouldn't want to do that."

"No, it's kind of frowned on." She studied him, still a great-looking guy. Lean and tending toward tall with lighter-blue eyes than his sons, intense but compassionate—broke some hearts in his day. He could be a bit distant and removed but that was okay—he knew how to give people their space. Unlike his wife, always so sure of herself and not afraid to let you know it. What a strange match.

"I thought you were working today," she said.

"I am."

"So?"

"Oh, you mean why Kevin didn't come? He had some kind of appointment or other, you know how it is with these young guys, girl probably called or something."

"Yeah. Probably a girl all right."

She kicked the sandal-heels across the room. "Haven't worn them much—cutting my heels."

"That's the way with new shoes."

"They're not new."

They both stared at the offensive heels spread-eagled against the wall. Finally she shrugged. "Whatever."

"He'd have come otherwise."

"No big deal. I got someone dropping by in a little while."

"Oh yeah? A friend?"

"Something like that."

"That's okay, I can't stay long."

"No rush. You sure you won't have a coffee?"

"Nah."

"A beer?"

"I'd love one, but it slows the hell out of me during work."

He glanced around the room, spotless for a change, the smell of Pledge still wafting from the recently polished furniture. The only thing out of place was the picture of Brian and her turned toward the wall. What's with that? Though he often had the same instinct at home.

"Listen, Jimmy, you don't have to stay because of me."

"I'm in no hurry, Rose, honestly. 'Sides, it's a bit of a break here—you know how things are."

"Maggie still the same?"

"Actually she's a lot better. It's just, well you know, it hasn't been easy on her."

"No."

"Jesus, who am I telling?"

"Oh God, Jimmy, can we please change the subject?" She had a mad urge to scrape off the mascara and eyeliner with her fingernails. "Excuse me."

She hurried across the room and tried to open the bathroom door but the handle came off in her hand.

"I thought he fixed it," Jimmy said as she stared at the handle, her eyes blurring.

"Probably just stuck again. I'll use the upstairs one."

"He said he fixed it."

"He did, as best as he could."

"He was never good with his hands like Brian. Jesus, lucky he didn't pull the damn thing out of the wall."

He wrenched the door open some more inches and peeked through the crack. "It's the hinge. Any idiot can see that. Fix it in a minute with a screwdriver."

On his way to the basement he tripped over a large metal object protruding from under the table. "Jesus Christ! He even left his toolbox here. What the hell was he thinking?"

"We had some beers, he must have forgot."

"That's all it takes—a couple of beers and that kid totally loses it."

"Yeah, that's what must have happened."

"Could never hold it like . . ."

"Brian! For God sakes, say it, Jimmy! I'm not going to crack up. Give Brian, *my* dead husband and *your* eldest son, a couple of beers and all he thought about was the next couple."

"Yeah, he sure could handle the sauce. Chalk and cheese, him and Kev, right?" He wrenched the door open another few inches, shoved the toolbox through, and slid in behind it. As soon as he was out of sight Rose fixed her running mascara.

"How's Liam?"

"I don't know what to make of him anymore. That's why I called you the other day. I can't even mention Brian's name now. As soon as the nice weather comes it's like he can sense the 9/11 commemoration is only months away and how dare I bring it up."

"Yeah, you were saying something about that on the phone."

"I just casually asked him if he'd like to attend this year with all the other little boys and girls. He freaked out on me, screaming something awful would happen, that his dad had warned him."

"Warned him what?

"I don't know, Jimmy, I'm too afraid to ask again. Today was the first day he'd even go to school."

"That's not good."

"Maybe you can come down some evening, take him out for a walk and find out what he's talking about?"

"I'll come tomorrow."

"No, let it sit for a while until he gets more back to normal. I mean the whole thing is crazy—Brian warning him—that's like Brian knew something was going to happen."

"Brian may have been many things, but he wasn't a prophet. He knew no more than the rest of us."

"So what was he doing down the Towers that morning? It's time we found out the real story. I don't want my kid turning into a total nut."

"Relax, will you. I'll find out what Liam was talking about."

"No! I want to find out everything. It's been nearly three years now and I'm sick of all this tiptoeing around. I can't even ask an honest question without people looking sideways at me like I'm some kind of a traitor or something."

"It's just the way it is, Rose. There's a lot of hurt out there still."

"And I don't have my share of it? The whole thing is screwed up. Liam doesn't even want me holding him anymore. And you know me, I'm not clingy or anything."

Jimmy halted, screwdriver in hand. He'd always liked green-eyed Rockaway Rosie, even as a teenager promenading the boardwalk she stood out.

"So, I sit with him at his computer pretending I'm into his video games, then I feel the tension building and all of a sudden he shrugs my arm off and says, *'It's okay, Mom, go watch some TV.'* I mean, a seven-year-old is telling me what's good for me. So I just sit in here with the TV on until he's asleep and go in and hold him. Oh, Jesus!"

He began to slowly turn the screw again. "Yeah, it's a bit like that with Maggie too. Only difference is—she got fifty years on the kid."

"Oh God. We're a right bunch, aren't we?" She sniffled then pressed a Kleenex to her mouth; the lipstick came off in a bright-red smear. She studied her face in the mirror over the sink.

"Thick as turnips, my father used to say. There." He gave the screw a tap of the hammer. "That should do the trick."

He tried the door. It moved much better, but was still a little stiff. "Hold on. Just one more screw! It always takes that one extra."

"Brian used to say that, remember?"

"Just one more screw—like a porn movie!" Jimmy laughed. "Maggie used to hit the ceiling. *'I hope no child of mine has ever attended such an event!'* Such an event?"

"I think I miss his jokes as much as anything."

"Corny as they were. Same ones over and over, but he had a way of telling them, big dopey smile on his face. Ah shit. At least we're laughing."

Her cell phone rang. She checked it out and rolled her eyes. "It's the lawyer, I'd better take it."

She climbed the stairs determinedly to her bedroom and slammed the door. Jimmy knew there was an issue with the remainder of the settlement; not wishing to overhear he strolled into Brian's study. She'd bring it up when she was ready. He'd always liked the room though

Brian had kept the shades drawn, said he could think better in the muted light. The study hadn't been touched since Brian last used it; hadn't been cleaned much either, Jimmy noted, as he ran his finger over a carefully stacked but dusty pile of *National Geographic* magazines.

He switched on the old brass office lamp that his own father used to keep on his desk and gazed around at the shelves of books. Unlike many collectors Brian actually read his. How often he'd seen one of these tomes out on the kitchen table or on the passenger seat of his son's car. But Brian had always been like that—ever since Maggie dressed the little boy in his Sunday best, walked him the couple of blocks to the library, and got him his first card. Jimmy had always been impressed, if a little daunted, by his son's wide taste in reading, particularly on religion. Here on his deep shelves Thomas Aquinas rubbed shoulders with Saint Augustine but kept a respectful ecumenical distance from the sermons of Martin Luther and the hymns of John Wesley. Spinoza stood in isolation at the far end of the bookcase—but the old leather-bound book now had a companion whose title was in Arabic.

Jimmy picked it up—an English translation of the Quran. He was just about to put it back when he noticed an inscribed card within: *To Brian, "From all I did and all I said let no one try to find out who I was," Yussef.*

Jimmy had twice taken Brian to meet Yussef at his falafel parlor in Brooklyn but his Egyptian friend had definitely not given his son a copy of the Quran on either occasion. Brian had never mentioned a further visit or a gift with such an enigmatic inscription. Why would he have kept quiet about it? He knew how much Yussef's friendship had meant to Jimmy.

He heard Rose's bedroom door open and her footsteps on the stairs. He placed the card in the Quran and the holy book back on the shelf just as she stepped into the study.

"Thought I'd find you here. Like father, like son."

Whatever the lawyer had said, her mood had darkened considerably. He would have liked to reach out and hug her. But her arms were folded tightly and he wasn't the touchy-feely type either. "You be all right, Rose?"

"Yeah, sure."

"Okay. You still going down the store?"

"What for?"

"You said you were going. That's why you were trying on the clothes, remember?"

"Oh yeah, the store—maybe I'll go later. I'm not sure anyone would notice the difference—thirty-one years of age, who'd be looking?"

"C'mon. You look like a million bucks."

"Yeah? Thanks, Jimmy. You always knew how to make a girl feel special."

"Well, if you need anything give me a shout. You got my cell, right?"

"Right here." She held up her own cell. "Jimmy, take the toolbox with you. And tell Kevin the door is fixed, okay? There's no need . . ." Her voice trailed off.

"Yeah, I'll tell him. Okay Rose, see you."

She spent a long time staring out the window after his car pulled away.

FIVE

He was standing next to Marcella when Richie Sullivan strolled into Dolan's. She'd been pondering a change in the menu and looking for input, but his mind was still full of Rose. He liked the sound of Marcella's voice, warm, rich, almost soothing with that lilt of the west coast of Ireland; you could almost touch the soft rain in its cadences, feel the cool mountain air. She was also very aware, for she looked up from the menu the moment he snapped into mental alert.

From his vantage point in the dining room, Jimmy could see Sullivan make his usual beeline for the bar, thus making it hard for his ex-partner to see him. That was Richie all over—street-smart and not a bad cop, but he'd have made a lousy detective. The brass knew that and never promoted him. The drinking had raised red flags, but when had that ever been a decisive factor?

Sullivan was off duty—dressed in a baggy suit, white shirt, and black tie—most likely on his way home from a wake or funeral. The joint was full with the pre-theater crowd and the bartender hadn't even given him the time of day.

Dumb Mick! Doesn't recognize a cop when it might as well be branded on his forehead. Too busy being the next Colin Farrell.

Sullivan didn't miss the oversight either; he unceremoniously shoved aside two revelers and rattled off a brace of quick-fire sentences. Colin Farrell's head shot back like a piston and he was instantly all attention.

Jimmy smiled. Sullivan's favorite introduction to preening bartenders used to be "You're an actor, right? Well, in this scene you're playing a bartender. So pour me a fucking Jameson's like your life depended on it—and it probably does."

Whatever the current introduction, Colin Farrell was now energetically gesturing in Jimmy's direction.

No wonder the suit was baggy—Sullivan had dropped thirty or more pounds from his considerable frame. He looked taller than his six feet, partly because he'd forsaken his old bullet-head style and let what was left of his red hair grow out. His face had cleared up too and seemed a size too small. Used to be bloated, blotched, and bulbous, not that such drawbacks harmed him in the sex department—he'd never married but got more than enough action from the working ladies of the West Side.

Jimmy had barely seen him since Brian's wake and missed him less despite their long years of friendship. Sullivan had made a show of himself. "The last person to see Brian alive," he'd bawled, with no notion of what he was doing to Maggie.

He did love Brian, but the feeling wasn't exactly reciprocated. Brian tolerated him and winked at some of his roguish qualities, but Sullivan was too old school and unsavory for someone on the fast track in the Department.

"Jimbo!" Sullivan smothered him in his still substantial girth. Marcella looked on with interest. She'd never seen her flinty head of security treated so informally.

"Richie, how are you, amigo?"

"*Menza menz*, you know the score."

"Yeah."

Sullivan gave Marcella the triple-X once-over. She blushed at the sheer leering nakedness of his appraisal.

"This is Marcella Fitzgerald, our night manager. My old partner, Officer Richard Sullivan."

Sullivan X-rayed her in even greater detail but made it abundantly clear that while two might not always be company, three was most definitely a crowd.

"Nice to meet you," Marcella murmured and retreated to the safety of the kitchen.

Sullivan raised his eyebrows then winked. "Not bad for a night manager," he said, expertly mimicking her accent and tone of voice. "Would you—or rather did you?"

Jimmy ignored Sullivan's shtick and ushered him into a booth. "What are you having?"

"You ain't heard?"

"I hear nothing no more. It's like I'm a leper, no one comes over."

"I been dry going on nine months. Be a year in September."

"You're kidding!"

"Yeah, the new me. Didn't you notice?"

"Thought you were running the marathon or something."

"The only thing I'm running from is myself."

Richie rubbed his face. He had a habit of doing that to his stubble, though for once he was remarkably clean-shaven. "I hadn't been feeling so good, went for a physical. Showed up late, I'd had a few. Doc freaks out. Takes my blood and all the other bullshit, and then I put it out of my mind. Come home one night after a session at The Landmark, go down on my knees with a large sized pain in the gut, see the answering machine blinking and think it's my mother after croaking down Lauderdale. Press the play button and I hear this nerdy voice: 'Officer Sullivan, on the slim chance you may still be alive, please call Dr. Feldman, your liver has suffered some serious damage. On no account ingest another alcoholic beverage.'"

He sat back and awaited a reaction.

"And that was that?" Jimmy finally ventured.

"Yeah, went to a couple, two, three meetings but mostly just clued into what Barney Rossiter said when he quit."

"Which was?"

"You don't remember?"

"A lot of things about Rossiter I don't want to remember."

"Yeah, I hope he's forgotten some shit about me too—like my name if Internal Affairs ever wakes up and goes after him." A shadow descended on Sullivan, if only for a moment. "But Rossiter's take on things alcohol was a real doozey—*every man gets a certain amount to drink in life and I gone way beyond my quota.*"

"Well, the both of yez sure had your moments. Anyway, it's good news, man."

"Yeah, you tried telling me often enough, right Jimbo?"

Jimmy nodded. "Still able to come into saloons though?"

"I don't make a habit of it, still get the yearning. That's why I ain't been in to see you."

"There's always out the house."

"Yeah, but you and me, when did we ever not toss back a few when we got together? And . . ."

"And what?"

"I don't know, man, needed time to figure things out, I guess."

Sullivan's eyes darted around the bar. In an instant he assessed the custom wood paneling, the silver napkin holders, the half dozen or so large flat-screens beaming ESPN from every angle, number of staff, class and mass of clientele, and summed it all up in an inflated estimate of Jimmy's salary.

"Nice situation you fell into."

"It sucks. I'm just a glorified messenger boy."

"Could be worse—Leroy Johnson's bouncing rock concerts. Gets to see all the big names down the Garden, 'cept he don't know who no one is no more." Sullivan looked away furtively and gave the room another once-over.

"Richie, what are you doing here?"

"I came to see my old compadre, what do you think?"

"Give me a break! You show up out of nowhere—not even a phone call."

Sullivan's jowly face dropped an inch but brightened considerably at the sight of two tipsy Lehman secretaries clip-clopping past on their way to the ladies'. "Now that's what I call class."

Jimmy waited. As ever, his old partner would take his own good time.

"Guess what?" Sullivan finally blurted. "Tony DeVito bought me a cup of coffee the other day. Just like old times. The two of us was shooting the shit and your name came up. Man, remember the laughs we had at the Academy?"

Jimmy studied him intently. Captain Anthony DeVito would walk a mile over broken glass in his stocking feet rather than hang out with a walking time bomb the likes of Officer Richard Sullivan, unless he really wanted something in a bad way—like send a message without printing his name on it.

"Oh yeah? Tony say I'd been in to see him?"

"Yeah, still thinks the world of you, man."

"Cut the bullshit! You know I'd have made lieutenant if it hadn't been for my *old friend* DeVito."

"You and me both! Motherfucker pulled the rug out on me ever making sergeant!"

It was an old hurt and it ate at Sullivan, but he had an agenda at Dolan's and he fingered the saltshaker while he looked every which way but at Jimmy. "Said you'd been asking questions—about Brian."

"Yeah, a lot of loose ends there."

"What kind of loose ends you talking about? I was the last one to see him. He ran back up the stairs like there was no tomorrow. To this day I blame myself."

Jimmy grabbed him by the wrist. "Spare me the hysterics. You already hummed that tune at the wake!"

Sullivan jerked back his hand. The weight loss hadn't affected his legendary strength. "What's the matter with you, man? What are you always so angry about?"

"Because my son is toast, and my wife is suffering like it happened yesterday! Now you tell me what the fuck Brian was doing down the Towers at eight fifteen that morning?"

"Hunting A-rabs, whacking towelheads, how would I know? Maybe the brass sent him on some lead."

"You never mentioned anything like that before."

"Just something that sprung to mind. Don't tell DeVito I said anything like that, you hear me!"

"Why not?"

"Because you know how he is! I'll never hear the end of it."

"If Brian was following a lead, the last thing he'd be doing is talking to a cop in uniform."

"What do you expect him to do? Walk right past me?"

The sweat was dripping off Sullivan's face onto the fancy place mat featuring the thirty-two counties of Ireland.

"So what did he say to you?"

"I don't know! He could have been going on about the fucking Mets, for all I remember."

"I think you had something to do with him being there."

"Jesus Christ, don't say that, man, I got enough on my conscience." Sullivan bellowed.

"What did he tell you?"

"He didn't say nothing—just ran back up those stairs when everyone else was running out!"

Marcella laid her hand on Jimmy's shoulder. He hadn't noticed her slipping up behind him. "Mr. Dolan is on the phone for you. I tried to take a message but he says it's important."

People at the bar had turned around and the babble of conversation had lowered to a sub-hum. Colin Farrell was fixing his tie, nervously staring across the room at them.

Jimmy pushed the table back and stood up. He felt beat up and exhausted. Still he straightened to full height before leaning right into Sullivan's zitless face. "You tell DeVito I'm getting to the bottom of this—I don't care how many careers I mess up!"

SIX

Yussef Ibrahim loved his Mercedes—its black-as-night hue, sleekness of design, style and comfort. He had worked hard for his success, and was pleased when the picture of him standing beside his car circulated with family and friends back in Alexandria. Of course he had no hand in this—his childhood friend Omar had been visiting and had taken the photo.

Yussef had provided well for his family and they enjoyed the comfort of the redbrick home on Shore Road in Bay Ridge. He had taken the subway to work for many years after his arrival in New York in 1977 and did not even own a car until he opened his fourth falafel parlor in 2000. It was then that he purchased the Mercedes and it had given him much pleasure as he drove to and from the parlors with the voice of his beloved Umm Kulthum seeping from the speakers.

There was the scraping of the paint in the week after the attack of 9/11, but had it been malicious or merely some drunken driver careening along Shore Road? He preferred to think the latter though his friends suspected a hate crime. After repair the Mercedes looked good as new but now he parked it in his garage at night.

Yussef drove some blocks along Shore Road to a clearing where he could view the Narrows and the ships passing. How lucky to live near flowing water. It hardly compared to the mighty Nile, yet there was a serenity to this part of Brooklyn that one could no longer find in Alexandria. It soothed his soul, and he had need of healing especially after the phone call from his friend Muhammad Rashid, imam of his mosque. Usually such calls were casual and pleasant affairs; after an uncomfortable silence, however, Muhammad inquired about Fatima. Yes, his daughter was in good health, Yussef had replied, now twenty-four and studying for a law degree at Columbia University, and

Muhammad was correct, there was hope of a match with the son of a cousin back home.

Then Muhammad took Yussef into his confidence. He had been examining some notes that Ahmad Damrah, the previous imam, had neglected to take with him on his sudden return to Egypt. Ahmad was of a tempestuous disposition and had not been a favorite of the two friends; a confrontational man, he had spoken often of his admiration for a radical faction in Afghanistan, something that did not endear him to the hardworking Muslim business owners in downtown Brooklyn. Some felt his views reflected badly on the mosque and had drawn attention from the authorities in the aftermath of the attack.

The notes, though cryptic, mentioned Fatima and her association with a police lieutenant in the year before 9/11. Could Yussef shed some light on the matter? The recent deportation of two young Islamic students had led to rumors of informers. While Fatima's name had not arisen, with the occupation of Iraq, tempers were fraying again in the mosque and who knew where such matters could lead.

A large tanker hove into view bearing oil, no doubt, from Saudi Arabia, Kuwait, perhaps even Iraq. How interconnected the world was nowadays—and how easy to turn such a vessel into a fiery floating bomb.

Yussef sighed: it had been almost three years since Fatima had disobeyed him. She had been young and impressionable; the girl had suffered much and he had hoped the matter was well and truly behind them.

He needed more time to think, but business called. The tanker moved on, guided by a tug that would lead it to its New Jersey refinery. In like manner Yussef would be guided—he would visit Muhammad but at a time when God's will became clear. He turned the key in the ignition and activated the CD player. Umm Kulthum began "Al Atlal," his favorite song; perhaps this was a good omen.

But as the familiar anthem of love and loss, desire and regret washed over him, the events of that awful September once again flooded his mind. Would God ever grant him peace? He sighed as he pulled the Mercedes out onto Shore Road and drove to his falafel parlor on Atlantic Avenue, determined to do all he could to protect his daughter.

SEVEN

Jimmy hadn't always loved baseball. More like a ritual he endured with his father two or three times a year up at the Stadium. All well and good first time through the Yankee lineup, and he always perked up when the Mick was hitting, but his favorite part was the seventh-inning stretch signaling the end was close at hand. It was sheer torture when games would go to extra innings. His father, Gerald the fire chief, along with being a diehard Bomber fan, believed in value for money and never left a game before the final out.

It wasn't until he had his own kids that Jimmy saw the bonding possibilities, a surefire way to connect with the boys when he'd been working nights or tied up in some drawn-out case. He couldn't believe it when Brian declared for the Mets but he went along with the program, just learned the Flushing guys' names, watched their stats, and even secretly rooted for them in the 80s when they owned New York. Kevin, true to form, maintained the Murphy tradition and followed the Yanks. And so it worked out that any teenage walls and resentments could be blown away with a simple "Any hits for Straw last night?" Or "What's Donnie B's average?"

Breakfast in the old days resembled a Talmudic study session with three heads bobbing over the sports section. Baseball was their means of communication, results and stats their nouns and verbs. What had begun as a way of connecting gained a traction all its own.

He was checking Jeter's average when Maggie freshened his coffee.

"The train was late again last night?"

"Nah, some of the kids live out in Long Beach dropped me off."

"Things go through your mind when you're lying there."

"I'll leave earlier in future."

"No, you have your work and it's good to unwind. It's just that when I wake up and you're not there, I still look at the clock. The nights seem longer now, every little thing surfacing . . ."

". . . Like driftwood in the foam." He completed the line of poetry.

"Do you think any of my tenth-graders could recite it now?"

"There's got to be at least one. You sure taught enough of them."

"Just one?" She smiled.

"You know, maybe you should try the teaching again. Laura Bianchi said they're only dying to have you back at Stella Maris—that you were the best."

"No, Jimmy. I don't feel right in myself."

She laid her hand on his shoulder but withdrew it almost instantly.

"I know we could use the money and that you could do with some time off."

"It's no big deal. I just figured I'd put it out there."

"Next year, perhaps."

Her voice trailed off. He stared out the window. A honeysuckle vine had fallen in the night and was swaying in the remains of the early morning breeze. The sky had turned overcast and heavy, though it had been such a glorious scarlet dawn. Often happened on the peninsula, a fog would drift in off the ocean, misting up everything until the sun burned it away toward noon.

"You must be tired." She emptied out his cup and poured him a fresh one.

The steam drifted up around his face.

"Nah, you know how it is—four, five hours is enough these days." He poured in some milk and a phrase from a song came to mind— "clouds in my coffee." Who recorded it? Woman singer. Never had to worry when Brian was around, knew all the names of the pop songs. Never liked anything heavy like Zeppelin or the Allmans, but the guy was encyclopedic about the frothy Top 100, from whatever era.

"I'm better up and around. The tossing and turning does a number on me," he added quickly.

"You should try one of my pills."

"Nah, a couple of beers do the trick. Where's Kevin?"

"He's not up yet."

"Guy still sleeps like a teenager."

"Talk about teenagers! He's been so moody lately."

"He should take up the guitar again—always got him out of himself. I was in his room the other day and there it was stashed away in a corner covered with an inch of dust. God, remember how particular he used to be about it?"

"That guitar was the love of his life.

"Yeah, always a shine off it. He could make it talk."

"He used to be so much fun. And what a dancer—no one moved like him, especially when Rose got him up on the floor. The whole room would stop to watch, remember?"

"Yeah." Jimmy shook his head. "He's never been the same since . . ."

He didn't need to finish the sentence. He watched her wash her hands again. How many times a day did she do it now? They'd all picked up some tic or habit. Rose with her smoking, Kevin barely talking, while he'd found himself staring out the kitchen window time after time—not looking at anything in particular, just gazing off in the distance.

"I never understood him like I did our Brian," she said while drying her hands. "We were just never as close."

Jimmy placed the tip of his finger under Jeter's name and followed the stats out to his batting average—197. So far from his usual flirtation with the big three hundred. Jeter said he rarely thought about it, that baseball was a game of failure: you just gave it your all and hoped for the best, to hell with stats.

Jimmy sighed. "Maybe you're trying to compensate too much with Kev. Just back off a bit and see what happens."

"But then he doesn't speak at all. If they take him away . . ."

"No one's taking him anywhere," he interrupted. "Just relax, okay?"

She nodded her head impulsively then sat down at the table and took his hand. "I know it's irrational, but when he's not here I get really anxious. Every time I hear a siren I think they're coming to tell me something."

"He can't stay home forever, Maggie. Life has to go on."

"At least you're here. I don't have to worry about you out on the job anymore."

"Yeah, I'm here." He tried to soften the resentment that almost spilled over; when she let go of his hand, he returned to the Yankees box score.

"Didn't you think that was strange yesterday?"

"What's that?" Jimmy said without looking up.

"Kevin just did not want to go see Rosie."

"I wouldn't make too much of it, probably off with some girl or other."

"When was the last time you saw him with a girl?"

"Yeah, I guess it's been a while."

"A while? More like three years. I worry about him, that's just not natural."

Jimmy sighed. He'd tried to soothe that fear a number of times with little result.

"Regardless," Maggie continued. "Seeing Rosie is a family obligation, and that's one thing Kevin was always good about. Not like Brian—I even had to remind him of his wedding anniversary."

"Not surprising." Jimmy laughed. "He drank so much at the reception he was shaking hands with himself."

"It was his only failing. And it never stopped him on the job. If he came in at five in the morning, I wouldn't even have to wake him. He'd be down here at seven with the coffee brewing."

As if by rote, she freshened his cup again, though he was on his third and had barely put a dent in it.

"There's something else. Kevin moved the picture again last night."

"What picture?"

"The picture over there of Brian and Rose—when he made lieutenant."

He realized his fingernail was jammed tight under Mariano Rivera's ERA.

"Why did he turn it to the wall?" she persisted.

"Jesus, I don't have a clue, Maggie. But coming home three sheets to the wind and knocking over a picture is not exactly a federal offense."

"It's the second night in a row he's done it."

He took a long gulp of his coffee. "Did it ever occur to you that when he's tied a load on Kev can't take Brian staring at him?"

Jimmy had never liked the picture. Brian's smile was beyond fake, and even though she was beaming, he could tell that Rose in her new hairdo and Lord & Taylor dress was the wrong side of happy.

"Lieutenant at thirty? Near the top of his class at Georgetown! Maybe there's a reason Kevin can't look at him."

"But they were so close and Brian always watched out for him. From the time they were little boys, don't you remember, Jimmy?"

"Yes, Maggie, I remember. I remember everything." The hardness welled up inside him and he might have said something he'd regret, but when she heard the creak on the stairs Maggie shushed him.

"Morning," Kevin said as he sat down.

"You're up," Jimmy noted while checking on Posada.

"You slept well," Maggie said.

"Not bad."

"I made batter for your pancakes."

"Nah, I'm not hungry."

"You should eat breakfast. Coffee?" Maggie hovered by his shoulder.

"Sure, thanks."

As they read the paper in silence, Maggie never took her eyes off Kevin. "What are you up to today?"

"I don't know," he answered. "Hadn't thought about it yet."

"When's your next tour?"

"Tomorrow. I just got the three days off this week."

"That's good." She smiled.

"Jeter got a hit," Jimmy glumly noted handing him part of the sports section.

"Yeah, he's been in a hell of a slump" Kevin agreed while holding his cup out.

"Why don't you go into Manhattan today?" Maggie asked as she poured.

"What for?"

"It's Wednesday. You could see a play."

"A play?"

"Well, maybe a show—*Phantom of the Opera* or something."

"That's still running?" Jimmy asked.

"I think so. But there's always something good on. When we were your age we went to shows all the time, right Jimmy?"

"Yeah, often enough."

"More than that. One year we saw absolutely everything, remember?"

"Sure, back when I was on the beat in the theater district. Got all the comps."

"You could take Rose. She hasn't been to see a show since . . ."

"No!" Kevin glared at her.

"Why not?"

"She probably has the kid to pick up," Jimmy interjected.

"I can do that. He can help me with the flowers down the church. It would be so good for her to get out. Get dressed up a bit."

"She was all dressed up yesterday."

"Oh, what for?" Maggie brightened.

"Said she was trying on some things she hadn't worn in a while."

"Well, that's good. Means she's getting interested in herself again. But it's not much fun parading your good things around the house."

"Said she had someone coming over later."

"A man?"

"I think she said 'some kind of friend.' I didn't pursue the matter."

"That's interesting," she mused but instantly dismissed the thought. "I doubt it's anyone special—we'd surely have heard. But she does need to get out more often. She and Brian were such a great-looking couple, weren't they? "

She picked up their picture and dusted it off with the hem of her apron. "Go upstairs and bring down your good suit, Kevin. I'll run an iron over it. Okay? And give Rosie a call—ask her what she'd like to see."

"I'm not going to a show, Mom, and, for the last time, I'm not calling Rosie. Okay?"

Maggie removed her apron, carefully folded it, and without looking at either of them climbed the stairs.

"What a fucking life!" Kevin muttered on his way up the hallway and out the front door.

You're only as happy as your unhappiest child. Maggie sighed as she sat down on her bed and gazed out the window in the direction of the ocean. But what happens when one of your children is gone forever? All logic flies out the door and you're left alone and clueless. Kevin was always my main worry; he seemed to stumble on every path in life.

Of course I fretted about Brian too and some of his choices, but his compass was always set, even his ridiculous decision to become a cop was finally paying dividends. It just never occurred to me that God would snatch him away.

Only then did I realize just how flimsy are the foundations on which we set our hopes and dreams. I saw the remains of my family in a whole new light. Kevin sent reeling without the support of his older brother; Rose unable to deal with the emotional demands of her son; and Jimmy on a fool's errand to get to the bottom of a mystery of Brian's own making.

Jimmy still resents me for insisting that he leave the job. But I wasn't the only one—Brian also felt the day of the two-fisted cop was over; younger men who could tackle the problems of poverty and lack of education were the future.

Now Jimmy stews in Dolan's while basking in the admiration of young women half his age. His vanity is hurt because Tony DeVito and others have far outstripped him; but is that their fault or his? He never tipped his cap to anyone or tried to better himself, just grumbled away in the shadows while even his own son rose above him.

I'd hoped that time would ease his hurt but no, he's determined to know what Brian was pursuing in his last months. But he never knew Brian like I did. Brian never confided in him. And so Jimmy roams far and wide looking for answers to questions that are so much closer to home. Answers that I won't give him, for fear he'd tear our family even further apart.

My duty is to protect our remaining son, our daughter-in-law, and Brian's living image, young Liam. I wish I could help Jimmy. He's a good man and deserves more. Time and a love of God are the two things that could ease his soul, but he has no faith in either. And so he blunders on, with little idea of the damage he may cause. But what do men know?

It surprised Jimmy when Brian joined the cops. Even in the year after Nam when he had nothing particularly steady in the way of work, Jimmy never thought of joining Fire. That was his old man's world and he wanted no part of it. Chief Gerald Murphy's shoes were far too big to step into, much less stagger around in.

Then again it stunned just about everyone when Brian entered the Academy after graduating from Georgetown. Could have written his ticket anywhere down Wall Street, gone to law school, whatever. Sullivan said he needed his head examined. Brian never felt he had to explain anything—knew exactly where he was headed.

Straight out of the Academy they sent him to East New York—one of the toughest beats in the city. He spent his downtime working at a youth center with kids more used to cursing out rookie cops than dunking balls with them. He even persuaded LL Cool J to show up at the center, and got down with hip hop though it was oceans away from his vanilla pop tastes. Just over a year on the beat, the *News* did a profile on him and how one cop could "make a difference" even while studying nights for his master's. The golden boy was on his way.

Kevin was the other side of the coin. Dropped out of St. John's. Hung around the boardwalk with a loose crowd. Got collared for a dime bag. Jimmy was down in Miami bringing back a celebrity bail-jumper. Lucky the cop recognized young Murphy and called DeVito. That was it. Jimmy read the kid the riot act—enough wasting time, apply for Fire or get the hell out of the house.

Kev wasn't particularly happy with the new gig but on his first post, to Harlem, he got in with a heavy-drinking posse and that kept him occupied. After 9/11 with all the publicity about Brian, strings were pulled; they transferred him to his grandfather's old command, Engine 268 in Rockaway, so he could be close to home and his grieving mother.

Jimmy had a good idea where'd he be hanging, seeing Kev wasn't the cappuccino type, and The Inn didn't open early Wednesdays. But he needed time to think, time to get a handle on his son—they had drifted so far apart. He stepped out down the boardwalk toward Beach 103rd in the bright May morning.

Though it was long gone, Irish Town continued to spawn memories. As he drew closer it was like retracing childhood steps past narrow alleys of bungalows that the families from Brooklyn, Queens, and The Bronx used to rent in the summer. He could still call to mind the faces of girls he had crushes on, their brothers that he downed six-packs with. Some of those families had loved the beach so much they'd bought the little houses, winterized them, and moved there full-time, but he'd lost track of them when the pubs and boardinghouses closed their doors and the last ballad was sung.

Life seemed so much simpler back in the shot-and-beer days of the old Irish saloons but that was just memory basking in its usual warm glow. After all, he'd been drafted, sent to Nam, and much of the beach was already drifting away from its doo-wop working-class simplicity into a cauldron of drugs, alcoholism, and urban despair. The 70s and 80s had been bad news, and the area had just been getting back on its feet when the attack, with all the local losses, shattered the progress it had been making. So many things seemed to stem from that September morning.

Whatever, he'd been neglecting Kevin. Difficult as their father-and-son talks had always been, Jimmy knew he had to reach out, and so he shrugged off the memories, strode back up the boardwalk into the glare of the sun until he reached the bustle of 116th Street.

The older men were inside the firehouse playing nickel poker. Kevin was lounging outside with the young bloods checking out the girls in their summer dresses. No problem for the NYFD since 9/11. Proletarian chic—the new in thing with the ladies around town, and the firemen played their cards to the hilt.

They all knew Detective Sergeant Murphy—what civil servant on the peninsula didn't? He bantered with them about the Yanks and Bloomberg and whatever good old days any of them was old enough to remember. Still, at the first lull in conversation he signaled to Kevin and they did the "walk and talk" down toward the bay.

"What's up?" Kevin said as they watched a sailboat skim across the lazy waves toward Cross Bay Bridge.

"Your mom's been through a lot."

"And we haven't? Anyway, why don't you take your own advice? I was on the stairs five minutes waiting for a break in the action before I could get a cup of coffee."

Jimmy ransacked his memory. How much had the kid heard? What were he and Maggie talking about?

"I'm not saying I'm any better. But she is your mother."

"She's your wife."

"What's that supposed to mean?"

"Nothing."

"Well, watch what you're saying!"

"What are you so jumpy about? I'm just stating the obvious."

"Oh yeah?" Had someone seen him getting out of Marcella's car? Making a big deal over nothing. But the kid looked confused, even guilty.

"What's the matter with you, Kev? You're out on such a limb these days no one can say boo to you anymore."

"Oh man, I don't know. I'm losing it around here."

"It's just something you're going through. Give it a bit of time."

"Time, my ass! Why does everyone keep saying that?"

"'Cause you're just so stuck in your own little world."

"And you're not?"

"Listen, I'm fifty-seven years of age. I got a wife and two kids . . . Ah shit!" He shook his head in exasperation. "I am what I am; but you still got a shot at being whatever you want. What's eating at you?"

Back down the street, with a blast of its siren, the fire truck nosed its way out. They both turned to watch it.

"I'm thinking of enlisting."

"No way, you hear me! Next thing you'll be dodging bullets in Baghdad."

"At least I'd know who the enemy is."

"You listening to that idiot Sweeney back there? You won't find that barstool patriot signing up."

"It's not just him. I want to do my bit for the country."

"Yeah! That was the word about Nam too, and look where that got us."

"This is different. We were attacked."

"Oh for Christ's sake, can't you see it's the same old story? Politicians do the talking; stiffs do the walking—and the dying! I still remember every second, sitting around Da Nang, VC lobbing mortars in at us. But what were we doing in their country? The domino effect or some such crap! Another twenty years we won't even remember why we went into Iraq. But I guarantee you one thing—there'll be no problem getting a Big Mac in Baghdad. Keep your good job, man. Don't end up like me."

"You ain't doing so bad. Got your pension."

"Yeah! Thirty years being a good cop and I chuck the whole thing in so your mom won't freak out every time she hears a siren."

He reached out and touched his son on the arm, but there was no budge. "You know, whatever you're going through, we could go out, have a beer—talk about it."

"For the last time, I ain't going through nothing, okay?"

He watched Kevin light a cigarette. When had he started smoking again?

"Okay, man, but quit turning that picture around, okay?"

"What picture?" Kevin coughed and the smoke billowed out of his mouth.

"Listen, sometimes I can't look at him either—it gets too much. But you're spooking your mom out, so leave that dumb picture of Brian and Rosie alone, all right?"

"Yeah."

"Jesus, look at the time! I got to run. Oh, by the way, I put your toolbox down the cellar."

"My toolbox?"

"Yeah, you left it at Rosie's."

"Shit!"

"Nice job you did with the door."

"Oh yeah?"

"The hinge just needed tightening, right?"

"Yeah, I guess that was it. Her and me—we worked on it together."

"You two should join the carpenters' union, go into business. Give your mom a call, okay? It'll mean a lot to her. Listen, be good—catch you tomorrow."

Kevin stubbed out his cigarette without looking up. Jimmy nodded and headed off toward the train but stopped dead at the shout.

"Dad!"

He might have been running late but he hadn't heard that plea in Kevin's voice since the day he was dropped from the high school baseball team. He walked back to his son.

"Maybe we can have that beer sometime?"

"Okay, big guy. You got my number. Name the time and place. I'm there."

Jimmy reached out very tentatively and touched him on the shoulder. Kevin patted him back on the elbow, a fleeting smile scudding across his face.

As he hurried to the subway Jimmy wished to Christ he'd thrown his arms around the kid. Why had something so simple become so difficult?

EIGHT

"Prick!" Sullivan muttered fiercely under his breath as he let DeVito's door slam behind him.

So his visit to Dolan's to find out what Jimmy Murphy knew was a bust? What had DeVito expected? When was the last time he'd shaken down a pro like Murph for info? Never, and it wouldn't be happening in the near future.

That was DeVito all over right from the time the three of them had hung out at the Academy. Talk big—do nothing; guy ended up a captain while real cops still busted their ass on the street. As for Jimmy Murphy, the less said the better, wasting his life checking IDs at Dolan's with a harem of stiff-backed Irish biddies mooning over him.

What was DeVito's game anyway? If he opened up and said what he was really after then they could talk turkey, but it had been the same ever since the big bang—What does Murphy know? What had Brian been up to?—the captain's beady eyes devious as a ferret's. But two could play that game, and so he gave DeVito just enough to keep the overtime coming—jack up his pension so he could quit his dead-end job with at least something to show for it.

In Sullivan's experience it all came down to the three P's—power, phunds, and pussy.

Forget about screwing around, DeVito would never risk crossing his upscale wife, lovely Rita in Pelham. As for Benjamins, guy was too squeaky clean to even contemplate a legit racket. Had to be power: either DeVito was afraid of losing his captain gig or some even bigger suit was putting pressure on him.

Given the years they'd known each other and what they'd gone through together, the three of them should have been as thick as thieves. Instead Sullivan was trapped between the other two. One slip and he knew DeVito could tighten the screws on his retirement prospects, while Jimmy would never give up until he hit upon some version of the truth that would ease his guilt about Brian.

"Fuck 'em both." Sullivan pushed through the gaggle of cops smoking outside Midtown North. When the chips were down Brian had trusted his Uncle Richie. He'd be damned if he'd give up the kid's secrets.

Colin Farrell winked conspiratorially as Jimmy hurried into Dolan's. What was the kid's name anyway, Conor something or other? Was every male under twenty-five on the island of Ireland named Conor?

Not a bad kid; cocky, but who wasn't at that age? Especially if you were getting laid at the rate he was? These new Irish were a whole different ballgame than the crowd who came over in the 70s and 80s. That generation would have scrubbed toilet floors with a toothbrush for the "shtart," as they called it. They came from little and were happy with whatever was thrown their way. This new Celtic Tiger breed were more like tourists passing through, pick up a hundred here or there for blow or weed, but most of them had Daddy's credit card to bail them out if they didn't care to break a sweat. Looked at you like you had two heads when you told them to hop to it. Of course it was all a facade and they cracked the minute you laid the New York real deal on them.

And then there was Marcella, calm and contained—came in a waitress, ended up running the joint. She might have had the background, her parents being in the pub trade back in Mayo, but command came easy; she created an oasis of clarity and everyone wanted to do right by her.

Well over an hour late, he searched the booths. She did her paperwork out in the bar in the quiet afternoons to keep an eye on things. He knew her strategy, same as his back when he was on the job. Show yourself as often as you could, that way when you had to go to ground they'd never be sure just where you were or when you might pop up.

Marcella didn't notice him approach. She was tall for an Irish girl and took herself seriously. Even at the late-night staff drinking sessions she rarely let her guard down. She was the manager and they were her charges though she could be friendly and solicitous. She was a little older than most of them—he guessed around twenty-eight—it was hard to tell, for her natural reserve and well-cut jackets suggested maturity. She mostly kept her dark-brown hair swept back from her face and tied up with a tortoiseshell clasp; she rarely wore makeup— why bother with that clear Irish skin?

"Dolan around yet?"

She smiled and her hazel eyes lit up at the sight of him. "Been and gone early."

She ordered coffee but didn't speak until the waitress had returned to her station. "Is everything okay?"

"Yeah." he took a gulp and wiped his brow. The train had delayed for an eternity at Broad Channel before meandering off toward Brooklyn. Too much time to think; it was always easier when you were in motion, the constantly evolving landscape or blur of graffiti in the tunnels kept you off-kilter.

"I don't know how to say this to you." She placed her hand on his. Her fingers were cool and she wore a slim silver Claddagh on her right ring finger. He noted that the crowned heart was facing outward to show she was unattached. "But if you ever need to talk."

He stiffened and she withdrew her hand instantly.

"I said the same thing to my son a few hours ago."

"And what did he say?"

"Oh, man, I don't know what's going on in that kid's head. Kid, what am I talking about? He's older than you."

"People grow up at their own rate."

"Yeah, I'd been and done with Nam by the time I was twenty-two. He's thirty now and still floundering. Well, at least he suggested going for a beer."

"It's good that he has you to talk to."

"He always needed me—unlike his brother. I just don't know if I was always there when it counted."

"Can I say something to you, Jimmy? You're very hard on yourself."

He liked the way she said his name—put a lilt to it, made it seem special.

"You always blame yourself first," she added with some emphasis.

"I thought that was a good thing."

"You can take it to extremes. You're always making sure the rest of us are okay. Even when we're having a drink, it's like you're there with us but really on your own."

He wasn't quite sure how to answer. So he grinned broadly. "Like a sheriff in a cowboy movie. I always fancied myself as a bit of a Gary Cooper."

She didn't acknowledge his joke, just nodded that she understood and returned to her papers.

He would have liked to talk but she had already picked out another bill. A moment had passed and he didn't quite know how he felt about it.

"Mr. Dolan asked me to apologize for not being able to meet you today."

She always used the formal when referring to the owner; she even called Jimmy "Mr. Murphy" to the staff and customers. He couldn't have cared less about Dolan missing their meeting—just didn't want to be late and under an obligation to him.

"How was the great man anyway?"

"Somewhat scattered."

Jimmy smiled at her descriptive powers—always terse and to the point. He could imagine the skinny little bastard blustering about in a reek of sweat and Old Spice, but he could tell that something else had gone down.

"You don't have to tell me, Marcella, if it's confidential. I'll find out eventually."

"You always know, don't you?"

"Believe it or not I used to be a good detective before I became a high-priced bouncer. Even more to the point, he'd be here to tell me himself if it wasn't going to be a problem."

She gave the most infinitesimal of nods and played with her pen. "He wants to reorganize management. He'd like you and me to work closer together—says we're a great team—our chemistry is *spot-on,* his words."

"I get all the good parts but what is it he wants me to do that you have so much trouble breaking?"

"He would like you to go beyond your security duties and act somewhat more like a maître d'."

Jimmy put down his coffee. "You mean he wants me to show people to their tables, right?"

"In a nutshell."

"From a detective sergeant to a glorified busboy."

"It's so much more than that, Jimmy, no matter how you put it."

"How the mighty have fallen."

She caught the unaccustomed note of self-pity. He could tell she felt it was beneath him and he regretted it.

"I'm breaking confidence because he doesn't intend broaching the matter with you until your contract comes up. I felt it only fair to inform you, give you time to consider your options, although I'd personally be upset if you . . ."

She left the thought unfinished.

"Yeah, you'd have to find someone else with new chemistry."

She stood up abruptly and gathered her papers. Colin Farrell was waving a credit card slip at her. "That's one way of putting it, Jimmy."

This time there was little lilt in the way she pronounced his name, little emotion either. She walked directly over to the bar, her back stiff, her heels clicking on the wooden floor. Two of the night guys from NBC turned to admire her. Colin Farrell leaned in close as he explained the credit card complication.

Jesus Christ, a maître d'! Suppose some of the guys from the job came in and saw him handing out menus. It'd be all over Midtown North in the blink of an eye. When was his damn contract coming up anyway? End of the summer or thereabouts.

More important, he had to deal with Kevin—and Rose? She wasn't dressed to impress her father-in-law and now you couldn't get Kevin over there with a bullwhip. He lied about fixing the door. He could have brought someone else over with him and then split. Jesus Christ, one of the morons from the firehouse! She had said she was expecting someone to drop by later. It had to be an issue of that nature—something had gone wrong and now Kevin, as was often the case, was shirking his responsibility.

Nothing made sense anymore. Both DeVito and Sullivan were hiding something from him. Brian was good at undercover. If he was following a lead he'd have spotted Richie Sullivan a mile away down the North Tower and would have steered well clear of him.

And Brian himself racing back into that madness a second time after leading those seven people out—anyone with a brain knew it was about to collapse. Brian had always been one of the bravest, but he was also one of the smartest, not some rah-rah lunatic ready any old day to go knocking on heaven's door.

After thirty years on the job, every bone in Jimmy's body screamed to him that something was out of whack. And yet if he kept pursuing it, what else might emerge about Brian? He and Yussef had obviously become tight if the Egyptian had gifted him a Quran with a personalized note. Yet Jimmy had met Yussef during the investigation into the first bombing at the World Trade Center back in '93, and as Brian had made patently clear, "there are no coincidences in my life, Dad."

NINE

Kevin knew he should have called first, but if Rose picked up, then what—iciness from her, mumbling from him, and in the end nothing less than a great big ball of confusion. No, far better go down to Breezy and start from scratch. Get it all sorted out with her before Memorial Day, not that it made much difference now that he wasn't gigging anymore. But old habits died hard and Kevin had always cleared the decks right before the peninsula went into summer overdrive.

He parked up the block and had a last cigarette as the sun sank in a fiery glow beyond Brooklyn and night began to gather out over the hazy Atlantic. Not for the first time he tried to figure out exactly how to approach the subject. Rose wasn't easy to talk to when her back was up, but there was no getting around what had happened on his last visit—he could no longer hide how he felt for her. Something had to be said.

He flicked the butt out the window then stomped on it when he stepped out. Little need to lock a car in Breezy—no thief with the least smarts would bother, too many off-duty cops and you still had to get it past hawk-eye Marty McCann in security. Kevin crossed the lawn rather than climb the steps—that way she wouldn't see him coming. Passing the kid's window he glanced in. Glued to his computer as per usual, little head glowing blue from the monitor. He didn't look up at her bedroom; the blinds were always closed tight. On the doorstep, he mentally reran his full argument then circled back so the first sentence would be fresh before he rang the bell.

She wasn't expecting anyone—barefoot, dressed in a faded black Jim Morrison t-shirt and blue jeans, hair unwashed and tied back.

"Oh," she said as if she had stubbed her toe.

"Rose, I'm sorry."

He was about to dig into his prepared speech but she fiercely shushed him and motioned down the hallway to the open door of Liam's room.

The fancy lines he'd spent over a week reviewing evaporated and he blurted out, "Listen, you and me got to talk."

"Wait!" She left him standing there with the door open and swept down the hallway into her son's room. "You okay, sweetheart?"

He didn't hear the kid's reply but a few moments later she emerged juggling plates of pizza crusts and a number of half-empty glasses of milk on her way to the kitchen. He could hear her dump the crusts in the garbage and rinse out the glasses. Only then did she beckon him to come into the living room and closed the door behind him.

Her arms were folded tight, face drawn and stern. This wasn't how he had visualized it.

"It's okay," he whispered. "You could have brought him out."

"Oh yeah?" she said crudely miming him. "You think he's ready for his mom and uncle going at it in a clinch?"

"Jesus! What are you trying to do to me, Rose?"

"Do to you? I seem to remember you were the one hanging onto me for dear life."

"I didn't know what was happening."

"You certainly felt like you were enjoying it."

"I'm sorry, I just wasn't used to . . . being that close to you."

"Oh stop acting like a teenager! One day you're plastered all over me, the next your father thinks I'm some kind of slutty housewife wait-ing for the Con Ed guy—especially after your mother was so kind as to call and say you'd be coming over."

"It was too much, Rose. One day you're my brother's wife, the next you're . . ."

How could he tell her about the joy he felt after finally melting into the only woman he'd ever loved, only to instantly be confronted by guilt. That's why he had to leave so suddenly; then when he got home to see Brian staring back at him from the picture!

But words had never come easy, so in the end he pointed across at the piano. "It was the picture."

"What picture?"

"The same one of you and Brian over there, the day he made lieutenant."

"Jesus, the Bensonhurst hairdo and that dumb dress your mother picked out made me look fifty! All because of Brian—*Can't you wear something fitting for a lieutenant's wife?* Your brother was so full of it sometimes."

"I thought you looked nice."

"You kidding me? I looked like an old lady. Maybe that's what Brian was really into." She picked up the picture from the piano and studied it for a moment before turning it away from them.

"I could never tell with the two of you. One minute you were all over each other, the next it's like you were on different planets."

That was Brian, especially after the promotion when he was hardly ever home and preoccupied whenever he was, forever checking his phone, slinking out to the porch to make calls, and when she finally questioned him about it, said he was protecting her and the kid. But was it real or all in his head?

"You know, lately I'm starting to wonder if your brother wasn't as lost as the rest of us—just knew how to hide it better."

"He was definitely hiding stuff that last year."

"Yeah, like why was he spending so much time on Atlantic Avenue? What was the attraction there? You think you know your husband then all of a sudden he's acting like a different person."

"You're awful hard on him, Rose."

"What do you expect? He was always so busy acting out his own movie he never thought about the mess he was leaving us extras."

She went over to the fridge, took a can of Bud for herself, then tossed him one.

"They never even came close to nailing him, did they?" Kevin cracked open the can. "The papers, the obituaries, like?"

"Makes you wonder about everything they write."

He took a slug, wiped his mouth with the back of his hand. "I can't really picture him anymore. I mean he used to be right here—in my mind's eye. Now all I see are the photos."

Rose nodded. Her life had been rocked to the core; but even as many things changed, others remained startlingly the same. The sun still rose and Brian's *New York Times* arrived like clockwork every morning. She couldn't bear to throw it out but likewise couldn't bear to read any more awful news, and so the copies lay in a pile in the hallway. It must have been October before she idly opened one and came upon the page that daily featured pictures and biographies of the dead heroes; she felt an immediate stab of guilt that she hadn't read Brian's. And so she lined up a month of papers and trawled through them, searching for him, instead often finding his friends, along with the husbands and brothers of the women she was being introduced to at funerals and memorials.

Yet all the tributes blended these larger-than-life figures into a generic soufflé of loving fathers, husbands, and brothers, solid citizens all—Little League coaches, churchgoers, and PTA members—when she knew from Brian's stories that some were also alcoholics, woman-izers, gamblers, and manic-depressives. Still, she saved Brian's glowing obituary and other relevant pages in his study. Liam might have need of them someday as he tried to piece together a father he'd never really known.

Off in the distance she caught the decaying drone of a foghorn. Brian loved that sound at night. He always drew closer to her, put his arm beneath her neck so she could sleep in the soft crook of his elbow. It still broke her heart to hear it.

"No matter what time I woke, he'd be staring at me," she whispered. "Never say what he was thinking."

Kevin stood up and gazed at the picture on the piano, the same one that had freaked him out back home. Those first months after Brian's death it was like the roots had been cut from under him, his whole world awash with an aching emptiness. He'd always looked to his brother for guidance, and when in trouble he'd ask himself, what would Brian do? But nothing seemed to fit anymore: his mother glid-ing around the house like a lost spirit, his father trying to hold things together and often making an impossible situation even more difficult.

He couldn't even go to The Inn, couldn't handle the pity. Just sat in his room with a six-pack but could barely cop a buzz. And then he began to feel weird, especially when he'd think of Rose down in Breezy alone; yet he couldn't dream of going to her, although she was the only one who'd understand.

"What is it, Kev, what are you thinking?" She took his fists and unclenched them.

"When Brian was alive, I could watch you and be with you, and it was okay. You were his and that's all there was to it."

"And you were his baby brother, always there with the big puppy dog eyes." She smiled. "Except when you were parading your girl-friends in front of me. Brian used to call them my rivals."

"He knew what I felt?"

"Are you serious? He had us all figured out. He thought it was so cute."

"And it didn't bother him?"

"Why would it? He knew you even better—safe as can be, just a harmless crush."

Brian knew a lot of things. But how well did he know himself? Often late at night she'd find him sitting on the couch, so wrapped up in his thoughts he wouldn't even hear her. She'd sit next to him, lay her head on his shoulder; she no longer asked what was troubling him because he'd waltz away her fears and make things even worse. And so they'd just sit there, he thinking, and she praying that whatever was troubling him would eventually work itself out.

And now three years later, she was sitting next to his equally silent brother. She loosened the band holding back her streaky blond hair and let it fall over her shoulders.

"Talk to me, Kevin. I can't stand any more silence. I can almost feel it trembling around me."

He looked anywhere but directly at her. "You know the real reason I didn't come around?"

"No. I don't know anything anymore."

"Because you might have thought I was trying to replace him."

"There's no replacing Brian, hon, he'll always be a part of me. But you were the one person I could lean on and you never came around. All I could think was: everything's broken apart, nothing will put us back together."

"Why didn't you say something?"

"By the time the shock was over I was too busy cursing him for run-ning back into that stupid building."

"He was just doing the right thing."

"Oh, spare me! You'd think he'd have given a thought to his family. And why was he spending so much time with all those foreigners when I needed him at home?"

"Brian was there for everyone. He was there for you too."

"And I wasn't there for him?" She stood up, knocking over the can of beer at her feet. "I loved your brother like it was going out of style, and I stuck with him through thick and thin. You hear me?"

He righted the can and looked around for something to wipe the spilled beer that was seeping into the thick pile of the carpet. She tossed her hair back to signal her indifference.

"But now I've got to figure out what I'm doing with my life. And when you stop sleepwalking down The Inn with Fatty Sweeney and the other idiots, you'll do the same."

He lowered his head and held it between his fists. "I guess."

"No! No more *I guess*! I got a kid in there who thinks his dad is some kind of superhero, and he's squeezing his way inside that friggin' computer screen so he can smell him and touch him and feel him again."

"I'm always there for you, Rose. You know that."

"You just don't get it, do you? I am so sick of this whole Murphymania. I had half a lifetime of 'always' and 'forever' with Brian and now I'm expected to mourn the rest of my life for him? In case you hadn't noticed I'm pissed as hell with you and your whole *I guess* attitude too."

"In case *you* hadn't noticed I'm doing my best."

"Sometimes you have to do better. I want to feel special again, Kev, don't you understand?"

He held her eyes for a moment before looking away.

"I thought so." She stood up abruptly and headed to the kitchen.

"Wait!" he said so loudly she cast a fearful glance down the hallway, but her son's door remained closed.

Kevin caught up with her by the kitchen sink. He grabbed her wrist and spun her around. When she glared at him he loosened his grip.

"I won't break," she said defiantly, standing so close he could feel her breath on his cheek.

He only hesitated a moment before he pulled her closer and kissed her in the way he'd always wanted to.

She held on to him, kissed him back fiercely, and this time he didn't hurry to the door.

TEN

Marcella was about to take their usual route down the East Side and through the Midtown Tunnel when Jimmy said, "Let's go down the West Side."

He'd been feeling weird all night at Dolan's—one idiot after another asking stupid questions that he answered on remote. He had managed to duck many such people in his detective days, melting into any shadow and letting some junior do the talking. Now from his perch near the reception desk it felt as though he had "Information" stamped on his forehead, repeating ad infinitum the same terse answers with a little imaginary addendum to preserve his sanity—"the bathrooms are downstairs, pal, don't fall on your fucking face!" Or, "take a right outside the door for Times Square, you can't miss it—or maybe you can you're so shitfaced!"

He needed a change—anything to shake his mood. Marcella didn't object though it was considerably out of her way.

It felt muggy as the dog days though it was still only June fifteenth and the dull breeze off the Hudson did little to ease either his restlessness or the humidity. He closed his window and she turned up the air conditioner. They drove in silence past the bulk of the *Intrepid*, a forlorn symbol of a war worth fighting, while across the river Weehawken and Hoboken shimmered like twin oases in the listless night. Once past the Holland Tunnel the traffic trailed off. Though it had been almost three years now many drivers still shunned the Lower West Side— who needed to be reminded?

All at once he knew he'd made a mistake. Even in the distance he could feel the power of the pit materializing. What was he thinking— going down there in the first place? And how could she be so calm? Had she no idea where they were heading?

The Financial Center loomed to the right, and beyond it the high-rises of Battery Park. Cars were backed up from the traffic lights on Vesey Street; she braked gradually and they took their place in line. Not a word out of her yet, even as his chest tightened. He wanted to roll down the window and take in a lungful of hot air but felt powerless to move, as though nailed to his seat.

Finally the light turned green, the cars began to move bumper to bumper, and there it was on their left, divorced from the outside world by painted plywood. Christ, was that the best they could do? Couldn't they at least erect a stone wall, keep the ghosts within? As the car edged by he scowled at the flimsy paling, while overhead floodlights blared down as if some alien spacecraft had burrowed deep into the heart of Manhattan and the authorities were taking no chances on what might emerge.

At least this time of night there was a somber hush, unlike the last afternoon he'd passed down Church Street, a veritable mall with hucksters peddling t-shirts and all the other bric-a-brac of commercial patriotism. Welcome to America—there's a buck to be made from everything, both the sacred and the profane, where the tragedy barkers cry high and low, inducing the tourists to purchase some star-spangled trinket so they might prove to the good folks back home that they had made the pilgrimage.

But don't hang out too long, buy your fake FDNY shirt and get a move on, there's dinner to be eaten at that cute little hip restaurant up in the Village, and don't forget the half-price tickets for *Mamma Mia!* where you too can be a dancing queen. The fuck with you all!

He stared beyond her pale face, dazzled by the hypnotic purity of the white light aimed at the pit, while she impassively drove on. Didn't she know what was in there? The swirling dusty remains of his son! Had she no idea that every fiber in his body was beseeching, "Why, Brian, for God's sake, why?"

A brace of National Guardsmen in desert fatigues nonchalantly observed the cars drifting by, counting down the hours in the hushed dust and decay of this catastrophe before they were heaved slam-bang into the self-induced American nightmare of Fallujah and Ramadi.

Jimmy stared back at them—just a couple of kids from some small town, somewhere, joined up in a rush of *do the right thing* after the big bang. Well, they'd made it to the unquiet grave of Ground Zero; next stop—a shot of the real deal in Anbar Province courtesy of Qaeda.

A plangent silence blanketed the pit. Wired New Yorkers for once didn't honk their horns or complain of delay, just glided slowly by in line, awed to be mere yards away from this floodlit crematorium.

She sped up when they passed Liberty Street and the white light began to fade in the distance behind them. She was about to exit left for the tunnel to Brooklyn but he said, "No, let's take the bridge."

He couldn't bear the thought of being underground. Couldn't face the claustrophobic silence in the tiled tube that linked Manhattan and Brooklyn.

An odd relief surged through him when they turned the tip of the island and headed north on the elevated highway. Up ahead the Brooklyn Bridge dominated the East River, a late subway train stalled amid its girded metal; while to their right the old sailing ships in South Street Seaport longed to quit their moorings for one last voyage to Rio or Taipei.

Brian had once quoted him some lines from Whitman about "tall masts of Manhattan" and "scalloped-edged waves"—funny how stray words stayed lodged in a brain even when the soul of the poem had fled and gone. Brian had a good head for poetry and could spout lines at will, especially when they related to New York and the life he was leading. Everything had a purpose for him; the irony was it had all come to a great big pulverized nothing, while life stretched on inconclusively for those directionless souls who had spun in orbit around him.

Jimmy had done his best not to obsess about his son over the last years. What was the point? He needed to fill the chasm left behind rather than dig any deeper, but fill it with what? He didn't like the man he'd become, aimless and unfulfilled, forever reacting to the covert strains of bitterness that had infected him. But on a deeper level he realized he had to hold on to the essence of his son, warts and all, and not let him be replaced by the heroic starred-and-striped plastic action figure that was being assembled for common consumption.

It wasn't just Brian. The city itself was unmoored. Life continued at its frenetic pace, but something ineffable had fled and hadn't as yet been replaced. Those twenty-seven hundred and more had been a breed unto themselves: firemen, financiers, cops, cleaning ladies, secretaries, assistants, maintenance crews, chefs, waiters, busboys—all unassuming, optimistic, driven New Yorkers doing their own thing without a notion that they were a tragedy in the making. It wasn't that the people who had taken their places were lesser in any way; the newcomers had, however, been touched by 9/11 and had less trust in the future.

The faithful departed were Whitman's children—they had gazed out across the masts and riggings, the scalloped-edged waves, and delighted in the throb of a bustling city full of life and magic—they never glanced over their shoulders in apprehension. They were Clinton's children too, long on hope and the belief that things would continue to get better. Jimmy keenly felt their absence and longed for the part of him that had fled with them.

In the first years after the attack everything was so different he couldn't nail down exactly what had changed. But as the third year dawned he began to sense that it wasn't only that so many people had perished, but that their very spirits had taken a hit. Perhaps it was just a matter of time until they'd settle into the disciplined ranks of the dead, but as yet that hadn't happened. He kept catching glimpses of departed friends in the distance but when he approached they'd merge effortlessly back into the anonymous crowd. The sound of the city too had changed. Where once the streets echoed to the melancholic promise of a Miles Davis horn, now the highs and lows seemed muted. He knew this had to be his imagination and he banished it as best he could. But then a familiar face would cast a backward glance in his direction and it would begin all over again.

Marcella was a good driver and had no problem taking the sharp exit off the FDR onto the bridge without braking. While she still didn't speak she did slow down to take in the view.

"Nothing like it, is there?" His words sounded hollow and coming from a distance.

"It's like a fairy world."

"I never thought of it like that."

"When you grow up surrounded by bogs and fields, you dream of this view and wonder if you'll ever make it here."

"Well, you did," he touched her fingers lightly. As ever, they were cool despite the humidity and the firm grip they had on the steering wheel.

She smiled but kept her eyes focused on the road, with quick glances beyond him at the receding view of Manhattan.

"It must have been so different growing up here—taking something the like of this for granted," she said.

"Most of the time you don't give it a second thought, and then all of a sudden you look up and it takes your breath away."

He glanced back to catch a full view and the Towers were there just as they used to be, glinting in all their brilliance; but the mirage was instantly swallowed whole by a gaping black emptiness. Without their ballast the island appeared to be tipping sideways toward the docks of Jersey.

They lapsed into silence again until they were on the BQE and passing beneath Brooklyn Heights. Manhattan still gleamed across the harbor but he didn't look anymore. He'd had enough of mirages.

"Do you mind if I ask you a question?" she said.

For once she misread him and took his silence for assent. "What were you doing that day?"

"I was going through something . . . ," he began.

It was the first time a silence had ever soured between them. She was deeply relieved when he continued.

"I had gone into town early to look for someone, sort out a matter. I wanted to clear the air, make everything all right.

"It was such a beautiful day. Even now I can almost touch it—the very texture, the feel. You get an occasional day like it at the end of summer and everything comes flooding back—the sky a big tent of blue, the air crystal clear with a bare hint of coolness, that particular New York it's-good-to-be-alive feeling, the whole nine yards. I felt certain I could fix everything between us, me and the party I was looking for.

"The minute I heard that dull almighty thump I could tell what had happened—just didn't think of the ramifications, especially the personal ones. I was off duty but I was a cop so I jumped into action. I knew what I had to do in an emergency. Totally forgot about what I'd come to town for. It was only later I remembered."

He had been gripping the dashboard without even noticing. She laid her hand on his knuckles. He could feel the silver Claddagh ring and wondered how could it be warmer than her fingers. He stole a glance, the crowned heart still faced outward.

"It'll get better with time."

"Do you think?"

"It always does, whether we want it to or not." She removed her hand and sped into the merging traffic from the tunnel. "We watched it over and over on television. So many of our neighbors had friends and relatives in The Bronx or Long Island. It was like we were all a part of it, worried about this one and that. But in the end they were all okay."

He didn't answer—just let the conversation lapse. From his years of interrogating he knew there was something on her mind, something else she wanted to say. The traffic had thinned and she was covering a lot of ground; he could see the large apartment building that marked the beginning of Bay Ridge. Soon they'd veer onto the Belt and pass under the Verrazano.

"I'd taken a year off after college and was all set to move to Dublin. I had a friend there, a man, and we'd made a decision. But after the planes hit, I couldn't go through with it. He was terribly hurt but I felt I had to come here, that there was something waiting for me, and if I didn't find out what it was I'd never forgive myself."

The Belt swept down toward the Narrows. The ships waiting to be piloted further into the harbor bobbed so high on the tide it seemed as though they might float over the seawall onto the roadway. Then there it was—the pearly glow of the Verrazano dangling in the distance; its lonely arrogance never failed to impress.

"Has he ever forgiven you?" Jimmy asked.

"I'm afraid not. He's a very thoughtful and practical man and I had no idea how I was even going to get here. He didn't know what to make of me. He thought I was throwing our lives away. And for a while I believed him and almost came around to his way of thinking. Then out of the blue I ran into Mr. Dolan. He was home in Dublin for Christmas and was over in Westport visiting a friend. We got talking in Matt Molloy's one night and he offered me a job, said I could work my way up and he'd handle the visa—you know how he is."

"Yeah, I know how he is."

He waited until they were close to Coney Island. "So, no regrets?"

"About coming?"

"Or leaving?"

"No, Jimmy," she took her eyes off the road and smiled at him. "I am so glad I'm here."

ELEVEN

Muhammad served Yussef hot tea in his office at the mosque on Atlantic Avenue. It was the first time Yussef had visited since his friend had been appointed imam. He often reflected that he might never have met Muhammad if they'd both remained in Alexandria and what a loss that would have been. Yussef's father was a wealthy importer until 1956, when the Suez Crisis ruined his business, yet all of his children attended Victoria College and were fluent in English. Yussef had hoped to teach English, but opportunities were few in Sadat's impoverished Egypt and he emigrated during the bread riots of 1977. Alas, New York provided even fewer opportunities for English scholars of Egyptian descent, and Yussef opened his first falafel parlor soon after his arrival. Still, he took great pride in his more than proper English and avoided polluting it with any unnecessary street slang.

Muhammad too had received a formal education but at a madrasa near his home on dusty Sharif Avenue. His imam, however, was a progressive man who believed his pupils should specialize not only in Islam but in subjects such as mathematics and English as well. Hence when Muhammad arrived in New York in 1978 he set up an accountancy service and prepared Yussef's first tax returns. A gregarious man of the people, the new imam was proud of his many sons and enjoyed their use of slang and interactions with Brooklyn street culture.

The old friends exchanged pleasantries and news from home but during a pause in the conversation Muhammad took a key from his pocket and unlocked the drawer of a formidable mahogany desk.

"I discovered these notes when I took possession of Ahmad's office. In his eagerness to fly the coop my predecessor apparently forgot about them."

Yussef expected some leather-bound tome but when he turned he found Muhammad peering at a child's copybook. There was no need for words; the friends had often shared their disapproval of the previous imam, Ahmad Damrah, and his slipshod way of conducting business.

"I must say Ahmad didn't spare the whip when judging our community. I had no idea he had so little regard for my talents." Muhammad laughed heartily.

"He was a judgmental man and easily given to anger."

"Ah, but you and I are like old mules, Yussef, another flaying barely raises a welt on our weathered backs. Your daughter, however, is another matter."

He placed the book on a prayer table and opened to a well-thumbed page where Fatima's name was linked by crude arrows to those of Lieutenant Brian Murphy and Officer Richard Sullivan.

"Someone in our community has been spying on your daughter, for dates and times of her arrival at your parlors and her college dormitory are noted."

"Why would anyone do such a thing?"

"I had hoped you might provide me with such answers. But let us cut to the chase—do you know this Lieutenant Brian Murphy?"

"He was the son of my dear friend Detective Sergeant James Murphy."

"Ah yes, I thought the name was familiar."

"Brian was killed in the attack on 9/11. *To God we belong and to God we shall return*," Yussef intoned and bowed his head before continuing. "Young Murphy had an interest in our faith and I attempted to answer his questions."

He silently begged God to forgive him for not stating the full truth.

Muhammad studied his friend carefully before cautioning, "There are more recent mentions of Fatima that you should be aware of."

"It has been almost three years! Why can't they let the past rest?"

Muhammad ignored the question and opened the book at a page further on. "She has been seen often in the company of a Morgan Bradford."

Yussef slammed his fist down on the table. "The young man attends her college. What would you have me do, lock her up as our grandparents did our mothers?"

"For your sake, I would gladly burn this trash," Muhammad said, closing the book, "but it may come in useful should the authorities question us again."

For three years Yussef had tried to banish all suspicions of his daughter and his anguish was apparent. Muhammad took his friend's hands.

"We live in difficult times and mark my words they will only get worse. Already some of my Shia friends turn their backs on me. This occupation of Iraq will breed trouble the like of which you and I have never witnessed."

"At this moment I care only about my daughter and her reputation."

"Which is why I invited you here. Now tell me, is there still hope of a match between Fatima and your cousin's son in Alexandria?"

"Yes, but my cousin is a woman of narrow intellect and even less discretion. You know yourself the mere rumor of a relationship with a nonbeliever could lead to an end to the proposed union."

"Your secret is safe with me."

"I rely on your trust, Imam, but as you well know I am honor bound to speak to my cousin of such an 'irregularity.'"

Muhammad bowed his head and sighed deeply.

"My patience grows thin with 'cousins in Alexandria' and their insistence on stultifying tradition. It is time for such ladies to 'get with it,' as my youngest son never tires of reminding me. We live in America now and must deal with these matters in our own way. Besides, I'm less concerned with Fatima's romantic affairs than her past dealings with a senior police officer. But seeing you have set my mind to rest, let us attribute these notes to Ahmad's ever present paranoia."

"Or some spurned suitor's jealousy."

"That too. Ahmad cultivated a circle of pious but unruly young men. If only they had fled with him. In the meantime, let us pray that Fatima is cool, as they say, with your cousin's son and that we will all return to Alexandria for her wedding—in the near future."

"*Inshallah*," Yussef murmured, even as he begged God once again to forgive him for concealing part of the truth from his friend.

Muhammad returned the book to the drawer then escorted Yussef to his Mercedes. The imam admired the gleaming car before his friend drove away. A mixture of emotions overcame Yussef on his way home. On the one hand God had indeed smiled on him—Ahmad Damrah had fled the country; but what of those who had been keeping watch on Fatima? Were they still plotting against her, and what might be their next move? And when would Fatima realize that a permanent relocation to Alexandria would be in her best interests?

After he parked the Mercedes in his garage, Yussef made his way into his kitchen. He passed a cabinet where he stored alcohol for his non-Muslim friends. The bottle of Irish whiskey that James Murphy had once given him caught his eye. How bitter to lose a valued friendship, especially during such a time of trial.

TWELVE

"If you don't want to do this, you don't have to," Maggie said, skeptically eyeing Jimmy in his plaid shirt, old jeans, and battered work boots. Amazing that those clothes still fit him; she remembered the faded shirt from back in their courting days.

"It's okay," Jimmy replied, leaning on the spade. "I just don't want to spend all day out here under the sun."

"It might do you good, put a bit of color in your cheeks. So let's try something. I love that *Rosa rugosa*, it's the only thing we kept from the old yard, but it's swallowing up my daylilies."

"It's going to be hard to move."

"No, we'll just cut it way back then dig it out. If it dies, so be it, but it can't stay there."

He sighed at the thought of the work ahead. This wasn't going to be the twenty-minute exercise she had suggested.

"So first of all dig a hole over there where the rose of Sharon used to be. Remember?"

"Yeah," he said. And he remembered the old toolshed that used to stand there before he tore it down, back when the whole yard was a wilderness. He'd had to dig up damn near the whole thing, mix in fresh earth and fertilizer before he could make a garden for her.

Still and all, those were happy days in their little white clapboard house. Brian and Kevin playing chase among the grasses. The Murphys had never built on an addition like everyone else, kept that garden for Maggie's roses, lilies, irises, and peonies. Their two lawn chairs taken out in May and stuffed back in the closet in October, watching the boys cavort and grow up in a house with little space but a surfeit of love.

"So what color were they?"

He hadn't realized she'd been talking. She was waiting impatiently for an answer.

"What color are you talking about?"

"The blossoms of the rose of Sharon?"

"Kind of blue, weren't they?"

"Aren't you thinking of a rather famous jazz musician? They were white as the driven snow and glowed in the twilight. I must have said that to you a hundred times."

"Jesus H. Christ!" he yelled.

"What's the matter now?" She turned in alarm to find him hopping around the garden on one foot, the spade stuck in the earth.

"My ankle is damn near broke!"

"Oh, come now, it can't be that bad."

"This earth is harder than concrete."

"It's not the earth, silly, it's the roots of the rose of Sharon."

She'd always been happiest in her garden. After the attack she lost faith, much like her people back in Galway after the Famine. The land had betrayed them and neither priest nor pope could do anything about it, her granny used to say; it took the sandy soil of Rockaway to heal their souls. Was such a thing happening again? Jimmy wondered.

"Were you late last night?" she asked quietly.

"I had a few beers after work. No big deal, all right?"

"No need to snap. You look a bit shook, that's all."

Truth be told, he was feeling somewhat the worse for wear—he hadn't mentioned the two or three shots he'd washed the beers down with.

"What time did you come in? I'm curious."

"Hey, you're the detective. You tell me."

"I was asleep."

"Maggie, we're nearly thirty-five years married. I could count on one hand the number of times you didn't wake up when I came home."

"I didn't hear a thing, honestly."

"Then why did you think I was late?"

"Father Clancy told me."

"How would he know? And how would you know that he knew anyway?"

"He rang while you were still asleep."

"What's he doing calling at that hour of the morning? Are you and he . . .?"

"I won't even dignify that with an answer. Besides," she said, giggling, "can you imagine?"

It would take a bit of a stretch all right to envision the hundreds of pounds of the local padre entwined around Maggie's slimness. "Stranger things have happened."

"Well, not to me! Bad enough I married a policeman but keeping company with a parish priest? God, what my granny would have said! Actually, we've been doing the First Fridays together."

"I remember them. Do nine in a row and you get first crack at the vestal virgins."

"To the best of my memory, Jimmy Murphy, handling one virgin was quite the task for you. Actually, Father Clancy was out running this morning, and who do you think he saw get out of a car over by 105th?"

"What else did he say?"

"Oh, don't worry. You were just a footnote."

"Well, hallelujah for that! I wouldn't want to be diverting the reverend from his spiritual endeavors."

"As a matter of fact, the reverend is feeling so inspired these days, he's considering an early mass for those on their way to Manhattan. He even felt that late-shift people like you might avail themselves of the opportunity on their way home, God help him!

"I wouldn't be counting on too much action from the bar trade," he said. "But he was on the money this morning. Some of the kids did drop me off on their way back to Long Beach."

"The least they could have done is brought you to the front door."

"I didn't want them to get lost—end up down the projects. And anyway, it was a soft morning and I felt like a bit of a stroll down the boardwalk."

A bird began singing in the distance. She listened intently. She'd always been interested in their songs and which one might be warbling. This time she didn't hazard a guess but turned her full attention to him. "I'm sure Father Clancy said there was just one person in the car with you."

"One of them might have been passed out in the back."

"Marcella?"

"No, she was driving."

In a flash of yellow the bird zigzagged across the garden saluting them with its distinctive melody.

"It's a goldfinch," Maggie said. "The first one I've seen this year and it's almost July Fourth. Oh my God!" She pointed upward. "There's the osprey I've been telling you about."

Jimmy looked up but it was too late. Still he had noticed the large shadow pass over the garden.

"I hope it's not hunting the finch. That would be bad luck." Maggie made a sign of the cross.

"Nah, I think ospreys only feed on fish. That's what my old man used to say."

Jimmy dug on, slicing into the tangled roots of the rose of Sharon. Eventually he reached down, pulled hard on one, and after some vigorous swearing and groaning, the root fractured. When he looked up in triumph she barely acknowledged him.

"Maybe we should leave the replanting for another day," she murmured. "I'm no longer in the mood for it."

"Just as well, there's something I have to do in the city before work."

He kissed her on the cheek but she was preoccupied. He shrugged, then went back into the house and changed into his suit. He caught a glimpse of her as he passed by the kitchen window on his way to the front door. She was deep in thought and he wondered if she'd noticed his lie.

How little I know about him anymore, what he does, what he's thinking. He's been a closed book for so long I barely know how to open it.

By the same token I've no idea what he thinks of me. He probably imagines my troubles began when Brian died, instead of when it first dawned on me that I'd never be more than an English teacher in Rockaway, never write books like Edith or Edna. But back then I had two lovely children and a husband who never strayed—more than enough to outweigh such foolish dreams. Then the world struck like a hammer.

I wasn't there for Kevin though I could almost hear him crying out for me as I'd pass him in the hallway. But my world collapsed along with the North Tower. Still, I'm doing my best to make it up to Kevin now, and my prayers are finally being answered—he's passed through his own darkness and is finally opening up to life and all it has to offer. Just as sure as I can feel Jimmy slipping away.

How strange that faithful Jimmy may be taking a leaf out of Brian's book with the young Irishwoman in Dolan's. Does he really think he's pulling the wool over my eyes? Brian never confided in me about his dalliances either. He didn't have to—ever since he was a little boy I could always gauge the depth of his relationships by the warmth in his voice when he spoke their names.

But there was something different brewing from the time he made lieutenant; I assumed it had to be a new woman, and I feared the worst—that he finally had found a soul mate and would leave Rose. Then what would become of little Liam?

In his last weeks I could tell Brian needed to talk, but just when he'd be about to confide in me his phone would ring or someone would interrupt. So I wasn't surprised to find his car waiting outside on my first day back at school after summer vacation. As usual he acted as if everything was under control, but I could tell he was in turmoil.

He finally admitted there was a problem. At first I didn't take him seriously when he told me he was being followed and was fearful about it. He wouldn't elaborate except to say that if anything strange were to happen I should immediately get in touch with Richie Sullivan—that Jimmy would go immediately to Tony DeVito and that would only complicate matters.

I called Brian a number of times in the last days but he insisted he'd been exaggerating, and that I should forget all about it. Then came the attack and the madness that followed. Whenever I'd try to concentrate on what Brian had said my head would start splitting. I should have told Jimmy back then; but even now I can't bring myself to mention it, he's so obsessed with his own imaginings.

There's that osprey again circling overhead. He'd better not be hunting the finch! He arrived the week after the attack along with all the doves and sparrows fleeing Manhattan. I first noticed him way up high over Brian's house, and then again circling St. Rose of Lima the day of the month's mind; it took him a while to work his way over here. But he's like a friend now—though a wary one. If I stand stock-still, pretend not to see him, he'll draw nearer 'til he ends up on the telephone pole outside. Oh, if only he'd build his nest there and find a partner, but he never will—I can tell he doesn't like to be that close to people, much like myself nowadays.

THIRTEEN

Jimmy hadn't been inside Midtown North since the last time he'd called on Tony DeVito. Although he'd spent a large part of his life within its walls, he no longer had the stomach for it after he retired—used to drive by, think of dropping in to look up old friends but instead kept right on going. Too many memories and unfulfilled dreams—why stir things up?

Accordingly, he kept his thoughts on a tight leash as he stepped past the group of uniformed guys smoking outside. Didn't recognize any of them—a couple gave him the once-over; they knew by his step and bearing that he was a cop of some sort—just wanted to be certain he wasn't some shoofly captain from Borough Command come for a surprise inspection or even worse Internal Affairs on some new warpath.

Joey Gallagher was behind the desk, once a promising welterweight Golden Gloves contender, now paunchy, splotched, and approaching Mike Tyson poundage. Crazy Joey with the thatch of dyed coal-black hair was casting his disapproving eyes over the throng of hookers, pushers, potheads, addicts, underage drinkers, bruised wives, handcuffed husbands—the flotsam and jetsam of every precinct house.

Gallagher didn't notice Jimmy enter in the wake of Madam Sheena, a tall trans woman in a billowing diaphanous gown who sucked up all the attention by demanding to know what the fuck the NYPD had done with her husband on his birthday of all days. Obviously accustomed to such imperious entrances Gallagher merely narrowed his eyes even tighter and nodded his approval when a rookie cop volunteered to deal with Madam's shrill inquiry.

Jimmy didn't make a peep, wondering how long it would take Crazy Joey to sense his presence. Would have made sergeant years ago if he'd he kept his nose clean. Jimmy had written the report—"a little too vigorous in his pursuit of information." Meaning he had beat the living shit out of a mid-level crack dealer from Avenue D who had decided to open a franchise at the back of Port Authority. No big deal in the grand scheme of things, except that a photographer caught some stills of the action and the *Village Voice* ran with the story. Gallagher had his fifteen minutes of fame in a *Voice* edition celebrating The Clash. He would have had a full hour if Jimmy had seen fit to let the precinct know that an inebriated Joey was the desperado who had fired the shots through the British flag flying over the Hard Rock Café one Saint Patrick's night.

"Jesus, Jimmy! I was half-afraid to look up for fear it might be the Angel Gabriel come announcing."

"What's the good word, cowboy?"

"You never gonna let me live that one down, right?"

"Another blow against the British Empire, Joey, you're right up there with Michael Collins."

"My old Donegal granddad would have been proud of me. I still owe you one."

He held out his hand. Jimmy slapped him five and winked. "How are things?"

"Ah, nothing like the old days—everything's by the book now. Even the whores got agents." He nodded over at some skimpily dressed ladies, one of whom with acute hearing gave him the finger.

Gallagher had finally found his anointed station in the NYPD—assistant desk officer—someone who kept his eyes open, knew every strand and fiber of the ropes, and was more than capable of handling anything that might barge into the precinct both by the book and beyond it if deemed necessary.

The phone rang, Gallagher picked it up, and Jimmy swept a glance around his old turf. If things had changed, the surface remained pretty much the same: big front desk, off-white walls with a green border, and the same old septic smell of little hope and much despair. Cops in all shapes and sizes came and went, on duty, off duty, uniformed, undercover, the whole gamut of law enforcement. At a glance he could identify the few on the way up, and the remainder just hanging on for the twenty years—do the time, get the pension, then happily outta there. He could tell exactly where each was career-wise by measuring against the arc of his own thirty years of service—the eager beaver stage, the studied nonchalance of early middle years, the recommitted period when he decided there was nothing else he would rather do, and then the closing stretch when he knew he was up there with the best but hadn't a snowball's chance in hell of going higher.

Jimmy drifted off into tangled memory, listening to Gallagher's reassuring drone while reporting some standard non-event to a superior half his age who wanted to make something more of it. His first sergeant, Bull McDaid, shuffled by in silhouette, dead these twenty-five years, a giant of a man feared by every pimp and pusher on Eighth Avenue, and yet a host of little cancer sticks had whipped his ass at Sloan Kettering.

"Hey, Drew!" Gallagher hung up and shouted across the room. "Someone I want you to meet."

A young detective in a suit too well cut for surveillance winced at the familiarity but strode over.

"Know who this is? You happen to be in the exalted presence of Detective Sergeant Jimmy Murphy."

"The . . .?"

"Yeah, the one and only. Call yourself a detective and you don't know the Big Murph?"

"Father of Brian," Drew marveled and stuck out his hand. "Your son was an inspiration to many of us, sir."

Bit of a Brian in him too, Jimmy noted. Though Brian had a lot more smarts, not to mention a sense of humor about the whole thing. Could almost tell this guy's pedigree—good degree from Rutgers, could end up captain someday, or mayor of whatever shithole he came from. Knew whose ass should be kissed and exactly how often and when it should be done.

"Pleased to meet you, sir." Drew hurried off in his loafers, the fast track calling.

"Been meaning to drop over to Dolan's to see you," Gallagher said. "But you know how it is. Cecilia wants me straight home nowadays."

"Yeah, I get the picture." Jimmy smiled. Although he knew full well that neither wives nor girlfriends had managed to keep their hooks in Crazy Joey when there was even the slightest chance of free booze. Why were all his old compadres icing him? The way things were shaping up they'd take a rain check on his wake.

"A different world, right, Jimmy?"

"As different as you make it, pal."

Gallagher noted the change in tone and inquired somewhat sullenly, "What brings you here anyway?"

"Come to see DeVito."

Gallagher stared down glumly at his desk, shoved around a mound of papers like he was interested in what he was doing before mumbling, "He's in with some brass dropped by from headquarters. Better come by another day."

Jimmy leaned right into his face so the cop could identify exactly what he'd had for breakfast. "If there was brass from headquarters in there, Joey, you wouldn't be sitting here on your fat ass, unshaved, tie loose, and running this dump into the ground in your usual fucked-up manner. Now you tell DeVito I'm here."

"Jesus, Jimmy, what's with all the 'tude? Haven't I always been straight with you?"

"Actually, no! But we won't even get into that, despite the fact that I saved your sorry butt on two different occasions."

"I know that, man, and I've always been grateful. But DeVito don't want to see no one right now—getting his act together for July Fourth or some such shit. I'll put you on to Trujillo, his assistant, he'll set something up, okay?"

"I don't talk to the engine driver's rag when I come to see the engine driver. *Capisce?*"

"Okay, but keep your voice down, all right?" He glanced around the room and lowered his own. "You don't know who's listening no more."

"So how come I didn't go through DeVito's assistant the last time?"

"What do I know, man? I just do what I'm told around here."

"You always did, but there was a time you looked out for your brothers too. So you tell DeVito's *assistant* to inform the great man that I'll be back, and soon!"

"Yeah, Jimmy, sure. Listen, how's Maggie?"

"She's tip-top. Now where's Sullivan jerkin' off today?"

Gallagher swallowed and looked left and right. He lowered his voice even further. "He's on vacation."

"Don't give me that shit! The only vacation Sullivan ever took was out the track and he charged overtime for that."

"He had days coming and took some sick leave, I swear to God."

"I saw him a month ago—there was nothing wrong with him then except that he'd lost some of his big gut."

"Guys who were down the Towers—they get cut a lot of slack. That's why they brought him back up here."

"I was down there that day and no one gave a goddamn."

"Yeah but you came through Nam in one piece. Sullivan ain't been right in the head since the big bang—slates hitting his ass when he was running out the door."

"At least he got out."

Jimmy knew he was hitting the old blue wall. No matter how many years he'd put in, he wasn't a part of it anymore but still he persisted. "You got a number for him?"

"Sure, but you know Sullivan's game. Leaves a number but changes one of the digits."

Jimmy knew Sullivan's game well. Knew Gallagher's too. The desk cop was sweating and overeager to please. Someone further up the ladder had whispered and it had turned into a roar—didn't have to be much, it was all in the delivery—thirty years' service had evaporated, Jimmy Murphy was now officially bad news.

"My bet is he's down in PR with some young broad. I got the names of a couple of love shacks in San Juan he could be at. You want the numbers?"

"Yeah, with one digit changed."

He didn't even say good-bye. Didn't turn around either when Gallagher yelled out his name, just pushed through the smokers outside then strode east along 54th and across Eighth Avenue. He was only yards beyond Broadway when he noticed. Just before Seventh he was certain. The guy doing the shading was good enough so that Jimmy only barely caught a glimpse of a figure melting into doorways, but there was no doubt. He slowed down and mingled with the crowd waiting for the light on Seventh, but as soon as it changed he wheeled suddenly down the avenue then stepped inside the awning of an electronics store.

As Drew turned the corner his face dropped. He froze until Jimmy beckoned to him; then he strolled over with studied Cagney nonchalance, making the best of an awkward situation.

"Listen, I'm sorry about Brian, he looked out for me, okay?"

"And that's that?"

"What else could there be?"

"You tell me."

"There's nothing to tell. I just wanted you to know that."

There was little purpose in asking anything else. This cookie-cutter detective wouldn't tell him if his life depended on it; so they nodded at each other and went their separate ways. But Jimmy knew there was more to the shadowing than mere condolences.

There was no point in going to Dolan's. No matter how light his duties, working security demanded a clear head. He called Marcella, told her to make whatever excuse she thought fit, and hopped on the A.

What the hell was going on? DeVito wouldn't see him, Sullivan had bumped town, and Gallagher had introduced him to a rookie detective who was now tailing him. It all had to connect to Brian unless he had stumbled upon something else.

By the time the shuttle was lumbering out of Broad Channel he was sure of one thing. He needed a drink and had little stomach for facing Maggie and her questions about blowing off work—the dark corner of a saloon seemed just the ticket.

It definitely screwed his plan for alcoholic solitude when he entered The Inn to unexpectedly find the just-off-duty Fire crew knocking them back. They had the joint to themselves except for two old ladies by the door poring over the lineups before pissing away their Social Security on the ponies at Belmont.

No one noticed him in the general uproar so he remained in the shadows and took in the scene. Nothing much had changed, a juke-box playing Archie Bell & the Drells and every summer hit for the last forty years. Half a dozen rickety tables sprawled over some slippery floorboards that doubled as a dance floor on New Year's Eve. And still the painting of Bobby Sands in pride of place amidst the Irish Tricolor and the Stars & Stripes, while faded photos of the clientele hung askew on the Sheetrocked walls. There used to be one of himself and Sullivan back when they were at the Academy, out of their skulls and still looking forward to life. He tried to locate it and in so doing stepped into the light cast from the television screen.

"Dad?" Kevin didn't seem particularly enthralled to see him though he recovered quickly enough. "What are you having?"

Jimmy was greeted fondly by the crew, not that this made him special. If a yellow dog in a red velvet jacket had strolled in on its hind legs he'd have been welcome too—nothing like a bit of alcoholic solidarity when you should be home showering, shaving, and getting civilized again for wives, mothers, and long-suffering insignificant others.

"Give me a Jemmy on the rocks."

This hard-man request for an Irish whiskey was greeted by whoops of appreciation from the Bud and Coors Light community.

"Yeah?" Kevin raised his eyebrows.

"Why not? But not a word at home, okay?"

"What plays in the pub stays in the pub!" a burly mustachioed probie wearing a Shilelagh Law t-shirt shouted, setting off a further cacophony of hoots and hollers.

"Give him a double!" Eddie "Fatty" Sweeney ordered the bartender. "I still owe you for that Yankees ticket, Mr. Murphy."

"Don't sweat it, Eddie, I couldn't go anyway. No point in it going to waste."

Jimmy didn't like being pushed into drinking, didn't care for Fatty's arm draped around his shoulder either; in fact he hadn't much time for the guy in general. Still he didn't make a big point of disengaging, just moved closer to Kevin.

After two or three sips, the Jameson's began to work its considerable magic. The doubt and confusion that had clouded his head all the way out on the A began to dispel. Was it ever any different? Whatever was bothering you became the fault of the distant city and dissipated in the warm company of your Rockaway friends and neighbors.

Even Fatty Sweeney began to grow on him, especially after the second double. It was nice to hang with Kevin, just bullshitting about nothing and everything at the same time. It had been a long time since they'd let their hair down together—something always got in the way. Or was Jimmy himself the problem, had he become too uptight, always looking back, trying to re-create something that was gone forever?

At one point Kevin announced that he was splitting, had to be somewhere, but after the jeers of his crew, he said to hell with it, there was nothing that couldn't wait, and called a round.

Everything would have just breezed along if the bartender hadn't switched over to CNN and the newsflash announced that two marines had been taken out in Fallujah. Just the mention of the city's name brought more jeers from the drinkers and conjured up visions of the charred corpses of the American contractors that had hung upside down from its old railway bridge a few months earlier.

"Fucking sand niggers!" Sweeney shouted," Coming over here and blowing up our towers!"

"Yeah! We liberate those people and this is the thanks we get!"

Jimmy clenched his fists; his palms had become hot and sweaty despite holding the icy glass. He could tell what was coming and he'd rather be anywhere than The Inn, but leaving suddenly, and unsteadily, would cause more of a stir.

He knew Kevin was watching; could he sense what was going on or was he just worried his old man might add a dissenting spoke to the wheel of this patriotic piss-up?

The face showed up at odd times, just like it had come at him out of the mist and the jungle, a shocked teenage North Vietnamese soldier. It had faded down the years like the semi-dormant malaria that haunted him all through the 70s, but while there might have been quinine to deal with the Asian shivers, nothing seemed to treat this particular soul-sickness. Brian's death had brought it back into focus; there had been whole days since then when that Vietnamese face hovered on the fringes of his consciousness.

Up on the television screen a group of young grunts ambled across a dusty landscape dotted with palm trees and rutted with irrigation canals, backs bent from the heavy gear, their faded fatigues not melding closely enough with the filthy sand. Sweat and grime streaked their young faces. Should still be home in their trashed bedrooms playing video games, not old enough to cop a legal drink in their own country but kicking ass in its name halfway around the world in some dump where they're not wanted.

Then a close-up of a kid removing his goggles, no sign of fear on his baby face, yet Jimmy knew that mask only too well and how it hid a quiet storm of tension, exhaustion, loneliness, and dread, all hepped up and held together by low-grade panic. It was a rare day in Nam that he hadn't been on edge, sweating, steaming, squirming, every moment of it accompanied by a distinct nauseous churning deep down in his gut.

And then one evening forty miles south of Da Nang it all came to a head when he and the young NVA soldier walked right into each other in the eerie mist, that first nanosecond of silent adrenalized recognition, then each of them screaming and shouting, flailing and falling, and doing their level best to rip the other guy's eyes out.

"Brian would be alive if it hadn't been for those bastards." Sweeney's voice cut through the TV chatter and the white noise inside Jimmy's head.

The face of the Vietnamese kid pulled into view and hovered inches in front of him. There was no escaping the odor even above the beery smell of The Inn—the stale stench of jungle rot mixed with sweat and blood, and the sweet-and-sour smell of fear. Jimmy pitched backwards and grasped the bar counter. Kevin reached out to steady him.

"You know what I'm talking about, Mr. Murphy, right?" Sweeney's words pounded in his eardrums. "You gotta protect this country when it's been attacked!" Sweeney punched his fist in the air and then began a chant that was taken up by the others. "USA! USA! USA!"

He had battered that NVA face, dug his Ka-Bar into it and screamed until the sergeant dragged him off the bloody mess, slapped his ears, and brought him back to reality before punching him in the chest for giving away their position. Mortars were ripping big holes in the foliage, bullets were raking the muck; everyone was scattering and shouting and trying to find cover.

"USA! USA! USA!"

A kid from Omaha who had just joined them that morning cried out for his mother as he sank to his knees, his face twisted in pain, before toppling over facedown in a fetid pool. Only yards behind, Corporal Perez from East LA was yelling "Motherfucker!" and slamming his fist into his jammed M16.

"USA! USA! USA!"

They'd called in air support, and Hueys for the wounded, but it was too late. There was nothing to do but fight back and hold on, and pray that when the jets came they wouldn't blow the shit out of them too.

"USA! USA! USA!" The chant grew and the old ladies down the front banged their glasses in unison, Belmont and the ponies for once forgotten.

The jets did eventually come, but the NVA and their VC scouts heard them and had already retreated to their tunnels where they could listen to the jungle erupt all around them. And when the last echo of a jet had expired in the distance, there was an electric silence broken only by the stray cries of the wounded, and the sound of the rain chattering on the fallen leaves and the bloody pools of mucky water.

They lay there for minutes before regrouping and waiting for the comforting *whup-whup-whup* of the Hueys that would ferry away their dead and wounded—another meaningless skirmish over a useless strip of jungle that no one gave a damn about. And then they pressed on, their only objective to reach the end of the valley, turn around, and head back the way they had come, in search of a ghostly enemy who only emerged from their tunnels to kill Yankee devils in the mist and the rain.

"You were over in Nam, right, Mr. Murphy? You tell 'em, you gotta protect the homeland, right?"

Then it was gone. Just like that. The face faded, the static cleared, the room swung back into focus; the TV news morphed into an ad for toilet paper. All that was left was an ice-cool rage that would take a lot more than a skinful of Irish whiskey to subdue.

"No, Fatty. That's not the case."

The pressure dropped inside the bar at the casual mention of the hated nickname. Even the old ladies looked up from their racing pages.

"I was over in Nam invading another people's country. Just like those kids on the television are doing in Iraq. And those gooks and towelheads or whatever shit name you call them were fighting back, just like we would if they were here telling us how to run our country."

Sweeney's face was contorted with humiliation and rage. But it was too late to turn back and Jimmy didn't have any desire to do so anyway.

"I hated every minute I was over there because I was scared shitless and I had no idea what I was doing there except that some chicken hawk politician down in DC sent me. And thirty-five years later I still wake up in a lather of sweat at the sound of mortars and shells exploding in my ears.

"But you know what scared me more than anything else? A little runt of a North Vietnamese soldier fought me to a standstill, and that bag of bones would have killed me if I hadn't been able to dig my nails into his eyes until he couldn't stand the pain. And you know why he almost kicked my ass? Because he believed in what he was doing and I didn't. And there's hardly a day goes by but I don't think of that kid and wonder if he'd have children of his own now if I hadn't beaten the life out of him for no good reason. So you think long and hard about that before you dare use my son's name again."

He didn't expect Kevin to follow him out of The Inn but as Jimmy strode past he couldn't help but notice the look of frozen concern and dismay etched on his son's face.

FOURTEEN

At the Westport train station Morgan had been beaming. He didn't say it, but Fatima could tell—she had passed the Bradford family test with flying colors. It would have been hard not to, given his intensive coaching.

All eyes were on her at dinner in the beachfront house but she answered each question to everyone's satisfaction, and asked some of her own to show that she understood the intricacies of finance and had her own ideas about the market. She even managed to playfully deflect randy Uncle John's question about her father "selecting Miss Ibrahim's future husband."

Her only cultural faux pas was in wearing her hijab to the Congregational church. The whole community turned in tandem when Morgan escorted her to the family pew. She could hear the whispered comments on how striking they looked, he tall and blond, and she dark and statuesque in her "Muslim scarf."

Still, everyone in the family was charmed, and his sisters took turns "styling" the burgundy headscarf in their bedroom. How little these silly girls knew of her traditions or the reason for covering one's hair.

At drinks around the pool Morgan droned on and on about his favorite sapphire hijab that "matched" her skin tone. Surely he meant "complemented"? Brian would have known better. But then a margarita or two had little effect on Brian. Funny that she should think of him on such an occasion. Brian could fit anywhere, be it old-money Westport or her father's falafel parlor on Atlantic Avenue. Morgan, for all his saccharine merits, understood little beyond his own severely circumscribed world.

Still he was cute and her boyfriend, and she returned his good-bye kiss at the station. On the train home, however, doubts began to gather. While her father and his British affectations might pass muster with the Bradfords, she shuddered to think how her mother would freeze under their scrutiny. The etiquette and chitchat of the club would be so beyond her.

Brian still came to mind with any stress regarding assimilation, no doubt because he had been a bridge to many new experiences. She had felt a rare comfort in his presence for he instinctively understood the depth of her beliefs. That's why she had given him the information he requested. How important was it anyway—the names of some men who no longer attended the mosque, men who cared nothing for the rights of women, or anyone else for that matter? Her father said she had placed her whole family in danger and had no idea of the consequences of her actions. He insisted she live at home for months after the attack, drove her to and from Barnard, forbade her to leave the house at night, and warned her not to speak to strangers. With time the shock passed and life went on, but now there was no Brian, just a dull ache where once there had been a warm expectation.

She had read about the "month's mind" they were holding for him at the church in Rockaway and had taken the A train out on that blustery October day when the whole city was still in mourning. But though she stood outside the forbidding Christian building clutching her flowers she couldn't bring herself to go in, fearing the same reception her father had received at the wake. Instead she walked down the boardwalk and inhaled the same air Brian used to—watched the same gulls, and on an impulse hailed a car service to take her down to Breezy Point.

At the security gate she flashed her student card and smiled innocently at the burly guard but he waved them on for he recognized the driver. The sad-eyed Haitian man drove her to 220th Street and parked on the corner—she had told him she was writing an article about 9/11 heroes for her college newspaper and wished to soak in the atmosphere of a community that had suffered much loss.

Sure enough he pointed up at a big house with blinds drawn and informed her that was the home of Lieutenant Brian Murphy, "one of the martyrs." She rolled down the window though a fine mist was seeping in from the Atlantic. The Haitian stared straight ahead, obviously a man of some discretion. She felt empty and bereft, and so terribly out of place. And then she remembered a line that Brian often quoted, written by her father's favorite, the poet of Alexandria: "From all I did and all I said let no one try to find out who I was."

Had Brian some idea of the tragedy that would befall him? He understood so much about other people—including her. Did he have similar insights into his own life?

"I took two others of your people here." The Haitian broke the silence, lilting softly in his island patois.

"Oh?" she replied, but felt like saying, Where did they hitch their camels?

"Yes, but that was some months before the conflagration. They said they were friends of Lieutenant Murphy's though they chose not to go in."

The flowers that she'd brought for the church lay on her lap. She picked them up and opened the door of the car. The Haitian watched as she strode toward the big house. A large osprey, not unlike those she'd seen in Alexandria, glided high above. She paused at the gateway; what would she say if Brian's wife had chosen not to attend the month's mind? But knowing the Haitian was watching, she opened the gate with a clang and climbed the steps to the front door. A sudden gust caused her to pull her hijab tighter, obscuring most of her face. Just then a sound at the window caught her attention and she turned to see a very pale young boy stare out from behind the blinds. His eyes filled with fear at the sight of her and in shock she dropped the bunch of flowers by the door. The blinds clattered once more against the window, the boy disappeared, and a light went on in the room. She turned and hurried back down the steps to the car.

The Haitian eased out of his front seat and opened the back door, took her by the elbow, and gently helped her into her seat. She sat for a moment wondering if she should go back and leave the card she had inscribed. As if in answer she heard the low comforting moan of a foghorn that Brian had described so well. When the sound finally faded away they sat in silence. Then the Haitian caught her eyes in the mirror and saw that she was crying. He stared ahead until the first drops of rain meandered down the windshield then he started the car and once more looked back at her. When she nodded he pulled out into the enveloping fog and drove her back down to Rockaway and the train at Beach 116th Street station.

FIFTEEN

"That's the first time I've heard you singing in a long time."

"Go on with you. I'm always singing to myself." Maggie laughed.

"Maybe," Jimmy said. "But not out loud. Anyway, it's nice to hear it again."

"Shows what a good night's sleep will do for you."

He had been surprised to find her sitting on the front porch when he stormed back from The Inn. He felt decidedly alert, not his usual disassociated self after an episode. His mind darted this way and that—a ball of nerves anticipating every eventuality. It had been a bad scene but he'd gotten off lightly for there was a moment when he might have done serious damage to the flabby firefighter. He badly needed a beer to come down; not to mention Maggie hadn't smelled the hard liquor yet. His hand was trembling as he opened the fridge.

"Pour me a glass of wine and bring it out here, will you," she called. "It's such a lovely afternoon."

A half-empty bottle of Chardonnay stood in front of the six-pack. She was taking a drink again? Strange, she never mixed pills and booze. He fought to steady his hand as he poured the wine and cracked his beer; inadvertently he caught a glimpse of himself in the sink mirror. His face was pale, almost gray, rigid and creased. He forced himself to smile in order to loosen the muscles but he still looked like a hangman after a hard day at the gallows.

"I slept so soundly last night." She took the wine from him, stretching luxuriously before curling her bare feet beneath her.

"You get some new pills?"

"Where have you been, Detective Sergeant Murphy? I emptied the whole kit and caboodle down the toilet weeks ago."

How could he have missed that? Back when he was on the job he'd have noticed such a change instantly. Maybe he was losing his chops. Still, pride caused him to lamely inquire, "You don't think you might be needing them again?"

"I'm hardly going to be mixing them with wine like those degenerates down on the boardwalk. Anyway, it was the best thing I did in years. It must be well over a month now because I stopped taking them right after I began the First Fridays."

As she sipped the wine she stared off toward the ocean, her eyes alert, chin thrust slightly forward. He could tell she was listening for the sound of the breakers. She always did when the winds blew offshore and the waves pounded the beach. The ocean bound them together and they had never seriously contemplated moving away from Rockaway; as dramatic and treacherous as the waves could be, at some level they both recognized that even after the worst storm order always returned—though with their own troubles they'd been waiting almost three years now.

She had begun to hum; at first he thought it was one of her granny's ballads but then he recognized "Tantum ergo" from the benediction. He had liked the tune himself as a boy but now it bothered him.

"Maggie, I don't mean to spoil the party or nothing but what's with all the religion? There was a time I'd have to drag you to church for a funeral."

"It's working, Jimmy. Come with me on Friday, it would be good for you—good for us too."

She reached out to him but he didn't take her hand, afraid she might notice his tremor.

"Nah, you know me. I'm a midnight Catholic. Things go wrong, I pray with the best of them." He shrugged. "But, hey, if it got you off the pills . . ."

"It's more than that, love. It's just like a whole weight has been lifted off me."

"Well, it is going on three years."

She took a longer sip and savored the wine for a moment. A monarch landed on the clematis that wound around the porch railing. It was a rare occasion when she didn't comment on such a sighting, as she feared for their lessening numbers; instead she frowned. "You know I cursed God the morning He took Brian, and I would have taken it to my grave before I'd have forgiven Him."

Jimmy looked away. This was the last thing he needed. He stuck his hand in his pocket.

"No, Jimmy, please." She leaned over, forcing him to look at her. "I don't know where this will end up, but it has something to do with the First Fridays."

"Maggie, listen to me, will you? The thing with religion—it's like a drug. Once it kicks in you got to keep using it. But if for some reason it stops working, the original problem can seem a whole lot worse."

"I don't care. I feel like God is finally listening to me."

"God is a big word for guys like me. I just don't want you to get hurt again, that's all."

She gently touched his cheek. "Things do change, Jimmy. You have to believe that."

"Yeah, Sullivan gave up the sauce and you take it up again."

"Richie Sullivan?"

"Lost about thirty pounds and remember all those purple veins? His face is as clear as a baby's bottom now. Jesus Christ! Remember him at the wake? Shit-faced and making a show of himself."

The house thick with people, everyone knocking back the free booze—bad news galloping down the Beach to Breezy and back again. Fire Department had taken huge hits, cops, EMS, and young financials too. No one could believe Brian hadn't made it out. Rescuing the seven people, that was par for the course for the golden boy, Rockaway's best running back, the last-gasp hero who dived over the line with seconds to go. His death just didn't make sense.

Maggie stone-faced and ashen being comforted by the old biddies and holding it together as best she could. Kevin dazed in his black suit, surrounded by his Fire homies, still unable to take it all in. A loud hum of conversation that periodically peaked as more bad news arrived. And then a crash in the hall as Sullivan arrived and knocked over a picture of the boys as kids. Didn't even bother to sweep up the glass, just staggered into the room, a survivor with the white dust still clinging to him, the center of attention, he held the floor and gave a blow-by-blow account of the morning's drama until he came to Brian whereupon he upped the ante and his tears flowed like twin rivers. Down Sullivan went on his knees begging Maggie's forgiveness for not stopping her eldest from sprinting back up those smoky stairs.

"Poor Richie, he always meant well," she said quietly.

"Poor Richie, my ass! He was the last one to see Brian alive and the bastard could barely remember a word he said."

"Please, Jimmy, let the matter rest. It does no good anymore."

"No, Sullivan knew more than he was saying. Even if it wasn't something any of us might want to hear."

She looked up sharply, razor-edged again, remembering Brian's instructions that she should talk to Sullivan should anything happen to him.

"What are you implying?"

"I don't know, Maggie. Brian wasn't even on duty. It's just too much of a coincidence that he and Sullivan ran into each other."

"They were friends, these things happen," she said unconvincingly.

"Brian didn't hang out with losers, especially at eight fifteen on a Tuesday morning."

"You're letting your mind run away with you again."

"Jesus, Maggie, I was on the job thirty years. There's something wrong with the picture, maybe Sullivan had something on Brian."

"What are you suggesting?"

"Brian didn't always play by the book, know what I mean?"

"Whatever Brian was doing down there, you can be sure it was in the line of duty," she snapped.

"I'm not saying anything against him, but I can't get a straight answer from anyone—the whole department is shunning me, and I can tell Sullivan's hiding something. He can't look me in the eyes anymore."

"Jimmy, did it ever occur to you that this might all be in your head—that there's a perfectly logical explanation, and if Brian had survived we wouldn't be giving any of it a second thought? Please, let's drop this now. It just gets us all upset."

She put her arms around him and held him close. He could feel his body stiff and tense next to her warmth; he couldn't remember when she'd last held him like that. He surrendered to the fatigue. How easy it would be to drop all the questions and stop banging his head against an official wall.

"Yeah, I suppose you're right," he whispered.

She smiled and the old tenderness surfaced in her eyes if only for a moment and a vague hope arose. Maybe this was the time to introduce the matter. "You know, there's something I've been meaning to talk to you about."

She put down the wineglass and sat up in the chair, placing her feet firmly on the wooden deck. He'd always liked her feet—petite and slim. She'd recently had a pedicure and her nails sparkled with a golden tint. In an odd way this new look gave him the courage to continue. "It's going on three years now."

She looked past him but he gently persisted. "Do you know what I'm getting at?"

"You've been very patient with me."

"You know, it's not the . . . well, the sex or anything. It's just we might be losing other things."

She was quiet for a moment. "I know, Jimmy, I'm not unmindful of what's happened between us."

"I figured I'd better bring it up, not have it hanging over us, like."

"Yes, I'm sure it's for the best," she said with a hint of finality.

"Well, I guess that's the long and the short of it." He looked away. "There's nothing much more I wanted to say."

She stood up and retreated to the kitchen. He had overstepped, gone too far. But then he heard the clink of glass, the pouring of wine, and she reappeared on the porch.

"Can you give me a little longer?"

"Sure, whatever."

"It's just that, I don't feel right within myself. Do you know what I mean?"

"It's no big deal, okay?"

"No, I think we should talk about it and things are getting better. Trust me."

"Hey, maybe the old First Fridays will kick in." He smiled.

"I know it's been hard on you, Jimmy, but it will work out, I promise."

He nodded, eager to put the matter to rest.

"There are other signs too," she said, her eyes glinting with excitement. "Haven't you noticed Kevin? And Rose?"

"What about them?"

"Well, Kevin's not drinking like he was. He talks to me all the time now. He was even on the phone with St. John's, inquiring about finishing his degree. And Rose was over here the other day, done up to the nines. Maybe she is seeing someone. I mean as hard as it would be, she's not cut out for widowhood and there's many the nice catch out there."

"She'll be a bit of a catch herself with the money that's coming to her. That's what troubles me, a lot of losers might take advantage of her."

"Well, she'll have to sort that out herself. Liam needs a father, and we'll all have to be very big about it when she does remarry." She kissed him on the cheek and then took his hands. "I have a favor to ask you. Just humor me, okay?"

"Sure, whatever you want."

"Leave yourself open to what's happening, all right? God is good and He can work for you too."

"Well, bring Him on. Throw His best shot—I stand at the ready."

"Just have faith and everything will come out all right. Okay? Now I'm off to water the plants before they die of the thirst, and then I'm going to give Rose a call. Have her and Liam over for dinner soon. Maybe she'll break some news to us. You be good now, okay."

"I'll do my best."

He watched her stroll around her small garden, singing to herself. He knew she'd be thinking of her granny and how the old lady loved to describe the wildflowers back in County Galway. He knew she'd be comparing her own sandy oasis of roses, peonies, and daylilies with the untamed wonders of a rainy haggart three miles beyond Clifden. The verse she sang of the old lady's favorite song was a giveaway:

The people were saying, no two e'er were wed
But one had a sorrow that never was said
And then she turned homeward with one star awake
Like the swan in the evening moves over the lake

There was no mistaking the improvement in her mood, the way she moved, the rare sparkle that had returned to her eyes. He had waited a long time and it was beyond welcome, but thirty years on the job warned him that something else was also in the offing and wouldn't be long about arriving. That was the problem with the God Game. Jimmy Murphy had never trusted it—much less cared for its rules. Damned thing came with too many umpires.

SIXTEEN

The kid sure liked having a man about the place. He even spent time in the living room watching the big television, his little tousled head resting on Kevin's bare arm. He'd never dream of sitting out there with her even with the bait of his favorite treats. When they were alone he stuck to his room glued to the computer.

Rose was allowed in to deliver meals and fuss around for a limited time, but eventually Liam would glare at her, signaling that she'd overstayed her visit.

It was much the same when his father was alive. Rose would do all the work, taking him to and from pre-K and play dates, but the minute Brian came bounding into the house with candy or a toy, up the kid would jump and leap into his father's arms.

Was he sullen at all back then? It was hard to remember. Things tended to fog up whenever Rose tried to summon her previous life. He definitely had his temper tantrums—what overindulged kid didn't? It was so different from how she'd grown up—the middle of five, lucky to get a single gift at Christmas from a stressed-out mom and a rummy dad instead of a room full of bow-tied boxes arrayed around a huge Christmas tree with multicolored twinkling lights.

That was life with Lieutenant Murphy—so strobe-lit it was hard to distinguish one highlight from another. It had been exciting, there was no denying, getting dressed up, speeding into Manhattan in the back of a limo, meeting this one and that, faces you only saw on television. But in the end, much of it felt like froth splashed on the shore.

Now the kid's sullenness was an everyday occurrence. Only Kevin and Jimmy could pierce it. Did they remind him of his father? What did he even remember about Brian? He refused to talk about him. But she couldn't give up, and persevered even if it always led to tantrums from him, and silent tears later in her bedroom.

What was this whole thing about his dad's "warning" anyway? She had tried to bring it up a number of times and it always led to Liam punching her shoulder in aggravation. She'd asked Jimmy to come down and get to the bottom of the kid's fear but every time he suggested dropping by, Kevin was staying over.

To top it all there was Tiffany Walsh and the summer camp fiasco to deal with. Why did the little bitch have to say anything about Brian? Kids could be so cruel—and stupid! She should have made sure her ear was well out of harm's way; lucky they weren't stitching a piece of it back on after Liam chomped on it.

And then being forced to deal with Nancy Walsh who was never less than a pain in the butt growing up. She had never liked Rose, especially after Brian got sweet on her. Those Walsh women were always bad news—flaunting everything on the beach, and now there was a new generation of them to deal with. Well, Miss Tiffany would be careful the next time she made a remark about another kid's father.

"Mom, can I have one of them pizzas?" Liam's request snapped her back to reality. Life was almost normal when Kevin visited, particularly when he and the kid stretched out on the couch watching *The Simpsons*.

Rose smiled as Kevin laughed uproariously at Bart's antics, to be followed by Liam's chuckle morphing into a raucous imitation of his uncle. It might be a dumb show, but at least the kid was laughing, if only to impress his uncle.

"Mom, did you hear me, can I have one of them pizzas?"

"Had enough of *The Simpsons*?"

"Yeah, think I'll go in my room."

Kevin winked at her and she smiled back. He made little secret of what was on his mind. It definitely made for a change.

She tossed a pepperoni in the microwave and brought it to her son's bedroom. He already had his earphones on and was perched in front of his computer in rapt attention as some gross-looking figures hacked away at each other. He didn't even nod as she laid the pizza down by the monitor screen, but at least he'd just had some kind of human interaction.

She fixed her hair in the hall and strolled back in. Kevin was already engrossed in another *Simpson*'s episode and chuckling along to a Homer rant. She stood close to him but he didn't look up.

"Kevin?"

Nor did he respond.

"This is great," she murmured.

But he was fixated on Homer's last statement to a flummoxed Mr. Burns.

"I mean this is everything I've ever dreamed of."

"What's that?" Kevin replied.

"Well, I've got one kid saving Frodo and zapping the whole Orc population, while the other has his head buried in some cartoon."

"What's wrong with a little TV? And anyway, it's not a cartoon, it's *The Simpsons*."

"There's nothing wrong with a *little* TV. But we should be down the beach swimming, it is the middle of July."

"Jeez, I just got off tour two or three hours ago. Helps me unwind."

"Well, I can't think with it on."

"What's there to think about?"

"What's there to think about? Now, let me consider." She stepped in front of the television and considered this question before throwing her hands to the heavens. "Well, seeing you put it like that, I have to admit I don't know. Maybe the whole world should flop down on their butts and study Marge's hairdo."

"Shit! I just missed Homer's best line."

"How do you know it's his best line if you didn't hear it?"

"Because I seen it before. How do you think I know?"

"For some crazy reason I thought that when you'd seen a thing once you didn't watch it again."

"This is not just about TV, is it?" He flicked it off with the remote.

"Why don't you tell me?"

"Listen, I turned it off 'cause you said we should talk about things—not let them stew."

"So talk."

"Okay! How about I'm sick to the teeth of sneaking in and out of here like I'm something to be ashamed of."

"What do you want to do, make an announcement next Sunday at St. Thomas More's? We've still got to figure out the best way to do this."

"Okay, okay, so there's things to be worked out. But in the meantime if I feel like catching a little TV to chill out, I don't need a federal case made of it. And don't tell me my brother didn't watch *The Simp-sons*. He knew whole shows by heart."

"When your brother was here, he had other things on his mind."

She regretted it even as the words were tumbling out of her mouth. He sat rigid as though slapped in the face before bounding to his feet and heading for the back door. She hurried after him but he was only going to the kitchen for a beer.

"Hey, I got a couple of things on my mind too, but every time we start . . ." He pointed down the hallway to Liam's room.

"I'm sorry, Kevin. I didn't mean it like that. Brian was a lieutenant. Sometimes it seemed like the whole world had his number."

"Yeah, and he spent too much time with the world and not enough with us. Those Manhattan people made him think he was someone."

"He *was* someone."

"And I'm not?"

"I didn't say that. I only meant . . ."

He tossed the empty can into the sink and opened another. "Yeah, but they were using him—the men and the women."

"Oh Jesus." She strode right over to him. "You could be a little more subtle, couldn't you?"

"Subtle, my ass! I've had enough of this shit."

He slammed the beer down on the kitchen table and this time did head for the back door, but she got there first. "I don't want to fight, Kev. It's just—this is not an easy situation and we have things to fig-ure out."

She put her hand on his chest then slid it up to his throat and around his neck. She buried her face in his shoulder and pressed against him. At first he resisted but when she put her knee behind his thigh, he grabbed her hair back and kissed her hard on the mouth. He slipped his hand down the back of her skirt and dug his fingers into her flesh. But when he lifted her skirt she pushed his hand away.

"No, Kev, he might hear and I don't want him to get upset again."

"So the kid bites one of those dumbass Walshes! It's not the end of the world. Besides his door is closed and he has his earphones on."

"I'm just so scared since that happened."

He broke away from her. She heard him mutter about getting more action down the firehouse as he stalked around the kitchen, but she made no effort to stop him slamming his beer down or cursing. It was as if she had muted him but could still see the picture, though it was dull and barely noticeable against the nightmare clarity of her little boy cowering in the corner when she arrived.

What if Liam had heard them in her room? What if he did know about their relationship? He'd always been well behaved around other kids, even shy and withdrawn after Brian's death. She couldn't live with herself if she was the cause of what had happened with Tiffany—and with September and the commemoration less than two months away it might even get worse.

Suddenly the mute was off and Kevin was right in her face. "Listen, I don't know about you, but I got to get out of here before I go crazy! Why don't we drop the kid off with my mom, go down The Inn and get ripped?"

He took out his cell phone and flicked it open.

"No, Kevin! I'll tell you when."

"You're giving me orders again! This ain't the old days when you and Brian were kings of the hill and I was your fucking chauffeur."

"It's not like that. Please." She reached out her hand, but he refused to take it. "You're all I have now, you and my son."

It took a while for the words to sink in but eventually he reached out and touched the tips of her fingers with his.

"It might help if you told me more often."

"You know how I feel." She murmured as he drew her closer. She took his earlobe in her mouth and bit it softly.

"It doesn't hurt to hear it." He pulled her close again but this time gently. "I mean, what's the worst that can happen? A big blast of bullshit and gossip! Then it's all over and we can get on with our lives."

He surely couldn't be so naïve as to think it would be that simple—that Nancy Walsh would drop by for afternoon tea just to wish her a happy life with her second Murphy.

"You do love me don't you?" he demanded, his eyes blazing again as he grabbed her by the wrist.

"You know I love you," she whispered.

"So what do you want me to do?" He suddenly let go of her wrist and spoke casually as if nothing had just happened between them.

"You've got to set your mother up for this."

"Okay." He picked up his beer, wandered back into the living room, and sat down in front of the television.

"Then when you're finished I'll talk to her, okay?"

"Done deal." He flicked on the remote.

"There's so much to think about and work out."

"What's that?" He chuckled at Marge berating Homer.

"Well, whether we should stay here and add the new extension or go to Florida, like we talked about."

"We'll figure it out."

"We'd get a great price for this house. Add that to the settlement— we could get a really nice place down there. But then there's the schools and what will you do for a job? What did St. John's say?"

"What?"

"About finishing your degree?"

"Uh. They, uh . . ." He slapped his leg in delight as Homer did a swan dive out of a tall building, yelling the whole way down until he was yanked from flight by the branch of a tree. "Oh yeah, they told me to drop by and see a counselor."

"Did you make an appointment?"

"Couldn't find my papers—credits and shit—Mom is tracking them down."

When the branch of the tree broke to Kevin's accompanying squalls of delight she poured a glass of milk and brought it to Liam's room. She placed it next to the other glasses that circled his computer and made a note to wear long sleeves in the morning.

SEVENTEEN

Jimmy grimaced as he lurched down the boardwalk into the warm damp breeze, the stray grains of wet sand pelting him in the eyes. He nodded at the few regulars braving the weather, but he had no desire to talk to any of them. What was there to say—"Wet enough for you, George? Rough day for August, Mike?" Instead he made his way to a spot where the wind always blew harshest and stared out at the crazies in wetsuits balancing atop their boards, so many black seals waiting for the perfect wave even in the teeth of this squall. Not for the first time he wondered what was the attraction—a mad dash across the back of a wave followed by the inevitable undignified plunge into the pounding surf?

Just another junky compulsion, and God knows Rockaway had seen enough of those in his lifetime. He used to worry about his two boys and the beach drug culture—not very likely with Brian, but with Kevin there was always the chance of him skidding into darkness.

What's going on with that kid! Kev was a homebody who exulted in the security of the house. Yet he hadn't been around for days on end, and even when he did darken their door lately it was hard not to notice that some other force was pulling him away.

There was a time Jimmy might have confided in Maggie, but he was wary about raising any more red flags. He couldn't turn to Rosie. She knew Kev better than anyone, but she was already up to her eyes in Murphy issues—no point in putting any more pressure on her.

And anyway, you had to be careful on the peninsula. Loose lips definitely sank ships. Blab about something in Connolly's or The Circle and, before you knew it, your concern had swept up and down the west end between 95th and the Surf Club with stops for refueling at

Kennedy's and The Blarney until it bore scant resemblance to the original problem, except that your name was still etched all over it.

He knew he should have gone down to Rosie's weeks ago. He'd promised her he'd try and find out what Liam was so upset about. But every time he brought it up the kid was away on a play date, had been acting up or whatever. Although to his practiced ear it sounded more like she just had a bad dose of in-lawitis and needed her space.

Something else bothered him too—the fear that he'd lost it. His own son had zoomed past him up the ladder. Jimmy knew he was no Sherlock Holmes. After all, this was New York—not the movies! He didn't solve crimes smoking opium and wearing a deerstalker. Like everyone else he did it by following leads, putting pressure on people and praying they'd crack enough to give him some glimpse of what might be going on.

There was something even worse; could the toxic dust that had filled his lungs that morning down the Towers have seeped into his brain? All sorts of horror stories were being traded back and forth between first responders—coughs, cancers, cardiac arrests, brain tumors, and worst of all, the debilitating despair that more could have been done for brothers and sisters who didn't live to see another day.

Then another surly blast of damp sandy wind hit him full in the face and he muttered, "To hell with it!" and strode off to the subway. He knew he was heading to Manhattan, he just didn't know where.

The train lumbered across churning Jamaica Bay, the wind whipping up jittery sea horses atop waves that lapped against the stilted houses of Broad Channel. Talk about Rockaway being cut off—people on the Channel were a real breed apart. More like small-town Maine than New York City. Step off the shuttle down onto the narrow streets and you could almost hear psychic alarm bells go off—stranger in town! But most outsiders chose to wait impatiently for the A, noses in the air, rather than linger on this island fastness spread-eagled across the bay.

Lurching past Kennedy Airport, he idly watched the big jets gliding in and taking off. There were times when he wished he could just pack up and go, like he did for Nam, leave the peninsula and its muddle of cares behind. He hadn't been to many places in the world after his discharge. Felt he was lucky just to make it back in one piece and stayed put for years on end.

Ireland had been an eye-opener—worlds away from the old men pubs in Irish Town with their laments about moonlight in Mayo, and Mountains of Mourne sweeping down to the sea. Most people on the emerald isle were decent enough—they just felt that Yanks were far from "the full shilling." But once you got beyond their Paddy self-righteousness, Johnny Cash's forty shades of green were even more vivid than he'd imagined. Still, at the end of the day, Jimmy felt more at home in bombed-out Belfast than any of the four green fields—the Falls and the Shankill brought to mind Far Rockaway, different accent and color of skin, but much the same problems without solutions.

He heard the beat before the train even pulled up at Rockaway Boulevard. When the door opened the young man swept aboard in a swoosh of his oversized red tracksuit, sky-blue Dodgers cap pulled low, his boom box shuddering to a jackhammer kick and snare.

There was a time when Jimmy knew his Public Enemy, even had a sneaking regard for KRS-One—in fact he was fine with most old school—but new breed rap left him cold. And yet he recognized that young black men had little other way to make their voices heard except through their street poets, crass though the trappings of the message could be. And so he looked away when the brother gave him the hairy eyeball. When he was on the job he'd have flashed his badge and told him to "shut that thing the fuck up!" But hey, "fight the power, man," it wasn't his battle anymore. Let DeVito, Sullivan, and Bloomberg ride the A for a change and do their own dirty work.

And so 50 Cent bitched on through the straining speakers nailing the other passengers to the walls as Jimmy passed by Euclid and all the other broken avenues of East New York wondering why nothing ever changed for the poor even as the world shifted on greased wheels for those with means.

These rutted streets had been Brian's proving ground. The "cop who made a difference" had done more than that—he had changed lives. A handful of his former posse had shown up at his wake, serious young black men going to college out of town, come to pay their respects to someone who'd seen a spark in their eyes and taken the time to kindle it. The wake had been like a carnival, all the different stars from Brian's various galaxies coming together for the first time, nervously eyeing one another, no one with much notion of the others, drinking, jostling, vying for their place, who knew him best, who had worked with him, played with him, drunk with him, slept with him, until the whole dizzy cacophony sounded like a psychedelic Coney Island Saturday night.

Then into the midst of it stepped Yussef, the friend Jimmy had made during the investigation of the 1993 World Trades bombing. The man from Egypt who'd opened his heart and family to him, seeking only to hold on to the bedrock of his traditions while balancing the demands of the American dream.

He didn't even know who mouthed the insult though the nasally voice pierced the hubbub that had already drowned out any idea of decorum in O'Connor's funeral home. "What's a fuckin' towelhead doin' here?"

There had been many the "shush" and "shut the hell up," but the damage was done, even though Yussef allowed it to glance off his natural dignity. He offered his condolences and left immediately, head held high, looking neither left nor right as he strode out of that room and Jimmy's life.

There had been many times in the next months when Jimmy had meant to drop by, but he'd let it slide. And then the months turned into years, and his shame at what had happened deepened until he banished Yussef to a far corner of his mind, only to be taken out and dusted off on guilt-driven sleepless nights.

The young man had departed the train back on Nostrand Avenue taking his pumping boom box with him and leaving Jimmy to his memories and failed intentions. On an impulse he leaped up and caught the sliding subway doors as they closed on Jay Street–Borough Hall.

"What the fuck!" A tall black figure in a dashiki snarled as Jimmy brushed past him.

"Sorry, man." Jimmy wrestled with the door, holding on and waiting for it to slide back.

"Fuck you think you are?"

The door opened and Jimmy jammed his heel in it, his rage stirring.

"Detective Sergeant James Murphy," he growled. "Now you were saying?"

The man in the dashiki held his ground, as did Jimmy until he grasped the outcome of this no-win situation. The other passengers had frozen in anticipation of a confrontation, except for a young couple that edged further down the car, the guy shielding his girl.

Jimmy stepped out onto the platform then swung around. The tall man glowered back unrepentant. The door had jammed and the conductor leaned out the window some cars ahead; passengers on the train drifted away from the tall man, now a barbed island of defiance anchored to the sticky carriage floor. The door screeched closed and the train staggered forward. Mouth set, Jimmy watched it pull away before striding up the stairs and out into busy, bustling Brooklyn. Some blocks down Court he took a right on Atlantic Avenue, an artery to the heart of Muslim New York, and made his way to 144, a small, neatly painted storefront. In the distance he could see the blue of New York Harbor and remembered how the proprietor had once told him that he always liked to be within sight of flowing water as he had grown up on the banks of the mighty Nile.

Yussef stood the moment he saw Jimmy ease into the warmth and hushed conversation of his falafel parlor; though he didn't smile, his grave brown eyes brimmed initially with surprise and then welcome. They stared at each other across small tables full of late-lunching workers. From behind the counter Yussef's wife, Maryam, gave a startled little cry and raised her hand to her mouth. Then Yussef opened his arms and the two old friends embraced.

Nothing was said but for the first time since a desolate September night almost three years before Jimmy did not fight back the tears. Yussef gently patted his back and waited a seemly time. Then he called for tea and baklava as Jimmy took Maryam's hands in his and noted that the pain of Brian's passing had also been felt in this household.

The two men sat at a table toward the back of the room and spoke of this and that before Jimmy said, "Can you forgive me for what was said at Brian's wake? I should have found that coward and thrown him out."

"And brought havoc to what was already the most difficult of occasions for your wife and family?"

"I should have come sooner, Yussef."

"You came when the time was right, James, just as I knew you would. Sometimes we can only be as big as we are."

"Jesus, you always had a way of hitting the nail on the head."

"How are you, my friend?"

"You know how it is—been a tough three years."

"And your wife?"

"She's better, but I wouldn't say it's been easy."

"No. How could it be otherwise?"

He took Jimmy's hand in his and laid his other palm on top of it. Jimmy remembered the first time that happened and how embarrassed he'd been. Over the years he had grown used to the warmth of the gesture and welcomed it.

Yussef had changed little: his receding hair perhaps a little thinner, a few flecks of gray in his well-trimmed beard, but still a handsome, erect man approaching late middle age.

"Is there some way I can be of help?"

Such a simple question but no one had put it quite like that before. Jimmy struggled for words that might capture the storm that tossed inside his head. Yussef waited patiently, his deep-set brown eyes glowing with understanding.

"I don't know, man, I just don't seem to be able to come to terms with things. I guess I can't let go."

Yussef held his hand a little tighter. "I have no easy answers for you, James. It's all in the acceptance of God's will. When we resist we call down unhappiness on ourselves and those close to us."

"We've talked about this before."

"It's an ongoing battle, and each day we must pray for the strength to carry on."

"There are times I wish I believed like you."

"Perhaps someday you will, *inshallah*."

Jimmy smiled and took his hand away when Maryam poured more of the hot sweet tea. She brushed some crumbs of the baklava from the table and smiled at him. She looked older—a network of tiny crow's-feet webbed the skin around her kind brown eyes, while melancholia had dulled her customary effervescence. What sorrows had she endured in his absence? Her smile still flashed readily, but it now contained some strained element of concern beyond friendship and compassion that he was unable to place. The men were silent until she retreated back behind the counter.

Jimmy swept the small room—the usual downtown Brooklyn assortment of courthouse workers and North African immigrants mixing easily and enjoying the pita sandwiches and honey-sweet pastries. He wondered if Yussef had suffered more insults beyond that thrown at him during the wake. Thankfully, there had been remarkably little physical retaliation against the Muslim community in the wake of 9/11, but with American losses mounting in Iraq it could only be a matter of time. Yussef might love America, but his concept of the country was worlds away from the current DC model. Although he hated Saddam, he had not approved of American troops remaining on the holy ground of Kuwait after the Gulf War; apart from religious considerations, he instinctively understood that it would breed unrest in the region. Jimmy had little doubt that his friend would deem the latest incursion into Iraq to be unmitigated madness. As Yussef sipped his tea Jimmy studied him and was surprised to recognize the same odd concern that he had noticed in Maryam's smile.

Could it have anything to do with the Quran that Yussef had given Brian—the one with the card that contained his signature and the enigmatic inscription? Did he suspect that was what had brought Jimmy to the falafel parlor and not just a quest for forgiveness over a stray insult at his son's wake?

"I always liked the sound of that word."

"What word is that?" Yussef looked up.

"*Inshallah*, it covers so much."

"God covers everything."

"But God must want us to find the truth."

"His truth—not ours."

"Aren't they one and the same?"

"What truth is it you seek, my friend?"

"I want to know what Brian was doing down in the North Tower half an hour before the attack."

Yussef at first held his eyes, refusing to speak, but then a beautiful young woman strolled into the parlor causing men to glance up from their food. Tall, confident, and olive-skinned, her dark hair tumbling, down over her shoulders, she walked straight up to Yussef who frowned when she kissed him on the cheek.

"Father, I've just come from the gym," she said loudly, casting a defiant glance at two disapproving young Egyptian men who sat at a table near Yussef.

Yussef nodded his acceptance of her lack of a hijab as Jimmy stood and shook hands with Fatima.

"Mr. Murphy." She smiled back at him.

"I haven't seen you in so long."

"You came to our party here when I was accepted at Barnard."

"It was that long ago?"

"Five years," she said. "Though I often saw Brian."

At a severe look from her father, she blushed and lowered her eyes.

"She is studying for a law degree at Columbia University," Yussef hurried on, eager to sound like the proud father. He exchanged a cautionary glance with his daughter.

"Yes, I just dropped by to pick up something from Mother. I must be going."

There was an awkward silence before she held out her hand to Jimmy.

"I'm so terribly sorry for your trouble, Mr. Murphy. I went to the month's mind in Rockaway but . . ."

She looked at her father, as if for help in completing the sentence.

"Thank you." Jimmy noted the discomfort and took Fatima's manicured hand. She smiled in apology then went behind the counter and spoke with her mother.

"We are very proud of her and her academic achievements," Yussef said, but then sighed. "As always with families, however, there are complications."

He excused himself, stood up, then joined Maryam and Fatima behind the counter before all three retreated into the small kitchen. Jimmy checked his cell phone for messages; he could not help but hear the sharp exchange in Arabic leaking out into the main room. Some minutes later Yussef appeared carrying the teakettle himself. Fatima followed him and walked past Jimmy. She halted at the door, adjusted the hijab she was now wearing, but did not wave good-bye.

After Yussef had poured more tea, he seemed preoccupied and stared out into the street.

"Complications?" Jimmy said.

Yussef took a sip and carefully replaced the cup in its saucer. He sighed and stretched out his hands, palms upward.

"Fatima is a dutiful daughter but she is easily swayed by new customs and trends."

"I was never blessed with a daughter, but I would imagine that comes with the territory."

"Indeed, such is the way in America, but in my country she has reached an age where she should be considering marriage."

"That will probably come in its own time too. I can't imagine there isn't interest."

"From many quarters." Yussef smiled grimly.

Jimmy sipped his tea and waited for elaboration, but when it didn't come he inquired, "And the complications?"

"She is keeping company with a young Christian man."

"Probably inevitable given she's at Columbia. And the lucky man?"

"Morgan Bradford comes from a good family, though one lacking any familiarity with our religion or customs."

"That's America for you."

"Indeed. Still, my cousin in Alexandria has proposed a match with her son, also from a good family—Hassan, a doctor, recently qualified."

"Fatima knows him?"

"They met as children and . . ." He hesitated, obviously choosing his words while gazing at his hands. When he looked up he continued with confidence. "She renewed acquaintance with him this summer. She has just recently returned."

"So?"

"She is not, as she put it herself, 'exactly blown away by him.'"

"A complication indeed."

"But not necessarily a deal-breaker, as you might say, James. Maryam and I were less than enthused at our only meeting before our betrothal, yet we have lived happily as man and wife. But we knew no other way. Fatima does."

"As my father used to say, 'Once they've seen the city you can't keep them down on the farm.'"

Yussef nodded his understanding.

"She has adapted to American life in other ways from us. Yet she is still my charge and I must make this decision—and soon. My cousin in Alexandria grows impatient for an answer. What would you do?"

"Ah, Jesus, I don't know, man. I never thought Brian made the right choice. As nice as his wife is, I felt they would grow apart."

"Did they, my friend?" Yussef leaned forward with interest and took Jimmy's hand again.

"I'll never know for sure, but they were definitely heading in different directions."

Yussef nodded his sympathy. "I see the same in my own family and it breaks my heart that I have exposed them to such temptation. There is a madness over here, James, that I was unaware of when first we met—or perhaps I chose to avert my eyes—this hunt for profit that grabs you by the soul. Back home in Alexandria, I had little wealth, but I had pride of place within my family. Now I have money, my children go to the best colleges, but we have no time for each other and, in my heart of hearts, I am a failure: I cannot even be certain that my daughter observes the fast of Ramadan. She comes and goes at all hours—things I took for granted I no longer can."

"We can't look out for them forever, Yussef. They have to find their own path in life."

"That is the American way and I am well aware of it. But I must advise my daughter as I see fit. If she marries the Christian man, who knows in what faith or traditions her children would be raised. And what would happen to Fatima should her husband predecease her? Would she be abandoned as happens to many widows in this country? In Alexandria she would live in the home of my cousin's family. Perhaps even marry another of her sons."

"That's looking a long way down the road."

"But which father does not try to anticipate the twists and turns of this 'road'? Perhaps you will let this problem of mine take root in your mind then give me the benefit of your advice?"

"I will. But now I have a question for you. Actually two of them."

Yussef flinched. It was as if he already knew what Jimmy would ask.

"Who are those two guys hanging on our every word?"

Yussef did not even look in their direction. "Friends from the mosque. After the attack I hired them to help me protect my parlors."

"It's been almost three years since the attack, Yussef."

"They are no longer in my employment but I still provide them meals should they be passing by. Since the conflict in Iraq resentment is growing again—one never knows." He spread his hands out on the table in a gesture of futility.

"And that's all?"

"What else could there be?"

They locked eyes. Jimmy knew there was more to it, but Yussef was a formidable man and would speak only when he wished to.

He threw another look at the two young men; although they were scarcely in their mid-twenties, both men's foreheads showed signs of callusing from contact with their prayer mats. One wore a white *kufi*, the traditional skullcap, and a dark vest over an embroidered white *kurta*. Both scowled back, not troubling to mask their hostility.

"There was a time when you wouldn't have tolerated their behavior." Jimmy spoke quietly.

"Just as there was a time when a policeman coming to my parlor would have been welcomed without any apprehension or suspicion from my customers."

"I'm no longer a policeman."

"Perhaps not officially, but every Muslim in the room looked up when you entered; thirty years of wielding power does not fade away overnight. And now, James, it is time for my prayers so you must excuse me."

"There is something I have to know. Fatima said she saw Brian often—when, where?"

When Yussef stood up Jimmy reached out for his arm.

"It's important!"

The two young men leaned forward. The one in more traditional clothing rose slightly, but the other in a wrinkled dark suit restrained him. After a moment, Yussef too sat down and whispered. "My friend, your son is gone. You must let him rest in peace."

Jimmy loosened his grip and pleaded, "I need to know, for God's sake help me."

Yussef stared back for some moments then glanced at the two young men and delivered some discreet authoritative signal, for both sat back in their chairs; one opened a well-thumbed Quran.

"Very well. But you may not like what you will hear."

Jimmy let go of his arm and motioned for him to continue.

"Your son began visiting this parlor some years back."

"When exactly?"

"It was winter—the second year of Fatima's college."

Jimmy did a mental calculation. "The winter of two thousand?"

"Some time after Christmas. Perhaps late January or February of two thousand one. I was happy to see him, and I suggested that you accompany him on his next visit, but he was reluctant."

"Why?"

"I don't know."

"I said 'Why?' Yussef. Don't lie to me!" Jimmy's voice rose above the hum of conversation; the young man wearing the embroidered white kurta sat bolt upright again and spoke angrily to his companion.

Yussef once more glanced at the two men, this time openly reproving them. They instantly looked away and he continued quietly. "Your son had an interest in my daughter."

"You got to be kidding me."

"Had he not been a married man, I would have been happy to consider the possibility of uniting our houses."

"He told you this?"

"A man does not have to be told these things about his daughter."

"And she?"

"She was a girl. Not yet twenty. At first I don't believe she was aware that his interest was more than friendly. Then she was flattered as any girl would be, though I don't believe at the time that he mentioned such matters to her."

"How do you know?"

"I asked her. She told me I was 'imagining things.' That he was married. That they just liked to talk of the songs on the radio and poetry, but I could see where it was heading."

"Go on."

"Then one night, it was in the late spring, he drove her home from college. She arrived in our house slurring her words from the effect of alcohol."

"Did you mention this to him?"

"He brought her to the door but did not accompany her inside. I had seen enough. I called my mother in Alexandria, and Fatima left the following week. She did not return until September."

"Before or after?"

"Before."

"Did they meet?"

"I don't know. I refuse to bolt her door."

"Well, did they communicate?"

"Young people have ways of contacting each other now that we can only guess at. All I know is that she was grief-stricken when she heard the news of Brian's death. As were we all."

EIGHTEEN

After his conversation with Yussef, Jimmy couldn't bear to get on the subway, much less head back to Rockaway. Instead he made his way up Clinton Street, figured he'd stop for a beer in the Heights. There was a saloon up there he and Brian used to hit on occasion.

Nothing made sense. Brian might have had a roving eye, but putting the moves on a sheltered nineteen-year-old girl? And yet Yussef was no screwball—he wouldn't want to disturb Jimmy or his family with some outlandish accusation. Unless he was hiding something— like who were the two young men in his so-called security detail at the other table? And what was all the prayer talk about? Back in the day Yussef never struck him as particularly devout. Was he now experiencing the real Yussef, and had the secular one been merely a front to beguile the gullible detective sergeant? Not to mention that back in '93 after the first World Trades bombing Jimmy went to Yussef's falafel parlor on an anonymous tip that there was evidence to be had there. Had their ensuing friendship blinded him to any suspicions he might originally have had about Yussef?

It was hard to miss Eamonn Doran's glassy porch with its kelly-green decorations and Irish tricolor flags. When Jimmy peered in the memories came flooding back of an afternoon spent inside listening to Brian talk about the city, and how for the first time he'd come to view its roiling streets through his son's perspective. Then all at once he couldn't bear the thought of sitting at the bar without Brian, how he'd only end up arguing with some loser while longing for the particular sparks that used to spray from his son's eyes.

He turned on his heel and strode along Montague Street past the dark certainty of St. Ann's church unsure of his destination but heading toward the water; and everywhere he noted the stately beauty of

Brooklyn Heights and how it appeared to be so balanced while his whole world was toppling this way and that.

When he reached the Promenade he stared out across the East River at Manhattan. He could hear the cars moving close beneath him as they labored along the Brooklyn-Queens Expressway. Though the view was postcard perfect he could not get past the glaring emptiness where the twin towers had stood. On an impulse he headed up Pineapple Street, took a right onto Henry and strolled past the St. George Hotel where once he had staked out the leader of a drug cartel. Now that he had his bearings he decided that he'd clear his head with a walk across the Brooklyn Bridge to Manhattan.

It was cooler up on the wooden planks as the sun broke through the clouds and began to descend on the cranes and docks of New Jersey. Already the rush hour cars and trucks were jammed both ways on the bridge and a train rumbled underneath on its way to Manhattan. People jogged or strolled by, oblivious to the world around them. Twenty years before such nonchalance would have unleashed swift retribution from the muggers and the seriously crazy who ruled this aerial turf. Now jocks blithely ignored New York City etiquette, pounding up within inches of someone's back before switching suddenly into another lane—behavior that once might have cost them a week in the hospital.

As he neared the middle of the bridge he could pick out the ferry plowing its way across the swell from Staten Island, and in the distance the spires and domes of Ellis Island glowed in the fading sunlight. The setting sun was indeed working wonders, casting Manhattan's skyscrapers into coppery Hoppery shades and setting a myriad of windows afire. He'd never heard of Edward Hopper until Brian gave him a poster of *Nighthawks* with its moody nocturnal diner; after that he couldn't get enough of the guy, for to Jimmy's eye Hopper captured the unease of the city's silent soul.

What would Hopper have made of the gaping hole on the West Side? What shade of russet or brown would he have employed to depict the rattling void that refused to depart after so much else had been blown away?

Ever since boyhood Brian had his own agenda, but he always left clues, dropped hints and enigmatic smiles so that you could piece things together. Jimmy knew he was missing something but no matter how much he wracked his brains he couldn't identify it. A wave of weariness broke over him. Maybe he was washed up. He wondered if he should call it a day—surrender to the poison of that big scar in the ground over on West Street and let all memories and suspicions remain banked there. But he knew he couldn't, he had to persevere, and so he strode on as the watery sun lit up the sails and riggings of the lonely remains of Whitman's schooners, and with each step he became more in tune with the madness of Manhattan and the freedom it had always promised those who rejoiced in being different.

Had Whitman's legacy suffered when the world came to the conclusion he was gay? Or had that knowledge only added to the luster of the Civil War nurse, the intrepid printer, and the first great taker of New York's pulse? Manhattan had always been open to those who had tiptoed across some imagined moral fault line, those who strayed from the accepted path when pursuing a goal. Did anyone love "Beautiful Dreamer" less because Stephen Foster abandoned his wife and drank away his despair in the Five Points?

But Brian wasn't around anymore to lift the veil from suspicious eyes, he wasn't available to vindicate himself and crack a crooked smile as he murmured "*quod est demonstrandum*." If the word got out that he was chasing after a teenage Muslim virgin many would change their opinion of him.

The hell with it! No matter what had transpired between Brian and Fatima, Jimmy swore he would get to the bottom of what his son had been up to! With that vow taken, his mind cleared and he hurried on to the end of the bridge and into the depths of lower Manhattan.

He needed a destination, some familiar anchor that would bring reassurance, and he found it in Park Row near the exit from the bridge. He had been coming to J&R Records since it opened, at first to buy the beautiful big vinyl LPs, and later their less impressive digital cousins.

He headed straight for the Allman Brothers rack and picked up *At Fillmore East*. Even in CD form his heart lifted, for he and Tony DeVito had barged their way to the stage back on that unforgettable Saturday in 1971. Thirty-three years later he could still recall many of the licks that Duane and Dickey had coaxed from their Gibsons that blistering night.

DeVito had struck it lucky in the draft, and instead of graduating from the Ivy League of Khe Sanh or Da Nang had gone to City College and received whatever degree they were giving away in those days to heads, dopers, and anyone who showed for enough classes. Hard to imagine Tony DeVito rushing the stage back then, just dying, trying to get anywhere close to Duane, his idol; and how seven months later he cried his eyes out when the silvery slide guitarist punched a hole in a peach truck on his Harley.

"And now look at the scumbag," Jimmy muttered as he paid for the CD.

"Say what?" The young clerk looked up in alarm from the register.

"You had to be there, kid," he said as he pocketed the disc and change from a twenty.

"I guess." The clerk nodded.

"Yeah, that just about sums it up." Jimmy stepped out onto Park Row. The clouds had gathered and drooped low over the tall buildings of downtown Manhattan and it felt even more humid. Then the sky opened and the rain came pouring gloriously down.

"Just what I needed," Jimmy muttered then turned up his collar and marched up Broadway bitterly recalling that almost three years earlier he'd run up the same street, his heart in his mouth, the white dust clinging to his hair and clothes.

She'd never met anyone the like of Jimmy Murphy in Ireland that was for sure certain. In fact she'd never before met a man in his cups who didn't care to talk about himself. Almost anything she knew about him she'd learned from other people—and oh how they liked to rave on about the illustrious Detective Sergeant Murphy. Before Mr. Dolan even introduced them she knew Jimmy's son had been killed on 9/11 and his wife had yet to recover from the tragedy.

Marcella had grown up clearing glasses in her father's pub outside Claremorris. She was well used to bars and the people who frequented them—Mayo or New York they acted much the same and there were few surprises. What you saw was what you got. But with Jimmy it was like peeling back the layers of an onion. He had casually mentioned serving in Vietnam but not that he'd been decorated. Likewise when the whole bar was cheering the bombs dropping on

Baghdad the first night of the invasion she saw Jimmy shake his head then slip out in quiet disgust.

His was an imposing, though often silent, presence; things worked well and people behaved during his shifts. She felt drawn to him without totally understanding the attraction. God knows he was old enough to be her father and yet he drained the light away from the other men in the bar. She felt safe and opened up to him in a way she never had with anyone else. But he wasn't without contradictions; Jimmy might be unobtrusive and unfailingly courteous, still she could tell he was hair-trigger aware and judgmental, though he kept his temper firmly under control.

Until the night the two frat boys made fun of Philip Doyle the waiter and let it be known that they didn't want to be served by a fag. It was all over in an instant. Jimmy informed them that they were no longer welcome in Dolan's but that they first owed "Mr. Doyle" an apology. There was a smirking moment before they became aware of the suppressed fury in Jimmy's eyes and realized the danger they were in. Apologies were summarily given and Jimmy escorted them to the door.

When he noticed that Philip was too upset to continue serving, Jimmy sat him at the bar, ordered two straight whiskeys, and talked quietly to the young Irishman. Only when Philip returned to work did Marcella notice that Jimmy's right hand was shaking like a leaf.

Marcella looked up in surprise when he entered Dolan's on his day off, his suit and hair drenched from the sudden August shower. Was it his innate New Yorker timing or were they in some kind of synchronicity? He winked and she smiled back, but he headed straight to the bar.

"Bushmills!" he demanded.

"Not your usual Jameson's, Jimmy?" Conor raised his eyebrows.

"No, and make it a Black. I'm chasing a memory."

"And a water on the side, right?"

"Yeah but make the whiskey a large one."

"For a large memory." The bartender nodded his appreciation and filled the glass to within a centimeter of the lip.

"You got it, man. One hell of a large one." He took a decent sip of Brian's favorite whiskey and shuddered. After he downed a gulp of water he joined Marcella in the booth.

"A little early, Jimmy?" She frowned.

"Sometimes you need a jolt," he replied taking another heartfelt sip.

"Bad news?"

"Let's just say unexpected."

"It seems to be one of those days."

"Dolan giving you a hard time?"

"No."

He drained his Black Bush and the fake crystal chandelier began to sparkle. Did Brian drink his "Protestant whiskey" to stand apart from Jimmy's father and the old Irish Town republicans who favored Jameson's, or did he really like the stuff? Who cared anymore, Black Bush hit the spot.

Marcella smiled too as she spoke some encouraging words to Ramón, the new bar-back. And then "Dancing Queen" erupted from the jukebox. It was too loud for that time of day but he knew she wouldn't turn it down. She had told him that her father always played it at full volume when there was trouble in the pub back home. The room lit up even more when he remembered it was one of Brian's favorite songs. Conor did a little shimmy for some tourists at the end of the bar, and not for the first time memories of his oldest son were saving Jimmy's day.

Marcella encouraged Ramón to speak English as he swayed to the beat; he smiled back at the attractive manager's attention—two immigrants far from home. Jimmy drank her in; she looked beyond good, for once she was even wearing makeup, her lipstick the palest of pink. They must have been lining up for her back in Mayo—or Dublin. What had really gone down with the "friend" back there she'd had the understanding with? He'd seen her blush furiously when young Siobhán, the perkiest of the waitstaff, had called back to her as a bunch of them were heading down to the Village late one night, "Jaysus, Marcella, you're a terrible one for the auld fellahs! First yer man back in Dublin and now look at you!"

The implication being that she had her eye on someone similar in Dolan's—the head of security, for instance. Jimmy's first real connection with Marcella had occurred during the Christmas season. He'd been standing at the crowded bar, nursing a drink before heading home, staring in the mirror wondering what he'd be doing if he was still on the job. He felt certain she'd been studying him for when their eyes met in the mirror she blushed and looked away. He smiled and raised his glass, and was about to join her then thought better of it. Still, some barrier broke between them for on his following nightshift she sat next to him when the waitstaff had their closing-time drink. And from then on they always seemed to end up sitting together.

"Dancing Queen" was fading away and Ramón had gone about his duties. Jimmy hadn't realized that he'd been staring at her. Flustered by the raw attention, Marcella reacted impulsively by hailing a passing waitress and requesting an Absolut and tonic.

"That's a first," Jimmy said. "I never noticed you drinking on the job before."

"Sometimes you need a jolt."

"In the words of the poet."

After she'd taken her first sip, Jimmy said, "Anything you want to tell me?"

She stirred her drink with great concentration before looking up. "Officer Sullivan was in earlier."

This wasn't quite what he'd been expecting but he had no trouble covering with his cop cool. "Oh yeah?"

"He was asking questions."

"Like what?"

"What nights you worked? Had you taken time off recently? Traveled anywhere?"

"That was it?"

She looked away at first. "He talked about Brian. He was apparently very fond of him. He wanted to know if you were pursuing any investigation of your own into his death—that you had a 'condition,' and that any more stress could make it worse and lead to . . ."

"Lead to what?"

"Delusions—of an aggressive nature. He said there had been reports, a number of your ex-colleagues were worried about you; he asked if I'd keep him informed of any irregularities in your schedule, that kind of thing."

"And that was that?"

"He told me not to mention this to you—that he might be forced to inquire into the legal status of Pedro and Ramón if I wasn't cooperative."

"And?"

"He made a few personal comments—nothing alarming," she hastened to assure him.

"He was never exactly Prince Charming."

Back when they were first partners, he'd told Sullivan on the quiet about his struggle with the NVA kid and that he got flashbacks occasionally. Sullivan must have mentioned that to DeVito at some point leading to a big red mark next to his name—"Sees dead gooks' faces!" And bye-bye to his lieutenant's badge.

First Drew, the cookie-cutter detective tailing him, then Sullivan sniffing around Dolan's—DeVito was covering all the bases! He obviously knew a lot about what Brian had been up to, but he hadn't a clue what Jimmy had stumbled on, and he badly wanted to find out.

Marcella ordered a second round of drinks, but her revelations had put a dent in the day and all their attempts at meaningful conversations fell flat. He was just about to finish up and head for the subway when she said very quietly, "Conor asked me out today."

"And?" He said in as noncommittal a voice as he could muster.

"I said I'd have to think about it."

"Probably a sensible thing to do."

"Is it, Jimmy?"

He looked directly at her; this time she stared back and didn't flinch.

"Well," he said, "if you're asking is it a good idea for a manager to go out with one of her bartenders, I'd have to say it's not."

"Is there any other way of looking at it?"

When Jimmy didn't answer she glanced over to the bar. Conor was chatting up some actresses just in from shooting a soap. He leaned over the stick and whispered something; they laughed skittishly and he added a confident young man's chuckle to the hubbub.

"I don't know, Marcella. It's been a long hard day. I'll see you tomorrow."

He drained the Black Bush, stood up, and walked out.

"Hey Jimmy," Conor called after him. "You sure you won't have one for the road?"

He didn't answer, just kept on walking.

NINETEEN

Kevin liked to jog. He could drive himself to the limit, run 'til his heart was about to explode, the sweat flying off his face, t-shirt plastered to his chest, and still push himself even further. Up and down that boardwalk, feet crashing against the worn planks, idlers jumping to one side jamming themselves to the railings at the sound of his approaching thunder. In and around the bungalows, up and down the sandy streets, and then one last almighty burst for home back down the boards.

It was better early in the morning, no kids out yet, easier to weave among the sleepless seniors—he could sense their trajectory from a distance, they didn't break stride or change direction like the high school Romeos and Juliettas suddenly stopping to smooch or overreacting to a quicksilver slap on the face.

Running was good for thinking. Things became clearer with each stride. There was no doubt about it—he loved Rosie with all his heart despite the almost crippling baggage she brought with her. There was only one way to handle that—put his head down and bull right through all the crap that would be thrown in their faces. They could overcome anything now for in the last three months the bond that had always existed between them had become so strong and incredibly intimate no one could mess with it. And yet there were other factors that both of them had to deal with including the one that came around like clockwork once a year and battered the peninsula like a hurricane.

The mood might still be carnival cool on the boardwalk, but with September rearing its mournful head in the distance he could already feel the tension rising around Rockaway. The hell with it! Bring on the third anniversary and thirty more after that. He finally had the woman he'd always loved. With Rose at his side he could walk through walls and be none the worse for wear.

And so he pounded back up the boardwalk one last time, accelerating straight toward flocks of seagulls and sparrows quarreling over discarded crusts of pizza. But no matter how much or how hard he ran the memory of the awful day still rankled and didn't ooze away in streams of fatigue. In fact the anger only deepened and hardened inside him and he yelled "Watch your back!" at more than one person he had no trouble avoiding.

For Kevin Murphy had buried his own story about 9/11 and it was slowly tearing him apart. Hungover as all hell after his previous night out, he'd been off duty, but once he heard the news he immediately made his way downtown where he was assigned to move people out of danger when all he wanted to do was dive through the dust and despair and claw into the rubble in some mad hope of rescuing something, anything.

Instead, he and his crew entered offices and apartments and escorted the dazed up above Canal Street, past the barricades already manned by cops and the National Guard. At first he gazed up in horrified awe at the North Tower and the gaping hole that was belching out thick black smoke and tongues of fire, but after its collapse he bent his head and tended to his mundane task. And never once did it occur to him that his brother might be down there buried amidst the torn girders, splintered glass, and powdered Sheetrock.

He should have had some inkling, for he'd been tossing them back with Brian 'til all hours the night before. Much of it was a haze of shots and beer, though it had begun innocently enough—a call from his brother to have a couple and help him unwind. No questions asked, yet Brian had quietly informed him he was on to something important; but when was Brian any other way? He'd been like that since they were little boys, always some great mission on his mind, some secret that couldn't be told, some holy grail that he was searching for and only fingertips away from finding.

Kevin knew there was no point in asking—that Brian explained only when he was ready and expected his kid brother to be there for him. Brian liked hanging with Kevin's posse of young Fire guys—and why not? He was a hero among them. The youngest lieutenant on the job, and yet he remembered each of their names and particulars after the first introduction. Some of their elder brothers had gone to Regis with him where he was always top of the class, a budding legend in the incestuous world of New York's Catholic high schools.

The posse adored the fact that he could drink them all under the table and still quote poetry to beautiful women, or toss off stories that ranged from Georgetown to East New York, from Giuliani to Cool J. And that's what he was doing early on the morning of September eleventh as they piled in and out of taxis around the Upper East Side, each pub and saloon excitedly receiving them as they breezed in on a wave of adrenaline—the jukeboxes blasting, the long-legged girls on barstools shedding their cool and joining the crew as they inevitably moved on to greener fields where Jay-Z, The Pogues, and Black 47 were pumping ever louder in their honor.

But somewhere along the way Richie Sullivan attached himself to Brian; Kevin had never liked Sullivan or his effect on his brother. The older cop tended to corral the young lieutenant, and sure enough the intensity spiraled with the two of them confabbing head-to-head about some "sensitive matter," and though Kevin tried to step in and take the raw edge off things there never seemed to be time, for it was always on to the next bar in an endless odyssey of searching for someone, or for something to unfold.

Finally they made a stand at a joint in the 70s; Brian and Sullivan had found what they were looking for. But that's where things got really cloudy—the jukebox was hammering the inside of Kevin's skull, he felt like he was going to throw up, then he was outside sitting on the sidewalk, and Brian had his arm around him, and he was being put into a cab with young Frankie Visceglia who was even more messed up, they were going back to his place to sleep it off, and Brian was saying he'd take them home himself but he had to hash something out with Sullivan, take care of some unfinished business that would "make everything clear," and the last time Kevin saw his brother he was waving good-bye, and then striding back into that raucous Upper East Side saloon.

TWENTY

The sun finally broke through the rain and clouds over Breezy on the morning of the Feast of the Assumption. With the sky clearing and the seagulls diving, a lone osprey glided by on the Atlantic breeze as Jimmy swore at the busy tone on his cell. He knew he should have called before coming down unannounced—just figured that Rose would be up and around at nine a.m. But there wasn't sight or sound of movement within the big house. He guessed the kid had been on the Internet late at night and had fallen asleep without switching the computer offline. Rose's Jeep was in the driveway so she was home.

It had been months now since he'd promised her he'd get to the bottom of Brian's warning to his son. True he'd offered to drop by many times and there was always some reason she didn't want a visit. But a promise was a promise—9/11 was almost on them and no decision had been made on Liam attending the memorial.

Jimmy slammed the Caddy door to further announce his presence, took the steps two at a time, and rang the bell. It echoed throughout the house. When he heard no sound he rang again. Then a thump not unlike someone jumping out of bed. He waited but she still didn't come to the door. Now Rose would be out of sorts from the late start, and there'd be the inevitable to-do about Liam's breakfast—the kid was so picky about food.

He heard the bang of what sounded like a wardrobe door. Jesus, she didn't need to get dressed up—it wasn't the good-looking young Con Edison guy or the UPS muscleman, just her cranky old father-in-law come to wrestle his grandson away from the computer. And still no sign of her!

He walked over to Liam's window and swept the trails of raindrops from the pane. The kid was fast asleep, still dressed in his oversize Mets shirt, the computer screen throbbing with some revved-up screen saver, the bedroom door wide open; and then he saw Rose run by stuffing a denim shirt into her jeans with one hand, awkwardly fluffing out her hair with the other. She was obviously racing to greet him. He sprinted back across the soggy lawn and was waiting, a little out of breath, but smile firmly attached when she opened the door.

"Hey, sleeping in? I should have waited 'til later." Jimmy beamed through his embarrassment.

"No, no, it's okay," she replied, her face red from exertion, still doing damage control on her hair.

"Figured I'd take Liam down the beach. Let him run around a bit."

"He's not up yet."

"The phone was busy, so I knew you were home. He fell asleep on the Internet again? Gotta watch that, they charge you for it."

"I keep telling him."

She seemed preoccupied so when she didn't invite him in he stepped forward. She held her ground for a moment before opening the door fully.

"Something the matter?" he inquired, wishing he were a million miles away.

"Yeah, Kevin's on the couch." She swept her hand over toward the living room. "I was feeling a bit down last night. Gave him a call at The Inn and he took a car service over."

"That's good. Looking out for you, like."

"We had two or three shots of tequila and before I knew it he was out cold. I just threw a quilt over him."

Kevin's snore grew louder.

"Listen to him." Jimmy smiled as he looked in at his son. "Hey, one sock on, the other off. What a disaster!"

She adjusted the quilt to cover the offending bare foot and shook him heartily by the shoulder. "Kevin, wake up! Your father's here."

"Jesus Christ, Rose! What kind of liquor did you pour into me?" Kevin groaned, holding his head like it was about to come loose.

"Tequila. And no one was twisting your arm."

"Dad?"

"Kevin? Fancy meeting you here. Finished for the week?"

"Yeah, I was partying down The Inn. Rosie called. Oh man, look at the time!" Kevin squinted at his watch. "I gotta run. Supposed to help Sweeney move a couch—where's my sneakers?"

"Hey, Kev," Jimmy said. "You're missing a sock."

"Oh shit! Yeah, we were acting out down The Inn."

"You Fire guys have the life. Russian roulette with your socks, and the one with a hole buys the shots, right?"

"Yeah, must have left it down there." Kevin took off the remaining sock, stuffed it in his pocket, then tied his sneakers. "Okay, Rose. I'll give you a call tonight. Maybe we'll go out for a beer."

Jimmy nodded. "You should do that. Maggie'd love to have Liam over. Hasn't been at summer camp, right?"

"No, he had a . . . a bit of a fever," Rose said.

"Bad thing this time of year."

"Well, I'd better get going." Kevin yawned and stretched.

"You want me to drop you off?"

"Nah, I could do with a walk. Get Sweeney to pick me up. Least he can do for moving his couch."

"I'll see you to the door," Rose said.

"Take care, Kev," Jimmy called back as he strolled down to his grandson's room. "I'll check out that fever."

"No, no, he's over it now," Rose replied.

"Well, I'll take a look anyway."

He closed the bedroom door quietly behind him as Rose walked Kevin out to the front porch.

"Why the hell did you say it was a fever?" Kevin whispered.

"Shh," she hissed. "What did you want me to say, his grandson bit off a piece of Tiffany Walsh's ear?"

"He'll find out soon enough. C'mere." He grabbed her around the waist and pulled her close. "You didn't get your wake-up kiss."

He pushed her up against the wall and slid his hand through her unbuttoned shirt. He gave a little start when he felt her bare breast and pushed even closer against her. She could feel his excitement and shoved him away.

"For God's sake, your father's in there."

"You feel good."

"Ever think of brushing your teeth before you kiss a girl? No, don't do that!" She slapped his hand and pushed him away again. "And what did you do with your other sock?"

"I don't know. I guess you and me must have been playing striptease."

"I just hope your dad didn't see you run from the bed to the couch."

"Nah, I was moving like streak lightning! How about a kiss for the road?"

"Good-bye, Kevin!" She opened the door and shoved him out onto the top step.

"See you later, shweetheart." He did a bad Bogart imitation and then winked at her. "Remember you're dealing with Detective Sergeant Murphy—whenever he's smiling that means he's really suspicious."

She combed out her hair in the bathroom and brushed her teeth while Jimmy joked with her son. At first it was all a deep male cajoling voice, but little by little the child began piping up. How well Jimmy related to him—just being there, the way an eight-year-old needed. She hated lying to her father-in-law, but was there any other choice?

"What's the matter, Rose?"

"Oh Jesus, Jimmy!" She hadn't heard him standing in the open doorway. He reached out awkwardly as she brushed away the tears and held her gently.

"I got a confession to make."

"Come on. It's never as bad as you think."

"Liam bit Tiffany Walsh's ear at summer camp. I'm so ashamed."

"Yeah, Laura Bianchi called yesterday, remember Maggie used to help her out at the camp? She wasn't home so I took the call."

"You knew? Why didn't you say?"

"Probably the same reason you didn't. Figured I'd drop down in case you'd be brooding over it. Anyway, Tiffany's ear is fine. Teach her to go saying Liam's dad is toast."

"I don't want Maggie to know!"

"You know Maggie's not your worst enemy. But she won't hear, I told Laura not to mention it. Okay?"

"Yeah." Rose went into the bathroom for a tissue. She blew her nose then smiled weakly.

"Rose, you sure there's nothing else bothering you?"

"No, I'm fine."

"Well, if you ever need to talk I'm here, okay?"

"Okay." She turned away and picked up the quilt that Kevin had left on the floor.

"Oh, by the way," he said holding up a sock. "I found this in the hall. Guess he didn't leave it down The Inn."

"He never knows where he's left anything when he's drinking! I'll get Liam ready so you can take him out."

"Rose, I got something to ask you."

She stopped dead in her tracks dreading the inevitable question.

"Brian and Richie Sullivan? What was that all about?"

"Richie was like an uncle to Brian." She exhaled with relief.

"Yeah, yeah, I know, he grew up on Richie's knee and all that crap. But you of all people know that Brian didn't hang out with the likes of Sullivan unless there was something going down. What were they up to?"

"I don't know. They did seem to get closer toward the end. Richie even called me up now and then."

"Called you?"

"Yeah, to let me know if Brian had to go to DC in a hurry or do something with Giuliani—things like that."

"That doesn't make sense. Sullivan is a patrolman, not a private secretary—and why wouldn't Brian call you himself?"

"Sullivan used to say he was tied up. I wonder now why I never questioned it but a lot of things about Brian didn't make sense those last months."

"You think Sullivan might have had something on him?"

"That's what Kevin thinks—he doesn't say it in so many words. But I can tell he doesn't like him."

"No, Sullivan is an acquired taste," Jimmy said, sighing as he shook his head.

"Brian always took his calls out on the porch. There was obviously stuff he didn't want me to hear."

"To run into each other down the Towers before the attack? It just doesn't ring right."

"I keep asking questions too but everyone says I'm upsetting them."

"Rose," he said and then sat down, unsure what he wanted to say. "I know it wasn't always easy for you, with Brian."

"Please."

"I raised him for better or worse; but to be honest, some of the worst didn't sit right with me."

"Don't go there, Jimmy, please?"

"No, I suppose there's not a lot of point in bolting the barn door with the horse already gone."

"Maybe I was the one who should have slammed it," she said without trying to hide the bitterness.

They gazed at each other, each one unsure how to continue. The grandfather clock that Brian had been so proud of ticked away mercilessly as they listened to the short sharp bursts of childish laughter coming from Liam's room. No sooner awake than playing his video games!

"Rose, would you mind if I told you something?"

"Not today, Jimmy, I just can't handle any more about Brian right now."

"Nah, it's nothing like that, I promise you. It's just that, well, there's no one else I can really talk to."

She couldn't remember Jimmy ever asking a favor before. "Sure, Jimmy, it's fine."

"Well, there's someone I've been thinking about a lot."

"You mean—another woman?"

"I'm not that old, Rose."

"No, I didn't mean it that way, it's just—I never think of you like that."

"Yeah, well, I suppose you wouldn't, would you?"

"Does Maggie know?"

"No, I mean nothing's happened or anything. But anyway, I don't think she'd even notice right now."

"Women always know, Jimmy, even when they don't let on to themselves."

She fumbled for a cigarette in her purse then lit it. Before she took a drag, she opened the kitchen window.

"Who is she? Do you mind me asking?"

"Irish girl, Marcella Fitzgerald, works at Dolan's."

"Brian, well, I think it was with people he worked with too."

"I used to hear the odd rumor about him. Even tried to bring it up one night, but he filled me to the gills with whiskey and before I knew it we were on the street outside McGee's hugging good-bye. I remember standing on Broadway, watching him stroll off down into Times Square like he owned the joint, and wondering how he'd handled me so well."

"Thanks, for trying. I know there were harsh words between the two of you at times. But he respected you more than anyone."

"I don't know about that. Everything I tried to tell him he disagreed with."

"To your face, maybe, but he chewed on every last thing you said. *My dad is the one straight man I know. If he ever turned against me I don't know what I'd do.*"

Jimmy stood up abruptly, his eyes scalding. He moved to the open window and gulped in some air. Rose moved over to give him space and ran the tap on her cigarette. They stared out at a big gull perched still as a statue on the back fence; then in one graceful movement it stretched its wings and took off toward the ocean.

"Crazy world, isn't it?" Jimmy said as much to the rising wind as to her. "I was mad at Brian for what he was doing to you and now I'm hardly any better myself."

The wind picked up further in tight little gusts and a neighbor's yard door slammed. Rose turned away from the window and asked, "Do you love her?"

"Ah Jesus, what the hell is love at my age? I mean, I like seeing the light in her eyes when I walk in the door—that kind of thing. She has a way of draining all the lousy acres of loneliness out of me. Is that love, Rose?"

"I don't know, I wish to God I did."

"Anyway, it's all academic, I mean she's twenty-seven, twenty-eight, what would she see in an old guy like me?"

Rose looked at him and smiled sadly. "You've no idea the way a woman thinks, Jimmy, age is only a small part of it. There's a solitary kind of thing about you that I bet she can't stop thinking about—integrity too."

"Yeah?"

She nodded. "Yeah. She can feel the pain in you and would give the world to soothe it. She's never even dreamed of the likes of you where she came from, you can be sure of that."

"That's one for the books." He smiled back then put his arm around her and they gazed once more out at the morning. The wind had changed, as it did frequently down at the end of the peninsula, and with it the weather. It felt warm and sunny, the clouds and rain a vague memory.

"There's one more thing I've got to ask," Jimmy said without moving. "Just can't seem to let it go."

She reached for another cigarette.

"Did Brian ever mention a man called Yussef?"

"The falafel man?"

"Yeah."

"From time to time."

"Can you remember when it began?"

"Sometime after he made lieutenant, I guess."

"Did he ever mention his daughter?"

"No, but I did," she said angrily. "You're talking about Fatima?"

"How did you know?"

"I saw her name on Brian's phone and asked him about her."

He waited for her to continue. Instead she removed his arm and took a drag from her cigarette.

"One night he was sleeping I checked his cell. Worst thing I ever did. Saw the names of all the people he'd recently been in touch with—Sullivan, DeVito, Maggie, the falafel man, and his tramp of a daughter, some other women too."

"When was that, Rosie? It's important."

"How could I forget? The last night he was home—September ninth."

She angrily stubbed out the cigarette.

"I'm going out for a walk, Jimmy. I'll leave you with your grandson. You have a way with kids."

"If I do it came late, too many times I let the world get in the way of my own."

"Yeah. I guess you're right," she said quietly as she grabbed a denim jacket off the back of a chair.

"By the way, Maggie would like you and Liam to come over for dinner some night next week."

But she was already closing the door behind her. Jimmy watched her clear the corner of the house. He stood by the open window for some time, relishing the warm morning but hating the truth for what it did to people.

He always took Liam to the same spot, down past the Surf Club on 227th toward Jamaica Bay and on out toward the tip of the peninsula. Jimmy preferred the wildness of the ocean with the big waves pounding the shore, the surf and the sky colliding, the shelly beach reeking with the tang of the briny green Atlantic. But he'd learned a long time ago that kids preferred the gentler touch of the bay, especially when they had baseball on their minds.

They walked hand in hand over the wet sand and rough grass, stray raindrops still sparkling on the thistles, Liam swinging his bat and Jimmy holding the mitt, the softball bulging in his jacket pocket. He'd taken the same route with Brian over a quarter of a century before and later with Kevin, often with both. Only the players' names had changed. The gulls still screamed above them but the wind subsided the closer they got to Jamaica Bay.

Liam didn't give a hoot for the Yankees or their chances of making the World Series, and even less whether the Red Sox might finally whip the curse of the Bambino. All he wanted to talk about was Mike Piazza, and did his grandpa think that one day he might replace "Mikey P" when age and battered knees had finally forced the Mets catcher to shuffle aside?

After the last months of doubt and frustration, it was a breeze dealing with the innocent inquiries of a newly minted eight-year-old catcher. It brought him back to the days when he answered similar questions from his own sons about a different set of heroes. How simple the world when you measured it against the stats and results of the boys of summer. It was good to feel a little hand nestled in his own again, and luxuriate in the total trust only an eight-year-old can bestow.

Where had all those years in between gone? Lost in a daze marked only by an occasional flashbulb of memory. What kind of father had he been? Definitely not one of the doting, ever present ones, he didn't even carry the ubiquitous family snapshots in his wallet ready to be whipped out at the drop of a hat. But neither did he squabble incessantly with an ex-wife and barely show up at post-divorce birthday parties; no, he was one of the also-rans who wasn't particularly cut out for fatherhood—stumbled into it more or less. Gave it his best shot but had other things on his mind also.

Had Vietnam stuck its ugly, sweating head in the way? Jesus, he loved his kids, there was no doubting that, but it was often hard to still the pounding of howitzers deep within his skull. He also had to plead guilty that he could go on the job in the morning and not give a thought to either boy until he was walking away from Midtown North across 54th Street to the subway late that night. Even then, he'd often be lost in the details of some case and might forget to pick up a couple of candy bars until he got off the train at 116th Street. Most of the time, though, he did bring some little gift home to stick under their pillows when he was too late to say good night.

Brian had loved the candy but it was more an afterthought. Kev, on the other hand, needed his dad's reassurance and approval. Things never went particularly well for him in school, always striving, never quite making it, until the day he got dropped from the baseball team and came face-to-face with the reality that he'd never be a Guidry or a Mattingly, not even a Cotto or a Dent.

Jimmy wondered if it ever crossed Kevin's mind anymore. Or was it just another high school moment, like a broken-hearted prom night, something that surfaced idly and was effortlessly dispatched? Whatever his son felt, Jimmy could never quite blank out the utter pain of rejection in a fifteen-year-old's face when he finally realized he'd always be a watcher in the stands.

Liam had run ahead and was waiting for him at their little hollow by the beach. Across the bay Coney Island's Parachute Jump did its best to mask the Verrazano Bridge while off on the horizon the jagged skyline of Manhattan brooded over the loss of its two most prominent landmarks. The boy was oblivious to such things as he flexed his muscles and checked his swing, for he had become the mighty Mikey P and was staring down his grandpa—the fierce Rocket, Roger Clemens.

Was the Piazza-Clemens confrontation the first time Jimmy noticed that Brian was skating on a hairline crack? That nail-biting October night back in 2000 up the Stadium—what was eating his eldest son?

The whole city was going crazy. A subway series, the Yanks were a game up. The three of them with good seats, tossing down beers, Brian had a hip flask of Black Bush in his pocket, had flashed his badge on the way in, who was going to search a lieutenant? Yankees and Mets fans all mixed up together in the crowd, for the most part enjoying each other and the crosstown rivalry—knowing they were a part of history. Proud of themselves, how many cities could boast one great team? New Yorkers had two, and that night they were playing for number one!

Brian was still flushed from making lieutenant, the whole peninsula was talking about him, guys on the job congratulating Jimmy: "Your son's going all the way!" Already had two or three pictures taken with Giuliani, flying down to DC for conferences, doing cop things Jimmy had never even heard of let alone accomplished. He was proud of his boy, and it didn't trouble him that he wouldn't make it to the same level. Or did it?

The ballpark was electric. The Rocket was on the mound, pawing the earth like a big Lone Star bull, you could almost see the steam coming out of his nostrils, the spittle at the corners of his mouth. What inning was it—early in the game, Piazza's first at bat, and already so much bad blood between them! Clemens had beaned Piazza some months earlier concussing him so badly he had to miss the All-Star Game. This was the confrontation every baseball fan in the country had been waiting for. The whole Stadium could feel something coming. The Rocket raging, juiced to the nines—Pennsylvanian Piazza calm as ever on the outside but you knew every nerve end was twitching deep inside, that he'd give it all up for one big mighty swing for the rafters, rock Clemens's world and send baseball's biggest bully staggering all the way back to Texas.

Brian was talking up a storm, how Piazza was the greatest-hitting catcher ever, and that this night would be poetry in motion. He'd been joshing with a group of lit-up Yankees fans in front of them. Jimmy's antennae had risen; one of the Yank guys in a Clemens shirt had become surly and was giving back way more than was called for. Brian wasn't paying him much attention as Piazza stepped into the box; he had passed the flask around once already and took another deep swig for good luck.

And then Clemens threw one straight down the middle in the high 90s and Piazza swung for the fences. Ball and bat collided and the crack resounded throughout the crowded canyons, the bat splintered; ball and wood careened outward. While Piazza lumbered toward first base The Rocket was dazed and confused as a piece of wood flew at him. He picked up the handle and flung it at Piazza.

Brian was instantly on his feet screaming as was the whole Stadium, the guy in the Clemens shirt was howling, "Piazza is a fag! Piazza is a fag!" Then from out of nowhere, Brian hauled him back over the seats, had him by the throat, and was choking him, Jimmy and Kevin were trying to peel him off, then Brian shook them loose and headed toward the field and Clemens, before he was dragged down by two security men; Jimmy and Kevin tried to rescue him, and everyone in their area was staring and pointing, and then the three of them were being escorted out and badges were being flashed, until a couple of cops stepped in and stroked the feathers of the offended security detail, and within minutes they were down the street at Stan's tossing back more beers and soothing tempers, and wondering what the hell had happened.

Why hadn't Jimmy understood then that his son needed help: that he was at breaking point wrestling with something way bigger than himself? But that was Brian. The big gesture that disguised so much else. Beat up The Rocket, build the fancy spread down in Breezy, or run back into that collapsing nightmare fully convinced he'd make it out.

"You're not listening, Grandpa. Toss me a curve. Okay?"

"Can I tell you something, man-to-man, Liam?"

"Sure."

"I miss your dad so much, it just don't seem to go away."

"So does Mom. She cries when she thinks I'm not looking."

"Yeah, grown-ups aren't supposed to cry, right?"

"I've kept her safe."

"From what?"

"I never opened the door for anyone 'cept you and Uncle Kevin."

"Your dad asked you to do that?"

"Yeah." The little boy stamped the earth like Piazza and moved some offending leaves away with his bat.

"Did someone else try to get in?"

"A lady."

"What kind of lady?"

"A lady with flowers and a hood like Gramma."

"A hood? You mean like the scarf Gramma wears after going to the hairdresser?"

"Kind of, but it was hard to see the lady's face. Then she ran off."

"When was that?"

"The day Dad went to heaven."

"You mean the month's mind or the day the Towers collapsed?"

"The month's, I guess."

"Did you scare anyone else away?"

"No, but I saw two bad guys across the street looking at us."

"How did you know they were bad guys?"

"One of them was dressed weird and they were sitting in a big black car."

"What kind of weird?"

"I don't know, just weird like in a movie. Now throw me that curve!"

"Sure. You ready?" Jimmy wound up, but just as he was about to release: "When was that, before Dad went to heaven?"

"Yeah, back when Dad lived with us and everything was okay."

Jimmy let the ball go gently. His grandson swung for the fences and made contact.

The gulls were screaming overhead and swooping down on a school of minnows in the bay, but Jimmy was far from the sheltered side of Breezy with an eight-year-old who'd nailed a softball.

For the first time some things began to make sense. The lady in the hood with flowers had to be Fatima in her hijab out in Breezy for the month's mind. And Brian was right: he was being tailed—just not by DeVito. But who else was crazy enough to tail a cop—had to be someone who didn't care, someone from a different world.

He didn't dally when he got back to her house; nor did Rose ask if he'd got to the bottom of her son's promise to his dad. She was polite but made it clear that she'd had enough heart-to-hearts for one day. Jimmy felt much the same; not to mention he was beginning to see the ghosts of patterns taking shape. If Fatima had gone all the way out to Breezy a month after the attack it was because she had disobeyed her father and renewed acquaintance with Brian right before 9/11. Brian had also spoken to Yussef in those last days. What was that all about, and how come Yussef was blatantly hiding information from him? And who were the two "bad guys" stalking Brian's house before the Towers were hit?

All the way back to Rockaway he grappled with these questions and others, and the beginnings of answers began to materialize. He could smell the wood burning as he parked the car. Maggie had lit the first fire of the year—so early, yet it glowed cheerily in the grate. She was reading a collection of Seamus Heaney poems that Brian had given her his last Christmas; it reminded Jimmy of the game she and Brian used to play where one of them would choose a line at random and the other would name the poem. It amazed him how often they were correct. Occasionally he would silently match wits with them and inevitably come up wanting.

"I put the kettle on for some tea when I heard you pull in," Maggie said with a catch in her voice and her eyes moist with tears; she closed the book and put it away almost furtively, as if she didn't wish him to know what she'd been reading or how it had affected her.

"Thanks."

"How was the boy?"

"The usual, quiet at first, but he warmed up when we went to the bay and hit a few balls."

"He spends too much time indoors."

"Yeah, there's no denying that."

"Did you ask Rose about dinner next week?"

"I think so."

"Well, what did she say?"

"I can't really remember if she said anything. There was a lot going on."

"Oh, like what?"

The kettle began whistling and she went into the kitchen. She brought back a cup of tea for each of them. She'd already put in his one spoon of sugar and the amount of milk he liked, even though she never got it exactly right. They sipped by the fire and she awaited his reply.

"Kevin was there."

"Kevin?"

"Yeah, out like a light on the couch. She'd been feeling down last night and gave him a call at The Inn. They did some shots and he passed out."

"God!" she exclaimed. "Will he never learn? Well, at least he wasn't driving. And it's nice that he went over. I wonder why he was so brusque with her all that time before."

"I guess he had to come to terms with things in his own way."

"I don't know what to make of him of late. One day he has me ransacking the house for his transcript from St. John's, the next he doesn't have a whit of interest in it."

Jimmy put his cup down and stood up. He didn't seem able to sit still anymore.

"Maybe it runs in the family, Maggie."

"What's that?"

"Well, you can't put your finger on Kevin and I can't put my finger on you."

"That's a strange thing to say. What do you mean?"

"One day you're raving about the magical First Fridays and how they've changed your life, the next I walk in and the tears are streaming down your face over some poem or other."

"I was looking up some lines that Brian and I used to quote to each other about hope and history rhyming."

He could tell it bothered her that she couldn't quote the exact lines; he wondered at the unfamiliar harshness in his own voice. Perhaps it was from an old hurt—the way she and Brian used poetry to keep him at a distance.

"Was there something you wanted to say to me?" she asked anxiously, but in time with the ticking of the clock.

There was so much he wished to tell her but for the first time he felt it was too late. She waited for him to speak and when he couldn't find the words, he knew that the fault was more his than hers.

He put his coat back on. There was nothing more to say. Manhattan was all he could think of. There was someone he had to see before it was too late.

TWENTY-ONE

This time he strode right past Crazy Joey. Before Gallagher even looked up Jimmy had already barged in through Captain Tony DeVito's door. DeVito did look up, as did his assistant, some smarmy sergeant who had clocked more time studying for exams than he had on the street.

"What the . . .?" the sergeant demanded, judiciously avoiding the normal four-letter word as he made for Jimmy before being waved off by DeVito.

"It's okay, Trujillo, Detective Sergeant Murphy is noted for his unorthodox entrances. I'll call if I need you."

Sergeant Trujillo threw Jimmy the look you give an old doormat—useful in its day, but way overdue a trip to the garbage.

When the door closed, the two men eyeballed each other. Then Jimmy whipped a CD out of his pocket and tossed it on the desk.

"Thought you might like this—remind you of who you used to be."

DeVito examined *At Fillmore East*, his lip curling in disgust. He reached into the top drawer of his desk, pulled out an iPod and a set of earphones. "I don't need it, schmuck, I listen to it here—stored right between *Eat a Peach* and *Idlewild South*. Got any number of live bootlegs too I can send you if you ever stumble into the twenty-first century."

With that he pulled down the bifocals from his forehead and examined the small print on the back of the CD.

"The weekend before Saint Patrick's, seventy-one, and we were there the Saturday, right?"

"Right!"

"I was wondering whether it was the Friday or Saturday on the train the other day. Now I got that straightened out, the fuck do you want?"

"Last time I tried to get in here you got Crazy Joey tripping over himself to keep me out."

"There's ways of doing things, Jimmy. The real issue is what's your problem—existential and otherwise? You been badmouthing me ever since I buckled down and made captain. All I ever hear is Murphy says this, Murphy says that, I'm too big for my britches, I'm a rising star who don't give a fuck about anyone, when the truth be told every time I ask you to come up and see me and Rita in Pelham, you make any kind of deadbeat excuse but cross the Gil Hodges and hang with someone who knew you before you turned into a crazy, paranoid son of a bitch who'd swear the fucking sun rose in the west rather than admit he was wrong about anything. Well, you can say whatever you like about me but don't you ever suggest I don't listen to Duane Allman no more! You hear me, cocksucker?"

With that he kicked back his chair, slid on his trench coat over his rolled-up shirtsleeves, and strode toward the door. "C'mon, let's get the hell out of here. I'm going up the fucking walls with this Bloomberg asshole. I thought Giuliani was bad!"

"I'll be back whenever," he snapped at Trujillo who jumped to his feet as they swept by.

Jimmy almost had to break into a trot to keep up with DeVito who roared at the front desk when passing, "Gallagher, unless you want to end up back in the South Bronx where you belong, you check everyone who comes into this fucking dump."

They took a right outside the door and had to run across Eighth Avenue to avoid the traffic. They didn't exchange a word; they both knew where they were headed. It had changed a lot over the years, but the Irish Pub on Seventh Avenue retained some of the breezy informality that had first drawn them as kids the night they caught Hot Tuna at Carnegie.

Two off-duty cops straightened up as the captain barged in. DeVito sent them a round to show he wasn't on some brass warpath then he joined Jimmy at a back table with a couple of glasses of Powers and some chasers of beer.

"Salud!" he said, drawing a deep breath, as they clicked glasses. They both grimaced at the rough whiskey. When he had washed the firewater down with a slug of his chaser DeVito ran his sleeve over his forehead and said, "Where to begin."

"Why not try the beginning?"

"Rockaway?"

"My son."

DeVito fingered the chaser examining it this way and that before he sighed. "Brian was a loose cannon, Jimmy."

"I thought that was me."

"He was a lot more like you than you ever gave him credit for, despite him being another rising star or whatever other half-assed term you called him."

DeVito waited but when Jimmy didn't rise to the challenge he continued: "When Brian made lieutenant there was a lot of shit going down with the presidential campaign. The Clinton guys in DC didn't trust Giuliani, the last thing they wanted was anything blowing up in their faces right before the election. The Bush crowd would have been all over them and Gore. So they were in touch with us big-time—What was happening on the streets? What was the mood of the city?" He waved his hand despairingly toward Seventh Avenue as though King Kong and Godzilla might be strolling by arm in arm.

"The usual bullshit!" He scratched the back of his near-balding head. "We needed someone to talk to them—someone who knew their language. It was a no-brainer. Brian was Georgetown, Moynihan intern, and looked the part. Take the shuttle down to DC, give them a nice big fat report that no one would ever read, and everyone's ass was covered."

He drained his Powers. "Always hits the spot. Rita won't have it in the house no more 'cause of my blood pressure."

"And?" Jimmy asked.

"Everything was going hunky-dory until . . ." He closed one eye and looked up at the ceiling, as though laboring with some abstruse mental calculation. "It was just before the World Series, no I'm wrong— maybe the playoffs. Anyway Brian had some tickets for a Mets game but he'd come across *something important*, felt DC should know."

"And?"

"I told him he was crazy, go to the ball game, it could wait."

"Why?"

DeVito drummed his fingernails on the table in the same way that used to drive Jimmy crazy when they were younger.

"I didn't think it was necessary."

"And he did?"

"Do I have to tell you about your own kid—'no stone unturned'? Problem was, he didn't have anything concrete, just chatter that he'd picked up."

"Out in Brooklyn?" Jimmy broke in but DeVito ignored him.

"The feds would have been all over us and for what? It might have leaked to the press, TV. Then where would we've been at if we couldn't back it up?"

"What did you do?"

"I put a lid on him, what do you think? I had Louis Esposito check it out."

Jimmy nodded his appreciation of Esposito's experience in such situations.

"We looked into everything Brian said to the nth degree—nothing came of it."

"A dead end?"

"According to Esposito! Brian was all sorts of pissed off. Claimed Esposito had walked through the case in hip boots and the leads all broke for cover."

"So?"

"So, the election came and then there was the whole screw-up with the count in Florida and it was nearly Christmas before it all got settled. There was the usual other shit breaking, you know what it's like. As far as I knew, Brian was just going down to DC dropping off his big manila file with some receptionist and that was that."

The bartender arrived with the same again. "That's from Mancini and O'Connor up the end of the bar."

DeVito stood up and raised his glass to the two cops. Jimmy didn't bother. DeVito had to play the game, he didn't.

"Listen, Brian had a great gig—a night down in DC every couple of months courtesy of the feds, nice hotel, making contacts, and you know how good he was at that shit. Passed you as lieutenant. He would have eventually left me in his dust."

"But he couldn't leave it be, right?"

"Not only that—I dropped the ball. Change of administration in DC. Giuliani acting out his usual psycho bullshit! It was damn near summer before I realized Brian was running his own show out in

Brooklyn. Had your buddy Yussef snooping around for him. Fucking *Casablanca* on Atlantic Avenue!"

He shook his head in amazement as he reran some memory. "Must have been late June when I finally hauled him in on his ass, told him to drop the whole thing, and the guy went ballistic on me! Told me he was hearing all sorts of shit and still reporting it to DC, but no one was even reading the files down there, that the new gang in town was even stupider than the Clinton mob, didn't give a rat's ass what was going on in the country just as long as they could shake it down for every last buck."

So I said, "What do you got?" But it was just bits and pieces of fundamentalists coming into the neighborhood and raising hell in the mosques—and all in Arabic. When we had it translated it was just guys blowing off steam about the US being an asshole state, how we all hated Muhammad, and our day was coming, garbage like that! There was nothing you could hang your hat on. So I went to town on him, told him I'd have his ass suspended if he wasn't a son of yours."

He shook his head again in disbelief. "You know what he did? He stormed out of my office screaming that they'd tried to blow up the Towers in ninety-three and what made me think they weren't coming back—blow up the tunnels this time or some shit? Him barely a lieutenant yelling in my face for the whole store to hear! I could have had his butt back on patrol in East fucking New York. I had my finger on the phone to call you about it, but with the fed connection I had to be careful. Anyway, next day he crawled in on his knees. Apologized, said he was all stressed out, that things were on the slide at home with Rosie. As if I should have been surprised by that—with all the stories going round about him!"

He exhaled deeply, a mix of sorrow and exasperation. "Said he needed some time off, was going on vacation with her and the kid. He was drinking too much, the usual shit. Happened to us all. So I gave him a month off. I understood. Rita was breaking my own balls about vacations and never seeing me. It was all quiet around here—just the usual summer crap—so I took some time off myself. Went up to Canada, did some fishing, what with putting my own house in order I didn't give him much more thought.

"When I got back mid-August, it was one thing after another, Giuliani doing his Mussolini without a balcony, it must have been a week or more before I happened to run into Sullivan out drinking, and for want of something better to say I asked him where Brian had gone for vacation. Of course, screwball with a full head of Guinness said that Brian didn't go nowhere anymore except Atlantic Avenue, was working on something big. I couldn't believe my ears. So I dragged Brian in again, he said he was almost at the bottom of it. The bottom of what? I asked. As usual he couldn't put words on it, some of the hotheads had left Brooklyn, same thing out in Jersey City and Paterson, gone to ground and couldn't be traced—but something huge was about to break!

"I thought to myself, I'm dealing with a lunatic, his eyes blazing like he'd seen the Second fucking Coming. What was I supposed to do? I didn't want to bust him, but he was out there, man, way out there, eight goddamned miles high."

"But he was right?"

"No, he wasn't! Or maybe he was, for all I know. But he didn't have anything concrete. I went through it letter by letter with him, dotted all the i's, crossed all the t's, and it wasn't there. Just a big series of educated hunches."

"What are you saying?"

"I don't know, Jimmy. For Christ's sake, I don't know, man. Maybe it's like our grandparents used to say—'he had the sense.' He could feel something brewing. But what was I supposed to do, go to Giuliani and Kerik and say, 'Lieutenant Murphy is a fucking druid—he sees something in the stars'? They would have laughed me outta there and put a big red mark next to Brian's name."

"Why didn't you tell me any of this?"

"You think I didn't want to? But you know yourself what it's like, once you start digging into these things you just don't know what else is going to come out."

"Like what?"

DeVito took another slug of the whiskey. He gazed down at the table until Jimmy grabbed him by the shoulder. "Like what, Tony?"

"There was a woman involved."

"What else is new?"

"She was young."

"Fatima?"

"How did you know?" DeVito looked up sharply.

Jimmy gave him the hard eye just to let him know who was asking the questions.

"Yeah, your falafel guy's daughter." DeVito eyeballed him back. "I didn't want that shit getting out. I mean before that it was just regular with Brian—married women, one-nighters, whatever—but put yourself in my position; does Rose need to know about some college kid?"

"She already does."

"Ah, Christ, but Maggie don't, right? And there's no need for her to. Brian's a hero, man—and he deserves it. You start bringing up shit like that, you don't know where it'll all end."

"So what was he doing down the Towers that morning?"

"I don't know, Jimmy, and to tell you the God's honest truth, with all that's gone down these last years, I don't want to know."

"I bet you fucking don't," Jimmy said and walked out.

TWENTY-TWO

They made love in very different ways, and yet with the lights out she often drifted back in time. Once she almost said Brian's name. Sometimes she felt conflicted, other times she hardly gave it a thought—that was then and this is now, and if nothing else it was good to feel wanted again. She wondered how she'd been dealing with the world the last three years—had she been on remote? She'd never felt attracted to anyone else. Must have just put that side of herself on hold, and then how easily it had come flooding back.

She cursed herself for being careless. She knew Liam would walk in on them someday. Maybe he already had; she almost died at the thought. How could she explain it to him?

But he was in Belle Harbor at the Abramses' on a play date with young Seth. That gave them at least another two hours.

She caressed Kevin the way he liked and he woke from his shallow sleep. At first he was reluctant, but within seconds he had rolled over on top of her. He had the same bristly jaw as Brian and the stubble roughed up her face. Her cheeks would be flaming but she didn't care, there'd be time enough to rub some cream into them; her lips would be bruised, but so what? It was worth it.

They smoked afterwards. She felt guilty that he'd taken it up again. But it was something they shared; besides, they'd quit together someday soon.

"My mother called from Lauderdale yesterday."

"Oh yeah?" he replied while blowing rings at the ceiling.

"She looked into that apartment for us."

"What apartment?"

"The one I've been talking about in the high-rise with the full view of the beach."

"Oh yeah?"

"She thinks they'll come down and be well within our range."

"That's good."

He did blow top-notch smoke rings. Too bad there was no demand for such a skill in Florida.

"You still want to go, right?"

"Sure. I guess. It's just a big step."

"Well, what we're doing is pretty big."

"Only thing is I'll have to chuck the firehouse and find something down there."

"Well, we'll have money—"

"You'll have money," he interrupted her.

"What's mine will be yours—and the kid's. Okay?"

She could tell he was unsettled. But it was time for a talk; she reached for his hand and squeezed it. He shifted the cigarette to the other hand and intertwined his fingers in hers.

"We could stay here," she said. "Add an extension. Liam could use a bigger room, stretch out a bit."

She waited for him to give an opinion, weigh in on their future, but he always shut down whenever that topic arose. It made her anxious. She had to be able to count on him.

"One way or another, we've got to get our act together."

"Like what?"

"Like when are you going to talk to your mother?"

"Well . . ." He exhaled and a cloud of smoke rose upward and then drifted lazily toward the ceiling. "I was all ready to tackle her the other day, but the nutty priest dropped by; on top of that, my old man's been coming and going at odd hours."

"Why can't you talk to the two of them together?"

"Wouldn't work; Dad's acting weird. You know how he is when he's on a mission?"

"Yeah, that day after you left he was asking me all sorts of questions."

"About what?"

"The usual—Brian, and what he was up to those last weeks."

"He just won't let it go. It's like he's trying to rewrite history or something."

He lit another cigarette. He didn't usually smoke more than one unless there was something troubling him.

"He was asking me about Fatima." She found it hard to say the girl's name.

"Arab chick?"

"Yeah. The falafel guy's daughter; did you know her?"

He stubbed out the barely smoked cigarette then turned to look at her.

"Maybe."

"What do you mean 'maybe'? You either know her or you don't."

"I met her once—no, twice."

"When?"

"With Brian. He was driving her home from some college uptown. He dropped by The Kinsale with her."

"You're kidding me—with all the cops that go in there?"

"If you don't want to talk about it, don't ask!"

"Was he . . .?"

"Bangin' her?"

"Jesus Christ. You don't have to be so crude."

"I said don't ask if you don't want to know."

She pulled her hand away. She felt like turning to the wall and crying.

"Listen, I don't know! He could have been loosening her up. Getting information. You know what he was like! He asked me to look after her while he went outside and made some calls."

"Then what?"

"Nothing. He came back in. She threw her arms around him. They had another drink and left."

"And that was that?"

"Well, they definitely didn't live happily ever after, though I think she might have gone for it."

"What do you mean?"

"She had the hots for him, what do you think? But it was like a teenage thing. She was young, hadn't drank much. Going on about what a great guy he was, how nice he was to show her around town. Jesus, hot spots like The Kinsale!"

"And how about him?"

"Had something on his mind, same as he did all that time."

She shook her head—what a mess he'd left behind.

"Listen, Brian didn't need to be putting time into some Arab virgin whose father might show up here with a machete. He had the pick of the city whenever he wanted it."

"So nice of you to let me know that."

"Well, you're the one who brought up the subject!"

"When was the other time?"

"Other time, what?"

"You saw her?"

He reached for another cigarette but she grabbed his hand.

He lay back and studied the ceiling. "The last night. I was partying with Brian and some probies on the Upper East Side. A lot of drinks, a lot of chicks! I went outside to throw up. Frankie Visceglia was even more hammered. Brian put the two of us in a cab and went back in the bar."

"To her?"

"I don't know."

"What do you mean, you don't know? You said you saw them together."

"Yeah, to her, who the fuck else! We'd been looking for her all night and finally found her. He said she was important—that she was the key. The key to fucking what? Jesus Christ! I should never have let him go back in on his own! The whole thing might have turned out different." He got up and went into the bathroom, locking the door behind him.

TWENTY-THREE

It had been coming for months, edging ever closer, but with Labor Day in the rearview mirror it now picked up a head of steam. In the bars people either drank too much or barely nursed a beer, the knife sharpening as the peninsula braced for the upcoming commemoration.

The mood hit everyone in different ways: down the firehouse it was somber, after all they had well over three hundred to mourn. Everything gleamed beyond its normal spit and polish; the Department would be on display, all its members under the microscope, putting on the best face possible. But the loss ate through them and many a hard man could be seen staring at the wall, tears trickling down his mustachioed face. An occasional hug or squeeze of a shoulder but no one spoke—what was there left to say three years later? Just suck it up, and if bitterness occasionally broke the surface then so be it; everyone felt the same pain, it was just that the knife twisted at a different angle for each individual.

The priest was no longer there to comfort them—the Franciscan in his brown robe knotted tight with his white cincture had been a familiar figure in Rockaway through good and, more often, bad. But he too had taken a hit down the Towers; now they had to fend for themselves without the ready smile and compassionate eyes of Father Mychal Judge.

Kevin hated being home that week and made himself as scarce as possible. He no longer needed to hear his mother alternately talking like there was no tomorrow or silent for hours on end, devouring him with her eyes, as if to soak up his essence and keep him always safe by her side.

Nor did he wish to be in close proximity with his father—either lost in thought or spouting stats as if Jeter, Posada, and The Rocket were first cousins twice removed, when all the time Kevin knew it was just a game to keep some semblance of normality humming in another shattered household. What was the point? It only postponed the inevitable; and sure enough when the grief and loss had been contained for too long they would explode in an outburst of regret and accusation, and all the elaborate sand castles of domestic civility so carefully constructed would come tumbling down around them.

If the first two years had been a maelstrom, this third would likely be even harder. There had been whole days when he hadn't even thought of Brian. Not that he didn't miss his brother or feel the sledgehammer blow when he considered never seeing him again. But all that had been thrown into flux the day he went down to Breezy to fix Rosie's bathroom door; layers of pain and sadness had been anesthetized by holding her and granting himself the luxury of being with her. Those moments were the best in his life, but they brought their own trials and complications. They were still living behind locked doors and closed shades, a sham of an existence. When all he wanted to do was scream his happiness to the heavens, all that was allowed him was a new lie to live.

The tension built all week and by Saturday morning it was almost a relief when the 9/11 ceremonies began. The osprey watched it all from one hundred feet above, arcing on the air currents then hovering gracefully for minutes before occasionally swooping down. His white head and breast glinted in the sunlight while a dark mask-like streak highlighted his pitiless golden eyes.

Earlier that morning Maggie had cut sunflowers in her garden and carried a bunch all the way down to St. Rose of Lima. She kept her head low barely acknowledging the condolences she received from her neighbors and fellow mourners; she had no wish to draw attention to herself on this of all mornings. Though her heart was heavy as an anvil she could tell that the veil between living and dead was at its flimsiest and could feel Brian's presence in all living things.

Liam barely gave his father a thought except when one of Seth Abrams's relatives dropped by to marvel at Lieutenant Brian Murphy's son on a play date. He had grown used to adults patting his head or tearily hugging him when they discovered who he was. Right now he was reveling in Seth's collection of Pokémon cards instead of attending the commemoration, and as soon as the adults drifted back to their own worlds and worries he and Seth would again lose themselves in *Grand Theft Auto*. All would be well. His grandpa would protect him from weird bad guys and girls in hoods, and when he grew up he'd become a cop and look after himself.

Kevin tried on his shades in Rose's hallway mirror. They went well with the dark blue of his suit. He had chosen a red tie—two years in black was long enough. He nodded his approval of Rose's gray blazer and skirt set off by a turquoise scarf. He'd stayed over the night before, told his parents he'd be crashing at Sweeney's. Maybe that's why neither his nor Rose's eyes were red from crying this year. They kissed one last time then Kevin held the door for her as they stepped out into the sunlight. The driver ambled around and opened the back door of the limo and they strode down the steps. They could almost hear the click of blinds as the neighbors caught their annual glimpse of the wife and brother of a martyred defender of the homeland heading off for Manhattan. They had a full day of speechifying ahead when they would sit motionless next to the wives and brothers, sisters and mothers, fathers, sons, and daughters of the thousands of others now exalted on an altar of pride, pain, and patriotism.

Jimmy Murphy attended no ceremonies unless staring out at the stillness of the ocean counted. No one spoke to him either as he stood bristling and erect on the boardwalk, even old Artie gave him a wide berth. His mind was crystal clear. He knew what he had to do—but not today. And so he bided his time, there were still conclusions to be drawn, the reckoning would come soon enough.

High over Dayton Towers the osprey banked off toward the Atlantic. It was getting near time for the long journey south.

TWENTY-FOUR

Even before he got off the R at 86th Street, Jimmy could tell Bay Ridge had changed. The train swayed to the chatter of Hong Kong girls in downtown fashions holding hands with second-generation Cantonese working their way up to suithood on Wall Street. All mixing in like nobody's business with Caribbean nurses, home health aides decked out in working white, a healthy contingent of North African women, many in hijabs and the occasional burqa, accompanied by serious-looking men studying pocket-sized Qurans, while their secular sisters gossiped and gesticulated, the requisite silver and gold gleaming on their necks and wrists.

It was all a far cry from the small-town neighborhood that he used to visit back in high school. Mostly Irish and Italian then, with a strong spicing of Norwegian; he often made the trip from Rockaway to hang with Bobby Olsen. He winced at the memory. They'd been drafted together, only difference, Bobby never made it back from the Mekong Delta. Killed by friendly fire, they said. Another fuckup in a war no one gave a damn about anymore!

What would Bobby be doing now if one of his own guys hadn't whacked him? Probably drinking. Guy could finish a keg and still had the legs to go hunting for another. Talk about the Irish being good at tossing them back—Norwegians could drink any Paddy under the table. Could still remember Bobby's big innocent face— red as a beet after he'd chug-a-lugged four jugs of Rheingold in The Three Jolly Pigeons. It had been a whole new world for Jimmy, hanging out with Olsen and his blond goddess sisters. Riding across the Verrazano to Great Kills, making out on the beach, then back to the bars, before crashing on the Olsens' couch, their old lady cluck-clucking in the morning as she filled them full of buttery blueberry pancakes.

It was a far different occasion when he pulled up in the yellow Caddy to pay his respects. Bobby had been dead a year by then, but the old lady still pumped out fresh tears, wondering why her only son had to go halfway round the world to fight the Commies when there was a shitload of them at every college protesting the war. Now few remembered Bobby Olsen or the fifty-eight thousand other kids who had given it up for some politician's stupid idea.

He followed the Benetton parade up the subway stairs to Fourth Avenue. Still a saloon on the far corner and Irish too. Some things never changed. The twilight was fading and the night clear, though there were few stars as he headed down 86th Street toward the Narrows. The Verrazano loomed to his left. Man, how they loved to speed across it, teenaged girls hanging all over them, screaming, "Bobby, Bobby, slow down," though they knew it only made him drive faster.

Olsen had a girlfriend, Maria Giordano, a quiet Bensonhurst beauty that his family disapproved of. Whatever happened to her? Married someone else, probably had grandchildren now. Did she ever cast a thought back to Private First Class Olsen coming home in a box after saving the good old US of A from invasion by a horde of starving, bare-footed peasants from the napalmed rice paddies of Southeast Asia?

What a waste! But what was he whining about anyway? He'd made it home safely. Hadn't cast Bobby Olsen a thought in years. If he was so upset, why hadn't he gone back and visited Olsen's mother again?

He halted near Colonial Road, leaned against a wall, and gazed across the Narrows at the dazzle of lights on Staten Island. What was Yussef up to and why had he lied to him about Brian? Had their friendship been nothing but a facade since 1993? Had he lied to Brian too? Led him on in the months before 9/11? Was his old friend responsible for his son being down in the North Tower that morning?

On Shore Road he took a right and strolled up some affluent blocks to Yussef's house. Odd that he'd never been invited; even Fatima's college acceptance party had been held in the falafel parlor on Atlantic. Jesus, the guy had done well for himself, a three-story redbrick with a garage on Bay Ridge's gold coast! Before ringing the bell, Jimmy glanced around and envied the tree-lined street that Yussef gazed upon when he headed off to inspect his falafel empire every morning. The American dream, and one lucky Egyptian had hit the jackpot.

A light went on in an upstairs room seconds after he rang the doleful bell. No sounds from within. His hand automatically reached for the .38. What was he carrying a piece for anyway? Hadn't taken it out since he'd quit the job except to occasionally clean it. Something about the hostility spewing out of Yussef's two young security guys had spooked him.

He rang again and the light upstairs went out. Then he spotted the snout of the concealed camera above the door. A blind man could see the damned thing! Talk about stupid, now anyone watching would know he was packing.

He tensed as he heard the approaching muffled footsteps. Yussef betrayed no emotion when he opened the door, merely nodded and beckoned him inside. He held out his hands for Jimmy's coat and hung it on the ornate hall stand.

"I have been waiting for you, James. I had expected your visit last week."

Jimmy saw no necessity to answer and anyway he was engrossed in the elaborate furnishing and décor. Outside, the building may have been typical Shore Road redbrick stolidity but he was now standing within a carefully reconstructed Egyptian household. And it was all so eerily silent. Barely a murmur could be heard from the street.

Yussef watched him take in the rugs, carpets, and wall coverings, much of it decorated with Arabic calligraphy, the dark wooden trunks and polished ebony carvings, two large candles casting their muted light.

"Come, let me show you." He gestured upstairs and Jimmy followed. Each room had been furnished with care, each wall shrouded with drapes, a large bed in the center and around it cushions and pillows—except for one room he supposed was Fatima's, sparer with a Mac laptop occupying pride of place, and the sharp smell of modern cosmetics edging out the musky heaviness of the rest of the house.

On their way back down the corridor to the stairs, Jimmy paused to look inside the partially open door of a room wherein flickered a bright votive lamp.

"*Masjid al-bayt.*" Yussef motioned. "The mosque of our house."

He murmured some further words in Arabic, and when Jimmy silently questioned their meaning he said, "God guides unto His light whom He wills."

"What about those who choose their own path?"

Yussef glanced at Jimmy in dismay but ignored the question.

"After your visit, I spent much time in here seeking guidance. It would appear some of my prayers were answered for you arrived on a night Maryam and Fatima have gone to the movies."

All the better to have your security detail do a number on me and dump me in the Narrows. Jimmy banished the thought and to ease the tension inquired, "What are they seeing?"

"They share an affection for the actor Brad Pitt." Yussef smiled, but then intimated that such matters were inconsequential.

They gazed at the lamp for some moments before Yussef turned on the main light. Jimmy realized that he had been praying when the bell rang. Across the deep-blue-carpeted room, four mats were lined up and pointed at an odd angle to the walls. Who had been praying with him? Jimmy touched his gun for reassurance.

"To Mecca." Yussef gestured in the direction the mats were pointing.

"What is it with religion these days? You, Maggie, everyone I know is either up to their eyes in it or running like hell the other way."

"When doubt is everywhere, the one certainty is God."

"He seems to be really in style at the moment."

"We turn to Him when we have no other choice."

"Like after the planes struck?"

"When there is pain and suffering, God is there for us. Your wife had need of Him, as did I."

"I can see her need, but yours?"

Yussef switched off the light and the shadows cast by the flame of the votive lamp danced to the unanswered question. Jimmy followed him down the stairs into the hallway and out through the kitchen into a large room with French doors opening onto a garden that had at its center a small illuminated fountain.

Some couches faced each other across a marble coffee table dominated by two framed pictures. One he recognized as Fatima in cap and gown on her graduation from Barnard. The other was of Yussef's youngest daughter, Leah, wearing the more traditional attire of Egypt.

Jimmy picked up her picture. She stood arm in arm with a young man in a well-tailored suit, his eyes burning with all the arrogance and certainty of youth.

"God did not bless me with a son," Yussef said.

"It would appear you're about to gain one."

"*Inshallah*."

"I have not seen Leah since she was a little girl."

"No, and even then, as you might remember, she preferred to keep her own company, and devote herself to her studies and her family."

"Meaning?"

"She cherished the traditions of her home and not the customs of America as did her elder sister."

Jimmy didn't have to be told; there was a restraint and a walled-off nature to her quiet smile, unlike the beaming self-assurance of Fatima. Her fingers were intertwined with those of the young man, their lives already inexorably linked.

"She's not in the country?"

"No, after the attack she was the object of scorn in her high school. I sent her to my cousin's in Alexandria. She would have liked to continue her studies there, but I feared that someday she might wish to return here; she now attends the American University in Beirut."

"And the young man?"

"Ammar is the eldest of a good family from Baghdad that moved to Beirut soon after the invasion."

Yussef bitterly emphasized the last word, something he had never done in their many discussions about the Gulf War. Jimmy took one last look at the picture of Leah and the young man. There was not even a trace of accommodation in the Iraqi's face, only a blank and implacable conviction that could one day lead to trouble. As if by reflex, Jimmy swept the room for concealed doorways or closets, but all appeared aboveboard except for the remarkable silence so dense it could almost be touched.

"The world has changed, James, both here and back in my country. I arrived in the United States with great hopes and dreams, many of which came true. But I had no inkling that matters would turn out as they did. Should Fatima choose the right path and marry her cousin, Maryam and I will sell all our worldly goods here and move back to be with our grandchildren. Leah and her suitor will eventually move to Alexandria where we shall all be reunited, *inshallah*.

"What is there left for us in this country where people grow more ignorant by the day, nourished by the paranoia of their masters? Where my eldest daughter is forced to choose between the world she wishes to inhabit and her family, and where my youngest was mocked publicly for cherishing and practicing the traditions of her people?"

Yussef groped inside a cabinet and withdrew an unopened bottle of Jameson's. Jimmy put down the picture and smiled, recognizing his gift.

"You said that one day I might have need of this. You were right, my friend."

"You're sure I'm not leading you into temptation?"

"One day, God willing, I will be strong enough to renounce one of the finer things in life." He smiled.

"Until then."

Yussef opened the bottle and poured two ample helpings. Then he withdrew to the kitchen, fumbled in the refrigerator for ice, and ran the tap. When they sat down with the whiskey and iced water, Yussef raised his glass.

"To our families, may they prosper in health and wealth."

"*Inshallah*," Jimmy murmured.

"*Inshallah* indeed. You did not forget, my friend."

"No matter what God wills, to my way of thinking friends do not lie to each other."

Jimmy scowled at both the fieriness of the whiskey and the truth, but Yussef savored his, nodding his head in appreciation.

"Did I lie or merely withhold evidence, as your Detective Briscoe in *Law and Order* once suggested?"

Jimmy indicated his lack of interest in playing games.

"I needed time to disentangle the truth from so many varying strands, James, while the grayness in your face indicated you were not yet ready for its consequences."

"And I am now?"

"That remains to be seen, but one way or another it is time for you to receive it."

"I trusted you, Yussef."

"And for my part, I did not trust you."

They stared at each other across the lacquered coffee table, each considering the other's words.

"I understand you are retired, yet you are still a servant of a country I can no longer put my faith in. The United States imprisons my people and holds them without trial. It invades Islamic lands and desecrates our holy shrines. I know you are a good man and would guard my interests to the best of your abilities, still there are those above you who have no concern for me or my family."

"I came to your door with the sole intention of finding the truth about my son."

"Your son too came for the truth, but he brought with him a cloud that still hovers over my family."

"You know he wouldn't have done that intentionally."

"I accepted him in my home because of our friendship, but he compromised my daughter in the eyes of both my people and the authorities."

"If he did, I'm sure he never meant to."

"James, your faith in your son is admirable but if you are ever to accept the truth you must learn to listen."

When Jimmy unclenched his fists and sat back in his chair Yussef continued. "Do you remember when you first brought Brian to my door? He was still a student in your Police Academy—tall and handsome, like his father—and intelligent too, interested in our ways and customs; he could even quote lines from Cavafy, the poet of my city. Fatima was on the verge of womanhood, perhaps thirteen. I remember her peering out from the kitchen at this mighty young man in his uniform.

"When he returned alone he was a lieutenant, and she laughed and joked easily with him as would befit a student from Barnard. But he sought to spend time alone with me. He wished to know of the comings and goings in our community and about our use of *hawala* for transferring money—he spoke about rumors of large sums coming into the country from Afghanistan and Saudi Arabia, and wondered who was receiving these funds and for what purpose.

He also wished to know my opinion of our imam and the affairs at our mosque. I took him into my confidence. I told him of the young men from our country, and others of our brothers, who had arrived in New York, some of whom had extreme ideas on how the Word of the

Prophet should be interpreted. I also told him of imams from other countries who preached at our mosque, and how I felt their intentions were not in the best interests of our people.

"This was done in friendship and I trusted his confidentiality. Some of these people had not pursued legal entry to the country, but they were not criminals, they merely reflected the feeling in some of their lands that American troops should have vacated Kuwait as soon as Saddam was defeated, and not remained there as infidels desecrating our holy places.

"Your son felt there was a possibility that something catastrophic was about to occur; he used my name indiscriminately to approach and even harass some of my friends and acquaintances. When word reached me about such indiscretions I forbade him to do so again.

"It was then that he turned to my daughter and began to pay her attention, to wait for her at her college and escort her around the city. She was a young woman and impressionable. Through her eyes he wished to gain information on the activities of certain young men—two of them were at my premises when you visited, which was one of the reasons I could not be more forthcoming with you. These young men studied at the feet of a visiting imam who was far from an admirer of American ways. Does that make them criminals? No, they are entitled to their opinions, but as you could see they are of a rash disposition and could one day pose a threat to my daughter's safety—even to my own."

Yussef looked off into the distance as if weighing what he would say next. When he turned back to Jimmy his words were more measured.

"I have knowledge of one strand of your son's activities. Only God now knows of the other avenues he was pursuing. He was a driven man convinced that there was some great threat to his country. He was correct in his assumption, but this threat did not originate in my mosque and there was little sympathy for it within our community."

He reached out for the remains of his whiskey, but on second thought pushed the glass away.

"Perhaps he discovered those seeds of destruction in some other community that he was investigating. He seemed to think so. He called me the evening before the attack and begged for a meeting. He wished to discuss some 'new evidence' he had come by. My first instinct was to say no; however, he appeared distracted and there was great pain in his voice over something that had just happened. On account of my regard for you, I agreed to meet him on the following day."

He murmured a prayer before continuing. "Which tragically proved to be his last. And now we will never know what he wished to speak about."

He paused for a moment and then continued softly, yet with a rare hint of bitterness:

The days of the future stand in front of us
Like a line of candles all alight

"Your son was fond of those lines from Cavafy and quoted them to me. Now alas all his candles have been blown out in this life. Hard though your task may be, my friend, you must reconcile yourself to that."

He bowed his head. When he looked up again, there was an icy resolve in his gaze that Jimmy could not ignore.

"As a father and a friend I have great sympathy for you; however, your son compromised my daughter in the eyes of our community. How could she ever make a good marriage after such an association? There is talk in the mosque about her that continues to this day and, as this war in Iraq worsens and passions intensify, she may be in danger because she was seen in the company of your son and another police officer."

Richie Sullivan, no doubt, following through on some lead for Brian when he was out of town. Jimmy knew the paranoia over police in immigrant communities; it had been no different with the Irish, Italians, Jews, and so many others down the years.

"After Fatima returned from Alexandria, I did not believe she would break her vow never to see your son again. But I was wrong, and though it is over three years now I am still troubled by his rashness and her lack of discretion."

Yussef refreshed their glasses with a stiff pour of whiskey and at first stared into his. "I am faced with a dilemma, James. By the customs of my people, I should inform my cousin in Alexandria about my daughter's activities. In their eyes she has compromised herself by her association with a man outside our faith; that he was married is an even greater concern. But worst of all your son may have had physical relations with her."

Fatima's muffled cry shocked both men. Engaged as they were in the back of the house, neither had heard the car ease into the driveway or the front door open. They both turned in astonishment as she spoke.

"Father, forgive me for listening, but since you refer to my friendship with Mr. Murphy's son, I have to speak my mind."

Maryam had thrown her arm protectively around the young woman, but she broke free and approached them.

At first she gazed only at her father and did not even look at Jimmy. Any sassiness or hint of modernity had been stripped away; she stood in front of him as a supplicant, a dutiful daughter awaiting her father's permission to speak. Yussef's eyes had clouded in pain and confusion; when he finally regained his composure and nodded his assent, she walked over to Jimmy and took his hands in hers.

"Brian was the kindest and most beautiful man I ever met. His only interest in me was to save lives. I tried to help him as best I could for that reason—but also because of my feelings for him. If I have caused your family distress, Mr. Murphy, I am so terribly sorry. I would do anything to take back the past."

"Wouldn't we all," Jimmy murmured. He intimated that he would make his own way to the door but Yussef shook his head, bade him sit down and bear witness to what would unfold.

Fatima turned once more to her father and kissed him on both cheeks. "I will write to Morgan Bradford tonight and break off my relationship with him." She sighed bitterly. "I'm sure his parents will be as relieved as mine."

When Yussef was noncommittal she continued more forcefully. "I have thought a lot about my situation, Father, and I'm sorry for the pain I've caused you. I've decided to become engaged to Hassan in Alexandria if he'll still accept me, and I'll join him there after graduation. Please don't mention my friendship with Brian to my aunt. If I know Hassan the subject will not arise."

"And if he is not the man you imagine?"

"Then we'll face that problem when we come to it."

Yussef seemed pleased. For this family it appeared that Brian's liaison with Fatima had at least been put to rest for the time being. Yussef took his daughter in his arms and kissed her on the forehead. She nodded good-bye to Jimmy and said, "Come, Mother."

The two men watched them go, the daughter straight-backed and resolved, the mother loyally trailing her. Jimmy finished his whiskey. He held out his hand to Yussef who stared at it.

"I know you will not take my advice, James, and this may bring us into further conflict." Yussef at first spoke quietly. Then he brushed the still proffered hand aside and drew Jimmy near. "Who knows what the future holds. But I will treasure the friendship we had before the world came between us. God willing, it will flower again—no matter what occurred between your son and my daughter."

"*Inshallah*," Jimmy whispered as his host walked him through the hall. He took his coat from the hall stand and cast a last glance at the dignified splendor of the Egyptian furnishings before Yussef opened the front door.

"James, I believe you know why Brian's voice was thick with pain when he called me that last night. It was for your sake I chose to meet him."

It was the last thing Jimmy wanted to hear, but when he didn't answer, Yussef nodded his understanding. "Be strong, my friend."

And with that Yussef closed the heavy door behind him.

TWENTY-FIVE

Jimmy did not change to the express at 59th Street; instead he remained on the R train as it wound its tedious way through downtown Brooklyn. He needed time to think and take stock for he could sense that doors were closing. He had little doubt that despite her graduation plans Fatima would soon be on a plane to Egypt. Whether the two young men were working for Yussef or keeping tabs on him was immaterial; Fatima had crossed a line and with the war in Iraq heating up, matters could only get worse for the Ibrahim family.

Then there was Tony DeVito sheltering behind his blue wall of silence! Whatever cover-up he was involved in, personal or otherwise, obviously depended on Lieutenant Brian Murphy remaining a legitimate embalmed hero.

Sullivan might be in cahoots with DeVito but there was no love lost between them. He did care deeply for Brian, however, and was with him in the final minutes before the Tower came down. He knew more than anyone else. But would he talk?

With his mind finally made up, Jimmy could barely wait for the R to rattle into Manhattan's 49th Street station. He jumped off the train, pushed open the emergency gate, hurried up the stairs and across West 51st to the familiar building just west of Eighth Avenue. The light was on in Sullivan's third-floor apartment. He always left it like that when he went out, along with the radio blasting 1010 WINS to scare off potential burglars. All was quiet, so chances were he was home.

Jimmy knew he had to breach Sullivan's barrier of resentment—appeal to their old friendship but still project enough strength so that his ex-partner wouldn't walk all over him. Another explosion like the one between them in Dolan's, and Sullivan's door could slam, leaving Brian's secrets locked permanently behind it.

Jimmy hadn't been to the hovel, as it was known at Midtown North, since the mid-90s. The entrance had been redone—new door, bells, and wouldn't you know it, the protruding snout of a video camera; first Yussef, then Sullivan? It made sense for a Muslim after 9/11, but a veteran member of the New York Police Department?

Still in the same building though, Sullivan always said that, given the low stabilized rent, they'd take him out feet first. Jimmy smiled grimly as he pressed the illuminated bell.

Not a peep out of him! What was he pulling? Jimmy leaned into the bell. He could feel Sullivan's eyes peering into a video screen and taking his measure.

Then Jimmy looked up at the camera and flicked their old signal from the Academy—an outstretched finger, then a sudden click of the simulated trigger with his thumb. He nodded at the camera, laid his hands out bare signaling that he carried no concealed weapon, though he could feel the butt of the .38 hard against his hip.

A sudden buzz and he pushed in the door. Bastard had been there watching all the time. What was he afraid of?

The old flophouse had changed. The last time Jimmy had visited he'd had to shuffle up the stairs in shadow light, the dangling naked bulbs either half-dead on the vine or stripped from their sockets. Now incandescent flood lamps blared down casting a peroxide sheen over the electric-blue walls.

The smell was different too—fresh paint and organic cooking had replaced the old West 51st whiff of ethnic food and street-cheap perfume. On up to the third floor he trudged, nostalgic for an era he never thought he'd miss—or rather resenting the Bloomberg soullessness that had replaced it.

Sullivan's door was slightly ajar and Jimmy snapped into red alert. Had Yussef's security guys got there first and were now awaiting him? He edged the door open and gingerly stepped inside. He could have saved himself the anxiety. Sullivan was draped over the kitchen table, dressed in an old NYPD undershirt and sweatpants, a copy of the *Post* spread out in front of him. But instead of the big gut leaking out over the sweats, he looked even trimmer than he'd been at Dolan's. The hovel had changed too; what had once been closer to a bag lady's flop was tidy, even monk-like. Guy had even invested in a garbage can, replacing the half-full plastic bags that once had littered the floor.

On the gas stove a pot of some odd-smelling thin brown concoction was gently gurgling. Sullivan eyed him from the far side of the table then, noticing Jimmy's attention on the stove, strolled over, turned down the flame, and stirred the soup.

"Miso."

"Japanese?"

"Yeah, good for B vitamins."

"You used to get them from Guinness."

"Tell me about it, but this shit don't give you a gut."

Jimmy closed the door behind him and stepped further into the room.

"Don't walk on the mat!"

Jimmy vaulted over the rubber padding and made a face as he pulled a chair out from under the table.

"Yeah, yeah, yeah!" Sullivan muttered. "You could use some yoga yourself. Your goddamn shoulders are up around your ears."

"I didn't come here to talk New Age."

"What did you come for?"

Jimmy took another glance around the room. Even the windows had been cleaned, and framed by bright yellow curtains.

"Getting to be a regular Pollyanna?"

"My mother sent them—brighten up the place."

A picture of his mother beamed down on them from over the fake mantelpiece. A public school teacher, she must have had more hearts than a cat had lives, for Sullivan had shattered a dozen or more. By the look of the changes around the apartment, one old lady down in Lauderdale could finally trade in her rosary beads.

"Ain't gonna offer me a drink?"

"Nothing but O'Doul's."

"Whatever, it'll take the dryness away."

Sullivan threw open the fridge. It was filled with yogurt containers and bunches of exotic leafy vegetables. He had to fumble in the back for the six-pack of non-alcoholic beer. Despite all the improvements he hadn't yet bought an opener, for he expertly hammered off the cap against the table edge and passed the foaming bottle.

It was ice cold and tasted close enough to the real thing, but the thought that there'd be no delayed kick took away some of the pleasure.

"Never thought I'd see the day we'd be reduced to this."

"Listen, Murph, it could be a lot worse and I'm alive, okay? Now what do you want?"

"I just came from Yussef's."

"Falafel guy?"

"Yeah."

"What did he say that got you so wound up?" Sullivan lumbered to his feet, sprinkled some diced onions into the miso, and stirred the pot again.

"He said that Brian had been on to a posse of fundamentalists who were stirring things up at the mosque."

Sullivan sneered. "What else is new? You had your ear to the ground back then, you picked up all sorts of that shit."

"Yeah, but Brian was the only one who acted on it."

Sullivan plopped down on his chair again. His eyes darted around the room, anywhere but at Jimmy. His hands, spread out over the *Post*, began to move almost independently, fingers tapping the paper then wiping imaginary sweat from his brow, an alky dying for a drink no matter what improved face he was presenting to the world.

"He had us all buzzing around like blue-assed flies until DeVito told him to leave it the fuck alone."

"But he didn't?"

"You tell me. You're the one talked to the towelhead."

Jimmy had always disliked that side of Sullivan—the dumb built-in racism that no amount of miso or yoga would ever put a dent in. Sullivan smiled. He could tell it got Jimmy's goat and would have needled him further but the soup began to boil; he dived over and switched off the gas.

"Yussef knew more than he was saying, right?" Jimmy probed.

"What do you think this is, charades? You're shooting in the dark, man, trying to pin a tail on a donkey you know nothing about."

"He knew Brian was getting close, didn't he?"

"Did it ever occur to you that maybe Yussef had his own agenda?" Sullivan sneered again.

"Maybe, but he didn't have a clue what Brian was doing down the Towers at eight fifteen on a Tuesday morning and you did, Richie!"

"You got one thing right. Old towelhead would have flipped his lid if he'd known where Brian had come from." Sullivan cackled at his own private joke but didn't cut Jimmy in on it. Instead he went after his old partner like he used to when cranky and dying with a hangover in their patrol car days.

"Maybe your son wasn't the saint you thought he was. Hey, maybe he came early to shake down Cantor Fitzgerald or Windows on the World. That ever cross your Goody Two-Shoes mind?"

"A lot of things crossed my mind, particularly what he was doing down there talking to you."

"Maybe he liked me—liked being around me, particularly when he needed a favor."

"What kind of favors were you laying on him?"

"I was his eyes and ears, remember, that's what he used to call me."

"So what did you see, what did you hear?"

"Maybe I heard something on the street before any of you overpaid detective smart-asses, and maybe the golden boy Lieutenant Brian Murphy was down there copping the word from his Uncle Richie!"

"Brian was too good a detective to be depending on your drunken ass!"

"Oh yeah, well my ass ain't drunk no more, and now you're depending on simple old Officer Richard Sullivan to get to the bottom of this whole thing. So for once in your stuck-up, principled life, Detective Sergeant James Murphy, you beg, motherfucker, c'mon, beg, you hear me!"

He began to cackle, an exaggerated sound that rose in pitch as he enjoyed Jimmy's discomfort. Had he noticed his ex-partner's hand shaking and the wildness in his eyes, he might have taken a different tack. For without a word, Jimmy was over the table, gripping him by the throat; down they went in a confusion of chairs, rolling toward the gas stove and slamming up against it. Then the soup was spilling down Sullivan's shoulders and he was howling and kicking in all directions. But Jimmy held on because he was back in the jungle again, digging his nails into Sullivan's face and hammering his head off the floor until the stronger man recovered his balance, punched back, and finally threw him off. In a flash Sullivan was on his feet and had whipped his Glock out from under the *Post* before Jimmy was close to reaching for his .38, and Sullivan was screaming even as he tried to soothe his scalded back. "You crazy motherfucker! What's the matter with you?"

Jimmy was shaking and staring aghast at the two bloody slits on Sullivan's face.

Now that Sullivan had drawn a bead on him he began sobbing from the pain and the rage. "You fucking bastard! I never made sergeant because you put the word in with DeVito!"

The gun shook in his hand but he continued to point it at Jimmy.

"You just couldn't bend your dumb screwed-up principles, could you? Jimmy Murphy had to be right, even when it messed up the best friend he ever had."

Jimmy picked himself up off the floor. His hip felt twisted and out of joint but he made it to his feet.

"Now get out of here and leave me alone!" Sullivan yelled. "I'm doing the best I can, which is more than I can say for you, you fucking lunatic!"

Jimmy held up his hands to show he meant no further harm, but Sullivan was having none of it. "And take your sick fucking paranoia with you."

The gun still trembled in Sullivan's hand as Jimmy opened the door and stepped out into the hallway.

"You know something else, asshole? Even your own son thought you were crazy. You hear me? You turned the kid away from you— and you damn well know it!"

He strode over, slammed the door in Jimmy's face, and left him standing like some discarded pillar of salt in the newly painted hallway.

He must have just missed Dolan. The smell of Old Spice still lingered around the booth as he slid in painfully opposite Marcella.

"Oh Jesus, Jimmy, what happened?" She reached out and touched his face.

"It's nothing."

"Nothing? You have a bump on your forehead the size of a goose egg. Have you been to a doctor?"

"It's just a . . ." But he hadn't checked a mirror and didn't know exactly what he was referring to except that his forehead was throbbing like the hammers of hell, his hip was aching, and he was having difficulty collecting his thoughts. Nor could he fathom how his visit to Sullivan had spun out of control. Still, it was safe to assume that his ex-partner must have caught him with a pile driver when they were rolling around on the floor.

"Come! Let's go into the office and fix it up."

Nor did she let go of his hand as they walked through the kitchen, the immigrant staff first waving then gaping at him in his disheveled suit with the torn shirt collar.

She only released his hand when she opened the first aid box in her office and searched for a bottle of rubbing alcohol. She washed her hands then doused a cotton swab with some of the clear liquid.

"Don't worry, I did a year's nursing."

"You never told me that."

"Lots of things I haven't told you." She put her hand on his shoulder and bade him sit on the desk. Then she examined his forehead. He closed his eyes as her cool fingers probed the ridges of the welt. She was so near he fancied he could hear her heart beat. She smelled fresh and young, and her voice, as ever, was soothing as a mountain stream.

"Relax now, this will sting for a moment but then it will be fine."

She held his head with her left hand while cleaning the welt. He didn't flinch at the pain, just gave himself up to the touch of her fingers. It was nice to be looked after, to cede control.

When he opened his eyes she was staring at him. She didn't look away nor did she smile; she was waiting for him to say something.

He closed his eyes again, unwilling to end the moment.

"I thought you were asleep," she said quietly when he reopened his eyes; she smiled and removed her hand. "There's no point in me asking if you'll wear a Band-Aid, I suppose?"

"No."

"No point in inquiring what happened either, right?"

"Right."

"Oh, Jimmy, what am I going to do with you?"

If only I knew, he almost replied.

Still he felt better, somehow rejuvenated, and she smiled again, more content than she'd been in months now that she'd finally helped him in some small way. She was still standing close, and she gazed in his eyes one last moment before placing the first aid kit back on the shelf.

"You just missed Mr. Dolan."

"Yeah, I smelled him."

"He did somewhat overdo the Old Spice today," she admitted after looking around to make sure no one might hear.

"That's an understatement." Jimmy headed for the door.

"Wait," she said.

She appeared nervous, digging her thumbnail into her ring finger. "Someone must have told him you'd missed a night or two—he questioned me about it."

"And?"

"I said you had some family business to attend to, that you'd approached me about it, something to do with your . . ."

"Wife?"

"No, your son Kevin. I didn't want him calling your house and getting a different story."

"And that was all?"

"He wondered if you'd come to a decision."

"About what?"

She was really nervous and he wondered why.

"Your new duties."

"My what?"

"You know, whether you can go beyond being security manager and get more involved in running the actual restaurant—with me?"

"Oh Jesus, I'd forgot all about that."

"I thought so, with everything that's been going on."

A fucking maître d'. No wonder he'd blocked it out, all the fireworks notwithstanding.

"Jesus," he groaned. "I thought when I didn't hear anything that it was just another of his brilliant ideas gone up in smoke."

"Actually he was very insistent about it and would like an answer 'in the immediate future.' Perhaps you should talk it over at home?"

She was studying him so intently he felt there was more to the suggestion than mere words.

"Well, it is a career move, of sorts," she continued. "Maybe you'd want to talk it over with your wife?"

"Yeah, I suppose."

He could tell she was probing—that she wished to know something but didn't know how to ask.

"Want to get a drink?" he finally inquired.

"That would be nice, but . . ."

"But what?"

"I don't think you should be seen in the bar with your shirt torn."

"Not to mention the bump on my forehead, they might think you're hanging out with a unicorn."

"Oh, Jimmy," she sighed in mock exasperation. "Even at the worst of times you see the humor in things."

"Yeah, they beat that into you in NYPD 101. I suppose I should call it an early night."

"There's something I want you to see first," she said, ushering him out to the service staircase. "Mr. Dolan showed me earlier."

"He has a secret room of delights where he entertains his night managers?"

"You don't know the half of it." She raised her eyebrows and walked ahead of him up the stone stairs. He admired her lithe figure and the sureness of her step. Despite the steep incline she stood erect and did not hold on to the banister, while Jimmy clutched onto it the full five flights up. He felt dizzy and a little winded by the time she reached the door to the roof.

"He's considering opening a rooftop bar for next summer and wanted my opinion on the layout. There'll be a special section for smokers that he thinks will have great appeal. He hoped it could be our first project."

She pulled back the bolt lock with some authority and he followed her out onto the roof.

"He's got a point, I'll grant him that," he said, raising his voice slightly to be heard over the cacophony arising from the street. "Smokers are tired of huddling out on the street especially in winter."

They were facing north over the city. The lights from uptown flashed and glowed turning the barren tarred rooftop into a dazzling oasis.

"He'd put the bar over there." She pointed toward 49th Street. "But that's not the real reason I took you up here. Close your eyes."

He idly wondered what she had in mind but a wave of fatigue swept over him and he was once again glad to cede control.

"Don't open until I tell you." She took his hand and slowly turned him around. "Okay, now you can do it—but slowly."

He'd taken care to avoid them yet the twin beams of light reaching up into the heavens were as magical and mystifying as the first time he'd seen them two years previously.

Still, despite their quiet majesty his turmoil began to surge—the familiar bone-deep emptiness curried by the pain of knowing he'd never see Brian again. She held his hand a little tighter for she could sense what he was feeling.

"I think of those lights as the eyes of those we lost—they see things we have no earthly idea of," she said.

The turmoil did not go away but for once he felt a strange inkling of peace begin to take form and surface. They stood close together holding hands and staring at the fragile pillars of light in the September sky. All around them the neon of the city flashed and popped but they no longer noticed. She leaned her head on his shoulder.

"There's something you should know before we go back downstairs."

He didn't answer, afraid to break the spell.

"I decided not to go out with Conor."

"No?"

"No. I just thought you should know."

TWENTY-SIX

Jimmy gazed out alone from the boardwalk. A day later the throbbing in his forehead was still constant, yet something to be ignored not dwelt upon. Maggie had been visiting her sister up in Woodlawn at the far end of The Bronx when he arrived home so all awkward questions had been postponed. He'd mooned around the house piecing together the events of the last days still wondering how he'd allowed the situation with Sullivan to ramp out of control. At Midtown North he'd always been known as the calm, collected one—not some enraged bull in Sullivan's china shop.

He gazed up and down the near-deserted boardwalk. The old-timers had already decamped back to the solace of their single rooms and unmitigated memories. Still, early twilight was one of the best times to view the pounding surf so he held steadfast and gazed out on the shadowy beach. The inky darkness was already threatening the horizon and the gulls had lined up along the sand, their static battalions facing diagonally into the wind, waiting for some secret sign to take off; going where, he wondered? He envied their certainty and marveled at their poise as they balanced on one spindly leg, waiting, waiting.

Then their leader, a big garrulous cock stretched his wings and without a glance behind launched himself into the wind before veering toward the water. He was followed by some lieutenants who, after screeching orders at the waiting squadrons, swooped into his slipstream, and within seconds the whole flock had erupted off the beach in a wild sweep of flapping wings. Some fifty yards out beyond the breakers they swung westward into the fading sunset and moved off toward the golden towers of Manhattan.

He liked this time of day, this melding of light and shadow, when out near the horizon the freighters and tramps steamed up the coast to New Haven or Boston, while the big jet airliners streaked above them, their lights winking as they headed north to Newfoundland and across to Shannon, or east over the Atlantic to Rome, Madrid, and other cities he'd never visit.

Behind him lights were coming on in the Surfside Apartments, the balconies still jammed with beach chairs waiting forlornly for the least sign of an Indian summer. But the weekend was approaching, and cases of Bud and Coors had been stacked next to the railings—no need of an excuse for a party in Rockaway, where the moon would soon rise and transform the fatigued beach into a subtle, silvery paradise.

He heard the pounding steps even before he saw the runner and within seconds identified them. Kevin might have gained weight, but his right foot still hit those boards in the same distinctive manner as when he was fighting to keep his place on the baseball team. That's when Jimmy had told him he needed to work on his stamina and speed if he was going to nail shortstop. Not that father necessarily knew more than son, but Ozzie Smith had said it in an interview and what was okay by The Wizard was all right with Mr. Murphy.

The kid had pounded the boardwalk all that long winter, but come spring he'd been dropped anyway and turned to smoking weed instead. Jimmy used to find roaches around the house. He knew it wouldn't be Brian—not that he didn't partake, he was just too smart to leave any evidence. Had to be Kevin. Still, he quit when he joined the Fire Department. Just a phase, though a pretty long one for his parents—five, six years of praying the kid wouldn't get caught doing anything dumb.

He got back into running eventually, but his fitness regimes were always initiated by crises. All that first year after Brian got hit, Kev pounded it out morning and night up and down the boardwalk. He was thin as a rail by the first anniversary then he quit one day, no reason.

Jimmy turned to watch his son approaching. He knew Kevin wouldn't see him, hood up, glowering down at the boards for fear someone had squashed a fruit or dropped some french fries that might send him skidding. What was it with kids, you were so tied to them; even years after they'd cut loose you could sense when they were in trouble or needed you.

Kevin didn't even come close to noticing his father though he was only yards away when he pounded by. Why was he running? Or what was he running from?

Kevin had been with Brian that last night. Tied a load on with him, had to be sent home in a cab. But there must have been more to it. Brian must have told him something.

Then, in a flash, as his son raced off toward Far Rockaway, the reason for Kevin's crisis hit Jimmy like a ton of bricks, and he swore to the heavens at his own stupidity. It was all so obvious and it had been right in front of his eyes.

"Jesus Christ," he muttered. "Of all the women in the world! What was that dumb kid thinking?"

No wonder Rose hadn't wanted him coming down to ask Liam questions about Brian's "warning." Kevin was shacking up there instead of spending nights at Fatty Sweeney's like he said.

Nothing for it but to head home and see what kind of damage control could be set in motion. This would not be pretty.

The house was lit up. Maggie had arrived back from The Bronx and was standing by the mantelpiece in the living room. The double-glazed windows trapped all the sound within, and though he couldn't see her face he could tell she was agitated.

She didn't look around when he entered the room. She continued staring into the unlit fireplace until he coughed.

Her face was pinched when she finally swung around. She was about to say something accusatory but stopped herself in mid-breath. "Dear God! What happened to you?"

"It's nothing."

"Were you in a fight?"

"Just some punk on the train last night—he said something."

"For God's sake, Jimmy, you're not a young man anymore. Why won't you face up to it before you get hurt?"

"It's no big deal, he caught me with a lucky one."

"Here, let me put something on it."

"It's okay, it's already been looked after."

"Are you sure?"

"Yeah, it's just one of those things!"

She turned back to the fireplace.

"I tried reaching you last night but you must have had your cell turned off."

He reached into his pocket and ran his fingers over the smooth surface of his phone. She was right, it hadn't rung since yesterday, must have damaged it in the scuffle with Sullivan.

"Guy on the train must have hit it. Was there a problem?"

"I wanted to talk," she murmured. "Something came up."

"What something?"

He took a deep breath anticipating the worst.

"Why didn't you tell me about Liam biting Tiffany Walsh's ear?"

Though he was relieved, the throbbing in his forehead intensified. The room was suddenly swimming and he reached out for the back of the couch.

"How do you think I felt when Laura Bianchi informed me about something that happened well over a month ago?" she said.

He felt weary and faint, and barely made it across the room to sink into his armchair. He was sure Laura had promised him she wouldn't mention it to Maggie.

"When did you speak to her?"

"Does it matter? Did it never occur to you I'd want to know if my grandson was in trouble?"

All the fight fled out of him. He couldn't remember why he hadn't mentioned it, what he'd been thinking.

"Or did you think I wasn't strong enough?"

Yeah, he figured, that must have been it. He buried his head in his hands to stop the pounding in his forehead. When he did look up she wasn't angry, more concerned, even compassionate. She laid her hand on the back of his neck then ran it through his hair.

"Jimmy, did you ever think that maybe it's you that needs the help? I know what you suffered in Vietnam, how it still haunts you. I should have done more at the time, but I was young and didn't know enough about life. The boys would have helped you too but they were always afraid to ask in case they'd drive even more distance between you."

She sat down on the arm of the chair and held him.

"I know I fell apart when Brian died. What else could I do? Put a brave face on it when my whole world caved in? But I'm better now. God has intervened."

She felt him tense but she held on even tighter.

"Look at you, Jimmy. You're too proud. You think you can sort out all the world's problems on your own. Well, you can't. Why won't you face up to that?"

His vision was blurred from the pain but when he identified the kindness in her eyes the years slid away and the young woman he'd loved materialized again; he remembered how he was so afraid he'd lose her if she knew what he'd done in Nam.

"Let it go, Jimmy. We can't bring Brian back. But we've got to hold on to the one we have left."

There were so many things he wanted to say, so many things he wanted to finally let go of. But he didn't have the strength. When he didn't answer she went out into the kitchen. He could hear her setting the table for breakfast. When she went upstairs he closed his eyes and dozed off.

TWENTY-SEVEN

Family dinners had always been a bit surreal, everyone putting on their best face, burying grudges, overconcerned with how everyone else was doing; not that they didn't care for one another, just that the sense of hyper-camaraderie never seemed totally genuine.

It wasn't anyone's fault, and Jimmy gave as good as he got. He often wondered if he wasn't responsible for the heightened jollity, going back to his early days on the job when he would blow in like Santa on steroids positively bulling to compensate for his many absences.

Brian had been no slouch either when it came to the big entrance, a bottle of good champagne in one hand, a box of Cubans in the other, kisses and hugs for everyone, raising the level of good cheer way up into the stratosphere.

Brian also knew how to handle Maggie. No matter what had been going on between them—and they had their issues—he'd sweep her up in his arms, lay a big one on her cheek, and present some little gift to demonstrate that he was eternally thinking of her, even if he hadn't called in a week. She'd pretend to scold him, and he'd play along mock-apologetically, but within seconds he'd have grand-slammed her mood right out of the ballpark and have her tittering like some tipsy teenager.

What was this dinner about anyway? Maggie never said. But she had taken down her mother's prized dinnerware and set the plates atop white lace on the kitchen table, lights were dimmed, candles glimmering, beer and wine served beforehand in the living room. Every glass in the cupboard was sparkling, every errant grain of sand swept from the floor, but there didn't seem to be an event—just her restless desire to bring them all together under the one roof.

Jimmy had picked up his grandson early and the boy squealed with delight as they peeled out of Breezy in the big yellow Caddy, blasting oldies and sending the seagulls scurrying. Soon as they hit Rockaway they went strolling hand in hand down the boardwalk, trading laughs and milkshakes while the healing waves swept across the late September sands.

But now, after a standoff when he had refused to eat Maggie's grilled salmon, Liam was upstairs playing with Brian's old toys, or more likely the Nintendo he had smuggled in.

Rose and Kev showed up separately, although Jimmy would have bet his bottom dollar that his son had galloped two or three times around the block to mask the fact that they had really arrived together.

The dinner staggered on under the weight of their forced gaiety and the gaze of the Sacred Heart whose light glowed brighter as the candles burned down. Eventually all that remained on the table were empty plates and refilled glasses of wine. Maggie and Rose, already on their second bottle of chardonnay, had loosened up and were circling each other like two boxers, feinting about doing the dishes, dodging about clearing the table, but there was a wild card bouncing around—Kevin at a benevolent level of tipsiness, choosing to ignore the posturing going on around him. He'd even playfully parried Maggie's rebuke when he mistakenly filled Rose's empty glass with red wine.

Jimmy's head began to tighten from his own unaccustomed excess of vino and his mind drifted to a night Brian showed up at the house with Sullivan in tow. For once the patrolman was merely merry instead of ossified, and the room shook with their laughter as they told censored tales of the riotous streets for Maggie's amusement. How long ago it all seemed.

Lost in nostalgia Jimmy missed Kevin's initial Yankees bantering but heard Maggie's reply: "Oh come now, Brian became a Mets fan because he had to do things his way. Same when he went on the job, he didn't want to be seen as making it on his father's name."

"Yeah, some days at Midtown North he'd barely give me the time of day."

"Oh Jimmy, you know he wanted you to be proud of him. That's another reason he made lieutenant."

"And I didn't. You never get tired of bringing that up." Jimmy snapped out of his torpor, his voice a little louder than he had intended.

"You just weren't as concerned with it, that's all," said Maggie, breezily brushing him aside. "Getting his master's, coaching the softball team in East New York. I used to get tired just thinking about all he was up to. You must have felt the same, Rose."

"Brian was Brian."

"That's for sure, always on the go, figuring out the next thing to achieve."

"Yeah, there were times it was like living with a souped-up résumé," Rose joked and Jimmy wished they'd change the subject.

"Oh come now, girl, there wasn't a woman around here who wasn't jealous of you." Maggie smiled back at her daughter-in-law but the mood in the room had subtly changed.

"Yeah, I was the real deal."

"You certainly were."

"Or rather, the real deal's wife."

"Aren't you being the slightest bit unfair?" Maggie sat up erect and blew out one of the guttering candles. A wisp of smoke rose between the two women and evaporated before she continued. "He always encouraged you to develop your potential. Go back to school, get your degree."

"As long as the strings were well attached."

"Well, he was your husband."

Rose cast her eyes downward at the irrevocability of the remark. She had been fiddling with the stem of her glass, tipping it back and forth; the red wine was now dangerously close to spilling over on Maggie's treasured white lace tablecloth.

"Maggie," Jimmy cautioned, laying a hand on his wife's arm.

But Rose no longer appeared to be listening as she twirled the glass ever lower until Jimmy could no longer take it. "Another beer, Kev?"

"Sure. Why not?"

Jimmy made his way to the fridge, took out a cold one, and unscrewed the cap.

"Don't you think you've had enough?" Rose demanded though her voice sounded small and tinny.

"What are you talking about? I got tomorrow off."

Rose winced at the edge in Kevin's voice and for a moment it seemed as if she might cry.

"There's a much nicer way of putting that, Kevin," Maggie said.

"Yeah, yeah, yeah." Kevin took the beer that Jimmy handed him and downed almost half of it before burping slightly.

Maggie shook her head in dismay but instead spoke to Rose. "Why don't you and I go upstairs and bring Liam down? Maybe he'll finally take a bite of that nice grilled salmon."

"No, it's okay, Maggie." Rose steadied her glass and pushed it away from her. "It had nothing to do with your food. He just never wants to be with us anymore."

"Reminds me of Brian."

"How can you say that, Kevin?" His mother swung around. "Brian was the heart and soul of this family."

Kevin shrugged his indifference and took another generous slug from his bottle. When he caught Rose's disapproving eye he lurched up from the table and headed for the fridge while downing the rest of his beer on the way. After he'd opened another bottle he finally answered Maggie. "Oh yeah, how about all the times he'd disappear into Manhattan—two, three days at a time?"

"That was the nature of his position in the Department."

"He was a lieutenant, Mom, not the friggin' commissioner. Guy had other pots on the boil."

Maggie took the napkin from her lap and folded it neatly. "Brian had his faults and his own life to lead, but he was here for every one of us when we needed him."

"I'm not running him down. Just telling it like it was for once," Kevin said.

How many times had Jimmy watched this same scenario over the last three years? How many times had he intervened, tossed some curve to give whomever a chance to step back. But before he could even wind up, Maggie shoved back her chair and brought her empty plate over to the kitchen sink.

"He wasn't a saint, Mom. Guy was human!" Kevin called after her. "It's just that the goddamn women wouldn't leave him alone, even the falafel man's daughter."

In the time it took his wife to return to the table Jimmy let go his curve. "You remember her, Maggie? Little black-eyed girl always playing peekaboo in the back of the store—going to Columbia now."

"Of course I remember. She was always very bright. I could tell she'd go places."

"Does anyone mind if I smoke?" Rose broke in. "I'd go outside, but I don't want to miss any more of Kevin's revelations."

Without waiting for approval she threw open the kitchen window and lit her cigarette. Kevin shuffled over and put his arm around her shoulders, but when she shrugged it off he lit one of his own.

"Well, we won't see much of her anymore," said Jimmy. "Yussef's fixed her up in one of those prearranged marriages with her cousin back in Egypt."

"That's hardly likely to work," said Maggie with a frown, "seeing as she's been raised in this country."

"He feels it's the best thing for her."

"He's obviously not concerned with a modern young woman's hopes and dreams."

"Are you serious?" Rose wheeled around on Maggie. "Do you think she ever gave a damn about mine?"

In the dead silence Maggie glanced at Jimmy for reassurance.

"That's all behind you now, babe." Kevin reached out for Rose's hand but she snatched it away.

"Oh for Christ's sake, they all know. What's the point in hiding it?"

"What are you raving about, Kevin? Can't you see you've got the girl distressed?"

"Sit down, Mom."

"I have no intention of sitting down with all these dishes to be scraped and washed. Don't listen to a word he says, Rose, as usual he's had way too much to drink."

"Oh yeah? Well, seeing we're on the subject, maybe you better pour yourself a stiff one."

When he put his arm around Rose she tried to squirm away but his grip only tightened. "Brian is dead, Mom."

"Why are you saying that?"

"It's the truth, goddamn it! And me and Rose got to go on living." He held Rose closer until her head was on his shoulder. "You hear me?"

As the truth dawned on her, Maggie tried to fold the tea towel but her fingers were at odds with one another. Finally she let it slide to the floor as she made her way out of the room.

Jimmy knew her movements—he didn't have to hear them. She would switch on the light, walk over to the window, look out toward the ocean, then lower the shades, walk back to the bed, and sit on the edge. She might stare at the wall or some picture on her dressing table; it made no difference, she was seeing a different world, one in which she knew her exact place, one in which her husband and boys fit the way she always imagined they should.

His daughter-in-law sat as if paralyzed, his son close by, chair pulled over, arm tight around her shoulders. If Jimmy listened he could hear the whispers, but they meant little; Kevin spoke to Rose like he would to a child, reassuring her that everything would turn out okay—that this distressful night was a mere bump on the highway to their eventual happiness.

He couldn't tell if Rose believed him. She allowed herself to be kissed and held, but she was in shock. She had stumbled into a conflicted situation and played her best hand, imagining that she would be granted the benefit of the doubt.

He ached for both women. He had tried to soften the blow, but he knew his wife well and was familiar with the world she hailed from. Whatever acceptance that world might ultimately bestow, it would not come easy. Like all closed-off societies the peninsula could be unforgiving, and there was a fascination with personal failings, especially when titillating or salacious.

Though Rose was devastated, he knew she would come to terms with the situation. He was more worried for his son. As a boy, Kevin had banged his head off the bedroom wall whenever the world failed to live up to his expectations. And when that same world passed judgment on him, he took the hurt and buried it deep inside. How would he deal with this challenge? Would his Rockaway roots help or hinder him? It was hard to tell, but this time Jimmy swore he'd be there every step of the way for his son.

"Rose, you want a drink?" Jimmy asked.

She shook her head, unwilling to surface from her daze. Nonetheless, Jimmy poured a glass of red and offered it to her. At first she looked right through it, but when he held it closer she took the glass in both hands and stared at it as at a communion chalice. Finally she took a sip.

"This is the last thing I wanted. Believe me," she mumbled.

"It is what it is."

"Yeah." She nodded.

Kevin pushed his beer away. "It's our lives. Mom couldn't run Brian, and she's finished running me."

Jimmy shook his head. "Jesus, guy, she needed to get the message, but not like an uppercut to the jaw."

"I've had it up to here with the whole carnival! I feel like some goddamned rag doll hanging in a store window for the whole world to look at."

"I get what you had to do and I'm behind the two of you, but there was a way of breaking this to her. She was just starting to get over Brian. Nutty priest, miracles, whatever."

"I loved my brother more than any of yez! But I'm sick of him being turned into a plaster saint. He's flesh and blood, or he used to be before everyone started making him out to be something he never was in the first place."

"Killing him was only half the story," Jimmy murmured. "They hijacked his memory too."

"Oh yeah, well, I'm taking it back! The little that's left." Kevin walked right up to him. "You know, Dad, when we were kids you used to drum it into the two of us that if we were honest everything would fall into place."

"That was a long time ago."

"Don't say that, man. You take that away from me, I got nothing."

Kevin allowed his father to touch his shoulder but didn't reciprocate.

"It still holds, Kev. It's just that maybe I lost the right to preach about it."

"Let's go home, babe." Kevin said quietly to Rose. "Things always get twisted in this house."

He went upstairs and carried Liam down. The kid had dropped off to sleep in the midst of Brian's old toys. Draped over his uncle's shoulder he looked even more like his father.

Rose fussed around, gathering the Nintendo, taking care not to trip over the wires and earphones trailing from it; then she put the boy's coat around his shoulders before realizing she couldn't find her own. It reminded Jimmy of the old days when he and Maggie used to bring

Brian and to her mother's house; invariably some issue would blow up, for the old lady had never reconciled herself to their rushed wedding, followed by icy protracted good-byes while they searched for a set of baseball cards or a mislaid mitt in the awkward silence.

On this night, however, farewells were brief and to the point, and when the door closed behind them, Jimmy sat down at the table amidst the greasy plates, poured himself another glass of red, and wondered if there was any chance he could patch the whole thing together one more time.

TWENTY-EIGHT

Captain Tony DeVito would have been glad if Officer Richard Sullivan just dropped off the face of the earth, but that wasn't how the NYPD worked. After the smoke of 9/11 cleared he was once more saddled with this "surviving hero" up at Midtown North; to add insult to injury, they'd been at the Academy together and worked the same precinct as rookie cops.

It wasn't that the lowly patrolman had anything on him—DeVito had always been clean as a whistle—just that Sullivan had been present at some awkward moments and, in his jocular but calculating way, he never let the captain forget it. Thus DeVito saw him pronto and even took the trouble to be nice; Sullivan, however, always on the lookout for patronization, sullenly resented it.

Sullivan had liked Brian—kid always made time for him—and why not? He'd bounced the little tyke on his knee, and taken the adolescent to ball games when his old man was too busy. It was a bit galling when Brian made lieutenant straight out of the stalls. Still, it was good to have a voice on the inside, someone who actually valued his street smarts, though Brian gave some of his other dealings a wide berth. But so what? The new lieutenant knew who to go to when he needed some extracurricular work performed. They might not have been related, but there was more than blood between them.

For that matter Sullivan still cared for Jimmy Murphy despite the two small parallel grooves his ex-partner had laid on his right cheek. Guy might be out of his skull and could use a straitjacket, but he wasn't a snooty rising star like DeVito who'd throw his mother to the dogs if a bone were lacking. When the chips were down, as they often were, Murph had always had his back. That meant something to a street survivor like Sullivan.

That's why he went to DeVito in the first place. Told him point-blank that they had to cut Jimmy in: Murph was a good detective and it was only a matter of time before he'd figure out what was going on and then—look out!

DeVito never even liked being told the time of day, let alone how to do his job. Still, for all his supposed analytical chops, the captain was just another brass moron who'd lost touch with the streets. He obviously knew more than he was saying, but he had no clue what Brian had been up to in San Diego and Sarasota, or that tips from the towel-head and his daughter had sent him there.

Who was DeVito protecting—a Department superior or someone way higher kissing Saudi ass? As usual the guy on the street just heard the white-bread half of the story. DeVito was like a big performing seal, always entertaining and everyone's best friend, but ultimately slimy and hard to keep a grip on.

"Here's the deal, Richie. Maybe we should have told Jimmy what Brian was up to from the get-go, but remember how crazy it was the weeks after the attack? Our job was to keep the lid on and get things back to normal, which is where they're at right now."

He pushed his bifocals back up on his forehead, leaned in, and lowered his voice. "For your ears only, I had Louis Esposito run a check on Jimmy and he came back talking up a storm about Mr. Happily Married Murphy playing footsie with some young Irish knockout down at Dolan's—something you never mentioned, by the way. She gives him a ride home every night and God knows what else—need I say more? If the full story about Brian breaks, you don't think some sleazebag reporter is going to throw that into the mix? You get what I'm saying, with Maggie and all? Is it worth upsetting the applecart again even for our old buddy?"

Sullivan had felt like saying "You mean the applecart of you and those above you getting the bum's rush when it comes to promotion? Because that's what would happen, asshole, if word got out that Brian had been onto something and the Department had not only turned a blind eye but put obstacles in his way."

Sullivan had held his tongue, but the whole situation was getting to him. Maybe it was time to get the fuck out of this business, go down to Florida, shack up with some rich widow, take up golf, play some canasta, and the hell with the rest of them. He'd put in the years, why not turn the screws on DeVito and get some extra overtime, come out of this mess with a jacked-up pension?

What had anyone in the Department ever done for Richie Sullivan? They all looked out for themselves. Brian had been the only cool one. The kid's face still haunted him. That fucking day had taken the joy out of life—the drinking, the sex, the good times, all gone up in a cloud of smoke, dust, and pulverized dreams. New York would never be the same; it wasn't just the bodies, those Saudi bastards had sucked the very spirit out of the joint.

On the other hand there was Maggie; he'd had a thing for her from day one. She'd always been kind to him, even when Jimmy was a dick. Did she need to be put through the wringer again?

In the old days Sullivan would have gone drinking—plowed his mind into a thousand furrows—woke up a week later too strung out to do anything. Sobriety was the pits! He had a pair of loaded dice in his hand—but when should he make his play?

He took an O'Doul's from the fridge and downed it. The familiar taste calmed him though it was like a dry ride—all fuss and no action. He'd have to supply that himself. Maybe do some yoga—a bit of meditation, calm his mind. The hell with that crap! He kicked out at his mat and sent it flying against the wall. Then he locked the door behind him and took the stairs two at a time, still uncertain what horse to back, but with the ghost of resolve beginning to materialize.

TWENTY-NINE

They might as well have been going to a PTA meeting so chatty and normal was Maggie on their way down to Breezy. She had been slightly more formal on the phone to Rose in the morning when she suggested a visit. Far different from the days immediately following the dinner when it had been back to siege mentality for Jimmy: act as if nothing was out of the ordinary, tiptoe around any emotional time bombs, and hang on for the inevitable calm—fair or false—that would follow the storm.

And so he joshed and chuckled and did his part to keep her mood ebullient even as he wondered about it. He stole an occasional glance at her as they cruised past Belle Harbor, Roxbury, and Fort Tilden just as they used to that lovely first summer he came back from Nam.

And always at the back of his mind, Brian going about his driven, furtive mission on those last days of the old New York. He'd definitely stumbled onto something suspicious out in Brooklyn, but was it just useless chatter fortified by that elusive sixth sense he seemed to possess—the *seanchaí* factor that the old Irish immigrants swore by?

As for Yussef, no two ways about it, he was hiding something. Brian would have copped on instantly to the two members of his security detail. Most likely they were the two "bad guys" that Liam had spotted outside his house, but three years later why were they still hanging in Yussef's falafel parlor? More than likely they were shaking him down over Fatima's association with cops; still, there was always the chance that they were involved in something more insidious.

Jimmy had seen much the same type in the Irish bars of the 1970s—shady men with thick Northern Ireland accents blending into the shadows of the ex-pat community after escaping from some British internment camp. As a young cop he'd cut them slack as long as they behaved, and for the most part they did—ended up respectable community members with jobs and grandchildren, just could never go home to Belfast or South Armagh. Terrorists or refugees—they all walked a fine line in a roiling immigrant city.

The osprey glided high above as Jimmy swung left on 220th Street; with the sun beaming down and the grasses and rushes swaying in the gentle late September breeze, Islamic South Brooklyn seemed a universe away.

Kevin greeted them affably at the door, holding Liam firmly by the hand and only letting go when the kid leaped into his grandpa's arms. Maggie hugged her grandson too but for once chose not to mention how closely he resembled his father.

How well they knew their roles. Even Rose had dusted off her best china and was pouring tea for Maggie within minutes. But there was an icy courteousness between the two women that would have taken a blowtorch to melt. Finally, one silence too many lasted just that little bit longer and Maggie declared, "I'd like to speak to Rose."

When neither Jimmy nor Kevin stirred, she added firmly, "Alone."

"There's nothing you got to say that I can't be a part of." Kevin crossed over to Rose and took her hand.

"It's okay, Kev," Rose murmured.

"No way! I know how she puts her own slant on everything."

"C'mon, man, let's get some air," Jimmy said, then shouted down the hallway to his grandson, "Hey big guy, let's go play some ball."

"I'll be fine, love, don't worry." Rose squeezed Kevin's hand.

Liam bounded into the room balancing bat, ball, and glove.

"Ready to do El Duque throws heat at Mikey P outside?" Jimmy gushed.

"Grandpa, you think we could have Uncle Kev play Mariano Rivera instead and you be umpire? He throws harder."

Despite a pang of regret at his demotion, Jimmy gamely trotted out behind his grandson. Kevin hesitated, but finally Rose pointed to the door. "Please, Kev."

Maggie made her way over to the window and watched Jimmy take his place behind the pint-sized hitter and call a very dramatic strike when Kevin threw the first ball.

"How many times have you slept with my son?" she inquired as matter-of-factly as she could muster.

"Which one did you have in mind?"

Maggie smarted at the rebuff; nonetheless, she poured another cup of tea and offered to do the same for Rose who pointedly declined.

"Pardon me for phrasing it in such a manner, but as I'm sure you've come to realize, you're the adult in this present relationship, and I want to make certain you understand the consequences for your family."

"Don't act so superior. Kevin loves me, and there's not a thing you can do about it."

"No, and when you were keeping company with Brian, there was nothing I chose to do either, though I knew he'd break your heart."

"Wasn't that considerate of you."

"Not really. Brian was strong-willed and followed his own convictions; however, he didn't always understand the consequences of his actions."

"And you did?"

"You learn about a person through observation and how they deal with crises. Brian was out of his depth in the last year of his life—whether that was over something that he had uncovered or another person."

"Don't you mean 'another woman'?" Rose interjected.

"He confided a great deal in me but that's no place for a mother to trespass. Brian had a restless nature but my own experience of marriage is that a wife will be the first to know if there's someone else in the picture—and why."

Rose looked away in anger. She'd always hated Maggie's school-marm lecturing. The older woman might have been close to her son, but she had no idea what it was like to be his wife.

Maggie poured a little milk into her cup, although the tea was already tepid. She appraised Rose, observing the ironed slacks and dressy shirt. She also glanced at her eyes and mouth for lines, and noted that her gleaming hair was long overdue for a shaping.

"You might find this hard to believe, but I was every bit as attractive as you. Yet it all fades, and there's not one of us who doesn't end up battling the mirror in the morning," she said with barely a trace of bitterness before taking a sip of cold tea.

"Kevin loves you—or is infatuated with you—for now. I know what you're thinking: Does Jimmy love me? I wouldn't blame him if he ran a mile—the hell I've put him through. Then again, men are weak and fickle, their heads easily turned by a good figure or a pretty young face. But if we don't accept, how should I phrase it, their *instincts*, nothing lasts and the family falls apart."

"That's why you always forgave Brian."

"There was little else I could do, for all it matters now."

"Well, I am doing something and I've got Kevin to help me."

"How sweet, and so very convenient. But do you love him? Unless I'm greatly mistaken you've already caught a glimpse of your life ahead with my youngest son."

"Yes, and it doesn't include you."

Maggie smiled at Rose's conclusion and for a moment took her measure. "You know, I'm not the bitch you think I am. With time, I'll get used to you marrying another man."

"You never liked me, did you? Never thought I was good enough for your darling. Well I was and I still am."

Maggie carefully placed her cup back down on the saucer; she hated to spill tea and remembered only too well the rings that Rose had left on her best coffee table the first day she visited with Brian. She smoothed down her dress and walked over to the window again. The remaining men in her life played on outside. Jimmy had taken to his role as umpire and each strike or ball that Kevin threw earned an increasingly more flamboyant gesture.

"Oh, I like you well enough—for all that matters. But I'm a realist, and someday you'll thank me for saving you and my grandson from further heartbreak."

"Why won't you just leave us alone, and let my son have a father who knows and loves him? Then maybe he can go back to being the little boy he was before . . ."

". . . His uncle became his new dad?" Maggie cut her short. "Just wait until Tiffany Walsh gets her teeth into that conundrum! You had the one hero in this family. We don't have another to spare."

She opened the window and watched her grandson—his face aglow with Brian's determination—swing left-handed for the fences. She waited until he had rounded the bases then called out, "Jimmy and Kevin, you can come in now."

Neither woman spoke as the men and boy tramped in, red-faced, out of breath and laughing.

"So, what's the good word?" Jimmy smiled broadly attempting to defuse the strained silence. "Hey, while you two were in here comparing nail polish, I was earning my spurs as umpire in the battle to the death between Mariano Rivera and Michael Joseph Piazza."

"Yeah, and Mikey P won, right, Grandpa?" Liam shouted back over his shoulder as he ran down the hall to his room.

"You said it, big guy!" Jimmy yelled, but the bedroom door had already closed and with that the smile faded from his face.

Kevin waited some discreet moments, time enough for the boy's computer to be fired up and headphones jammed into small ears. Then he went straight to Rose. "You okay?"

She barely nodded.

Jimmy studied both women, trying as best he could to read between the lines. "Hey, Kev, at least we got a plan to get the kid away from his video games. Don't forget those Mets tickets."

"Hadn't been for Brian getting our asses thrown out over Piazza we could take the kid up the Bronx," Kevin replied.

Maggie whirled around. "Why in God's name were you ejected from Yankee Stadium?"

"Some Yankee fan called Piazza a fag. Brian nearly choked him."

"It wasn't exactly one of our finest moments," Jimmy added. "Good thing Giuliani didn't see it."

Rose shook her head in disbelief. "So that's why Brian gave away those tickets? I can't even remember what dumb excuse he gave me."

"I should have known there was something wrong—the way he lost it that night." Jimmy spoke into an unsettled silence. And then piping up like one of the little plovers down on the beach, the muffled sound of Liam's earplugged laughter leaked through his bedroom door.

"But how much of it was real and how much in his head?" Rose said barely above a whisper.

"Hush now, girl." Maggie walked over to her. "He's still our Brian and any way you look at it—he's a hero."

"I'm tired of heroes. Just for once, I'd like to hear the truth."

With Liam's laughter now mocking them, Rose ignored Maggie's outstretched hand; instead she slipped down the hallway and made sure her son's bedroom door was still closed. On her way back her footsteps faltered—not so her voice. "He didn't come home the night before. I was sitting by the phone ready to tell him it was over. Wondering if I'd have the strength to go through with it, or let him talk his way back in again."

Maggie was about to say something but Rose silenced her.

"No, Maggie, you listen to me for once! Do you have any idea what it was like walking into the mayor's receptions, women whispering and smiling to each other, never knowing if he might have been carrying on with one of them?"

"Oh God, I knew his faults from the time he was a boy," Maggie said. "I used to pray that he'd turn a corner, and he had, he swore to me. He was a good man, Rose, if only he'd gotten out of there, things would have been different, I know they would."

"I used to say the same thing over and over to myself."

"The last time I talked to him it was all about you and Liam. You have to hold on to that, 'cause we have a chance to grow old and change and become better people. But our Brian will never be anything more than specks of dust down on Rector Street."

Maggie took her purse from the couch and walked down the hall to her grandson's room. Before she opened the door she called back, "Now, Kevin, you look after Rosie tonight and be kind to her. And if you don't mind, girl, I'd be forever in your debt if you'd allow me to take my grandson home for a few days. He might help soften the chill that won't leave our house."

Liam's presence was a blessing on the drive back to Rockaway, for Maggie and Jimmy had little to say to each other. Their grandson was unusually voluble and each was forced to answer his questions or respond to his observations. He sat between them, a small island in a widening gulf.

Rose would not have been happy—there were only two seatbelts; but Maggie had her arm firmly around the boy's slim shoulders to make sure he didn't shoot forward at a sudden stop. By instinct Jimmy would reach out when slowing down or taking a corner and occasionally their hands touched.

After a while he stopped noticing for his mind was elsewhere. Where the hell had Brian spent that last night after he'd put Kevin in the cab? Why hadn't he reached out? Was Sullivan right? Had his son turned away from him?

"Grandpa, are you and Uncle Kevin taking me to a Mets game?"

Oh, Jesus, the kid had overheard them back in the house. He could tell Maggie noticed too, though she stared straight ahead, lips pursed.

"I thought you wore your earphones when you played video games?"

"I do, Grandpa, but sometimes I take them off to make sure Mom is okay."

"And was she okay today?"

"She's happy when Uncle Kevin is there, so I usually leave them on."

"What did you hear, love?" Maggie asked.

"I heard you talk about Dad getting in a fight over Mike Piazza."

"Your dad loved you very much."

"I know, and he would have wanted me to see the Mets, right?"

"Yeah, big guy," Jimmy said. "Your dad sure did love those Mets."

"He loved Mike Piazza too."

"That he did."

"And he beat up some Yankee fan who called him a bad name, right?

"How did you know that?"

Liam smiled confidentially. "Can I tell you something, Grandpa?"

"Sure."

"Sometimes I open the door and listen."

"That's not very nice," Maggie said but Liam's attention was already elsewhere.

"So are we gonna go to Shea, Grandpa?"

"I'll check the schedule, make sure the Mets are in town. Season's coming to a close and they didn't make the playoffs."

He hated the very sound of those last words. Reminded him of Brian's disappointment almost every year.

"Grandpa, can we get another one of those strawberry milkshakes like the one you got me the night I couldn't eat Gramma's salmon?"

Jimmy waited for Maggie to comment but when she didn't he said, "Yeah, kid, I'll take you down the boardwalk tomorrow."

He was staring out the kitchen window when Maggie came downstairs after settling Liam into his father's old room. He didn't turn around. Everything seemed blank, purposeless, much like the emptiness he used to feel when he came home and couldn't reconcile Rockaway nonchalance with the adrenalized nightmare of Nam.

"Jimmy?"

She sounded much farther away than the mere distance across the room. He didn't even hear her walking toward him, just felt her hand on his arm, though it was as if she was touching someone else.

"What's to become of us?"

"I don't know, Maggie."

He felt old and weary, and was no longer in a mood to humor anyone. He idly wondered if he was about to have an episode; he didn't care anymore.

"You think you have everything covered and then . . ." Her words trailed off.

"Guess your God likes to keep a couple of aces up his sleeve."

"He's your God too, Jimmy, if you'll only open up to Him."

He laughed, but it rang hollow.

"Nah, my God got his ass kicked about forty miles south of Da Nang one steaming hot October evening, and the little that was left of Him went up in a pile of dust on a clear blue September morning."

After a while she murmured, "Are you okay?"

"You know, Maggie, I think we're a bit beyond that."

"Have I let you down, Jimmy?"

"You had your own problems to deal with."

"But your problems were mine too."

They stood close to each other, both now terribly aware of the distance widening between them.

"You know, something just occurred to me."

"What's that, Jimmy?"

"One of those poems you and Brian used to recite to each other, what was it? *Too long a sacrifice can make a stone of the heart?*"

"It's Yeats."

"Guy had a way with words."

Upstairs the kid jumped off his father's bed and the ceiling shuddered. He knew she'd be remembering that Brian used to do the same thing at that age.

"I'm sorry, Jimmy, I've been self-absorbed."

"Why does it always have to be about you, Maggie?"

"Because you never say anything. You never spoke about our Brian. I mean, really spoke. I've never even seen you looking at his picture."

He spun around to confront her. She was shocked at the bleakness in his face.

"I don't look at his picture because every time I do, he gets further away from me. And I don't need the papers or the TV talking about him either, because more likely than not it's some cheap politician using him to get reelected. I don't need that because I got him in here, deep down, every memory stored from the night the doctor pulled him out of you, until the day that big piece of shining shit fell down on top of him. I have all that, and it's rock solid, like he was. He's there when I want him, and he has the smarts to go away when I don't—just like he was in life."

"You never told me any of this."

"Talk is cheap, Maggie. I said some things I didn't mean and there's no way of taking them back. That's why I went into the city that morning. I had to talk to him, had to find him."

He began to move away again but this time she grabbed him by the elbow and stood between him and the window. "Tell me, Jimmy, please, for both our sakes."

Her fingers were pinching his arm. There was a desperation in her eyes that struck him like a fist, it reminded him of Brian, the few times he questioned himself for the world to see.

"Please, Jimmy."

He shook his head at the very thought of the thing that had been gnawing away at him.

"Please."

He was still of two minds. It almost felt too much, but the words were closer to the surface than he ever imagined.

"That last Monday morning, I was finishing up a case in the city. I'd promised I'd drop off some things for him down the house in Breezy. I was late. The train was running slow. I apologized. But all he could think was that I was still riding the A. He was worried about me, but I was in a bad mood and got up on my high horse. I told him that cops not riding the subway was one of the things wrong with the city.

"He just shrugged, he'd heard it all before. That really got me going. I started in about cops living out on the Island or Jersey coming into New York and lording it over the people who live here. He was in a hurry—I could tell his mind was elsewhere—but he listened to me like he always did. So I hit him with a cheap shot, said you can't live like a prince behind a gate in Breezy and then go to Bed-Stuy and not be prejudiced.

"I was totally out of line, but that got his attention. He just shook his head sadly. You know what it's like when your own son looks that way at you? I was so furious I turned my back on him and walked out of his dream house. He ran down the steps after me and called out, *Don't be like that, Dad. We can work it out.* And you know what my last words to him were? *Work it out your fucking self, Lieutenant!*

"That's what words do to you, Maggie."

THIRTY

Her granny used to call it "good harvesting weather"—those cool, clear, sunny days of late September. She had come directly from a poor farm in County Galway to the sandy streets of Rockaway, a seventeen-year-old girl. She'd never gone home, just kept the rocky fields of Connaught stored safely in her heart.

Maggie used to accompany her to this same church and listen to her mumble her Hail Marys, Glorias, and Our Fathers as she counted off her rosary beads all through the Latin mass. The old lady never cared much for priests—thought they were too full of themselves; she practiced her own custom-made version of Catholicism that needed neither parish priest nor papal approval.

Maybe that's why Maggie drifted from the church in her late teens, although she was married in this chapel and had both boys baptized in its slippery font. Unlike many who lost family in the Towers, she didn't have the bulwark of faith to comfort and guide her; it was more happenstance that she'd stumbled into St. Rose of Lima one sleep-deprived morning a year or so after the disaster.

Winnie Cleary, the beach gossip, had been dressing the high altar with fresh flowers that teary day. The church had become her second home ever since she lost her only son, Tommy the fireman.

But now two years later, instead of joining Winnie Cleary at the altar as she would normally have done, Maggie sat down in her favorite pew and watched the widow quietly go about her business, her weather-beaten face illuminated by slivers of blue light from the window behind the statue of Our Lady of Lourdes.

When they were little girls she didn't like Winnie Cleary—"very coarse and full of auld chat," her granny used to say. But on that first desperate morning almost fifty years later, Winnie had welcomed Maggie, and put her straight to work arranging flowers and cleaning the wax off the golden candlesticks. And when they were finished, she informed Maggie that she'd be there again the following day at ten o'clock sharp, and would be grateful if Mrs. Murphy could help, as she was expecting a delivery of fresh lilies.

Winnie had introduced her to Father Clancy, who she described as "very fussy but nice in his own way." And she was right. In fact, there was an air of overwrought gentility that pervaded the church. Neither Winnie nor she had ever mentioned Tommy or Brian, although their sons' spirits hovered just above the shoulders of both women. There were times in those first weeks when Maggie wanted to cry out to Brian in heaven, for the silence was often unnerving; Winnie appeared to sense her pain and would gently lay a hand on her arm, and point out a piece of wax that had spilled or some petals that needed picking up off the altar linen.

The beach gossip had not lost all her old sharpness and could be stealthily irreverent, raising her eyes heavenward when Father Clancy would voice one of his pet peeves or rattle on about some innovation that he wished to introduce; occasionally the two women would share a quick smile behind his back. All these little routines and confidences helped Maggie make it through her early days at the church, until there came a time when she began to feel some sort of accomplishment as she closed the vestry door on her way home.

Father Clancy had almost leaped for joy when Maggie told him about her granny's love of harvest weather. For some time he had felt that the ancient Christians must have brought gifts from their fields to their meeting places; accordingly, Maggie's news was, at the least, synchronicity and, perhaps, even a divine signal. He had positioned bales of straw at either side of the altar steps, and some sheaves of corn and baskets of apples around the statue of Saint Rose.

Maggie gave herself up to the earthy smell of the harvest melding with the comforting odor of incense and fresh wood polish. She watched the jowly priest emerge from his vestry and approach the willow-thin Winnie on the altar. Full of some new enthusiasm, he whispered effusively to the widow who merely nodded and continued with her tasks.

The men around Maggie had been closed off, that was Rockaway, and perhaps it was the same with men everywhere. Her father, brothers, husband, and sons had for the most part cordoned off their deepest fears and hopes from her. This simple but fussy priest wore his jubilant soul on his sleeve, and had somehow led her to believe that a spark of redemption would one day illuminate her shadowy tunnel of grief.

Why was it so hard for Jimmy to open up? He had a sensitive side, and was blessed with depth and understanding, but it was as if he took pleasure in his own reserve. Yet there was hope, he had confided in her that awful evening when they had brought Liam home from Breezy— told her the secret he'd been keeping about his last conversation with Brian, and how he'd been scourging himself for three whole years over it. Perhaps she should confess her own secret about Brian and how he had told her he was being followed in his last days, but that might only inflame Jimmy's imagination and do more damage than it was worth. She had come to the church to wrestle with this problem, but the choice seemed no clearer.

Her thoughts were yanked back to the altar. Father Clancy had raised his voice past his customary whisper. "For God's sake, Mrs. Cleary, the candelabra are at least three inches too close to the tabernacle, haven't I made that abundantly clear these many years?"

Although Maggie didn't hear Winnie's reply she rose from her pew, about to hurry down to the altar and intercede on the widow's behalf. Then something else her granny used to say in her thick Galway accent made her pause: "Only vestry widows make a fuss about dressing altars. The rest of us have husbands and families to look after."

There was little doubt—she had become a vestry widow. Winnie had lost a son, and years before her husband had run off with another woman, she had no one else; but Maggie still had both. To top it all, Jimmy Murphy was a good man that many women would have given their eyeteeth for; he had stood behind her through thick and thin and was still there, though it would be hard to deny that he was fast slipping away.

She tiptoed from the pew and genuflected then cast a last look around. Prisms of light from the many stained-glass windows—a mélange of purple, green, and amber—were now dotting the white marble altar; it was her favorite time of day in the church but she turned her back on it. In the transept, she dipped her hand in the holy water font and made the sign of the cross, then sprinkled the remaining drops on the tiled floor to help quench the thirst of the poor souls burning in Purgatory. She added her own prayer that these divine teardrops might soothe the spirits trapped in the specks of dust still circling around Rector Street.

One of her granny's words, old and out of use as it was, taunted her the whole walk up the boardwalk back home. The old lady had warned Maggie about her tendency to be "prideful" and predicted it would be her downfall if she didn't keep it in check. Now "prideful" echoed in the click of her heels and beat like a piston inside her head. She had allowed this inclination to fester beyond proportion until it drove her days. At their last conversation in front of the fireplace she could tell that Jimmy had already drifted away, their easy familiarity long gone, he tensed whenever she even brushed up against him. Was this what they'd come to? Even more to the point, did she intend to do anything about it or just let him go?

She allowed her mind to zoom back over the last three years. Apart from the grief there was little she could distinguish. She had lost whole swaths of her life—all gone by in the blink of an eye with nothing to show for them. Was it possible to pick up the pieces and start over again? Were the pieces even there to be picked up—or had some stranger stumbled upon them, dusted them off, and walked away with all her "might have beens"?

She clenched her fingers; they felt stiff and tired but her engagement ring glinted in the sun. It had belonged to Jimmy's mother, the fire chief's wife who had died young. Maggie had never known her but she loved the ring and admired the woman's taste. It was looser than the gold band that Jimmy had gone into debt for—such was their rush to get married with Brian on the way. Would she continue to wear their rings if he left her? What would it be like running into him at Liam's birthday parties? How would they greet each other? What would she say and in what manner would she say it? One thing she didn't doubt—she'd be as prideful as ever.

She picked up the phone on the hall stand the moment she walked in the door. She knew the number by heart and dialed it immediately for fear she'd lose her nerve. It rang six times and her heart began to pound as her resolve grew weaker.

"Dolan's!" some young man answered far too assertively.

"Could I speak to Ms. Fitzgerald, please?"

"Miss Fitzgerald is busy right now. Can I take a message?"

"If you could tell her it's Mrs. Murphy, Jimmy's wife, on a matter of some urgency."

After a moment's hesitation the young man said much more respectfully, "Could you hold on a minute please, Mrs. Murphy?"

He must have laid the phone on the reception desk for Maggie could hear people entering and leaving, the sound of midtown traffic leaking through then disappearing abruptly as the door opened or closed. The song from the jukebox was instantly familiar but she didn't identify "Dancing Queen" until the chorus. It had been one of Brian's favorites and she smiled at the memory of his out-of-tune version. Kevin had learned it for his brother's thirtieth birthday and surprised him by singing it at the party they threw for him at Connolly's on Beach 95th. What a night it had been and how wonderful to see the sheer love beaming between the two brothers when Brian joined Kevin on the final chorus—Brian about to become a lieutenant and Kevin so happy to be on stage serenading him. It seemed like forever ago.

"Hello?"

Maggie had almost forgotten whom she was calling and was startled to hear the Irishwoman's accent.

"Ms. Fitzgerald, it's Maggie Murphy, Jimmy's wife."

"Is everything okay?" Marcella asked, anxious and uncertain.

"I'm not sure."

"Jimmy's okay?"

"As far as I know."

"You gave me a fright for a minute. I'm sorry. He should be in around five. He always calls ahead if he'll be late or unable to work."

Maggie could hear the lyric "Having the time of your life" above Marcella's worried breathing but was at a loss as to what to say next.

"He was always good at that," she finally blurted.

"Yes, he's very thoughtful."

"Perhaps too much so at times."

"What I mean is he's always there to help any of us out—without making too big a thing about it. We think the world of him."

"And I don't?"

"I'm sorry, I didn't mean anything like that."

"Ms. Fitzgerald . . ."

"Please, Marcella."

"Marcella." Maggie tried the word cautiously without any of the irony she employed when enunciating it to Jimmy. "My problem may be that my husband thinks the world of you."

"I see."

"Do you?"

"He's come to mean a lot to me, but nothing of a physical nature has occurred between us."

Maggie noted how carefully the young woman had chosen her words, as if she had been expecting this conversation. She wondered if Marcella was sitting or standing. Was she alone at the reception desk or had the young man who answered the phone returned with her? What was she wearing—Jimmy had mentioned once that she favored well-cut jackets—one in purple was his favorite. It was probably mauve. For all his experience describing details in court her husband had never mastered the difference between those particular shades.

"Has it occurred to you that such feelings can be as dangerous to someone else's marriage as the mere physical?"

Across another silence Maggie could hear "You are the Dancing Queen" before Marcella answered haltingly, "I think so."

"So you see how it might concern me?"

"I'm afraid I have to go, there's a problem at the bar."

Maggie could tell she was crying.

"I think I've made myself plain."

"Yes, Mrs. Murphy, you have."

Maggie waited for some further elucidation from the young woman though she knew it wouldn't come.

"Well," she said with a sigh but then pulled herself together and curtly added, "thank you for your time, Ms. Fitzgerald."

She continued to hold the phone to her ear even after the line had gone dead.

THIRTY-ONE

The tide must have been way out; he felt like he'd been walking too long for the crash of the waves to still seem so distant. It was a dark night, no stars in sight; even the planes taking off from Kennedy were enveloped almost instantly in the low clouds. The lights from the boardwalk beamed dully behind him and his footsteps in the sand shuffled in time to the eerie pounding and spraying of night surf.

Then he stepped on the first clump of seaweed and his feet sank in the wet sand. He waited for the brine to sweep over his shoes, but it didn't, just lapped gently around them.

The salt would eat into the leather unless he went home right away, washed them in the sink, dried them, and added a decent coat of saddle soap then polished them in the morning. Maggie did that for him back when they were first married and used to walk hand in hand along the beach to Breezy. But he wasn't going home and she no longer thought to do it anyway.

He felt the old urge to go strolling on out into the waves, but knew he wouldn't. Too simple, too easy, and guys like him didn't do that kind of thing; they just tidied up the mess, made the best of things, and carried on. No point in causing problems for everyone else.

He walked back toward the boardwalk. Then he saw it glinting in the dreary light, a beach chair, close to the ground, deserted; someone must have left it with the intention of coming back and never got around to it.

He hadn't noticed his fatigue. It was beyond physical, more the head and the heart; it felt good to sink down into that simple chair and let his legs sprawl in front of him, dig his heels into the sand.

He knew it was coming. His hands had been sweaty even as he stood within range of the cool salt spray. He laid his elbows on the armrests and gripped the aluminum tubing. Then he heard the rumbling of artillery in the next valley and the reassuring *whup-whup-whup* of Hueys approaching. He recognized the different heavy pieces, his and theirs. He knew how his artillery got there, he had seen the roads the engineers cut through the jungle; but it never ceased to amaze him how the NVA and the VC could set up big guns on the sides of hills surrounded by towering vine-enmeshed trees for camouflage—must have carried them metal section by section all the way down from the North on the Ho Chi Trail and reassembled them, then moved them on again before the B-52s got a bead on them. What a people! And he and his teenage buddies were supposed to defeat them, when all they cared about was girls, beer, and getting back to the States with their asses intact.

Then the boyish faces of guys he'd served with shimmered in front of him: a kid from Missouri who swore he was going to kill the captain and nearly did, a bear of a guy from Texas who played poker better than anyone he'd ever known, a guitar player from Louisiana who might have caused a stir if he'd made it home—all of them melted back into the fog to the echoing shuffle of the waves.

When the face did arrive it seemed younger than his dead comrades'. He gripped the tubing but it just hung there in the salty air, calm and serious, before it too drifted away toward the Atlantic, taking with it the sounds of the battle.

He must have slept a considerable time for when he awoke a wave had splashed close by and drenched his outstretched feet and ankles. He also caught the repressed sound of teenage laughter, but for once he felt deliciously relaxed and didn't wish to move. Another wave broke over his legs and the laughter grew louder. He almost lifted out of the chair when the rocket went off right behind him. It rose into the dark sky shooting off red-white-and-blue trails that sank slowly over the ocean.

The boys scampered back to the boardwalk hollering to the heavens; Jimmy smiled and followed them, trudging through the sand, his pants wet and sandy up to the knees. He had an overpowering urge to talk, to connect, and he knew there was only one person he wished to be with.

She wasn't in the bar when he entered, not in her booth either. It was late; the theater crowd had gone, just a few night birds gazing into the big screen at a ball game out on the coast. Colin Farrell threw him a concerned look, so much so that he hurried into the bathroom. His hair was still askew from the breeze on the beach, while the wet sand clung to his trouser legs. He doused his face in hot water and shook the sand off his pants, but he could still taste the salt on his lips as he entered her office.

She was surprised but didn't smile. Her hair was down and a few strands had drifted across her cheek. He was overjoyed to see her. There were so many things he wanted to tell her about the last weeks and, even more important, the decision he'd made on the train. He began with the least consequential.

"I've been thinking about Dolan and what he wants to do with the place, and my part in it."

She didn't respond, just stared at him.

"I'm going to accept his offer and treat it like a promotion. The new rooftop bar is a surefire winner and there are other changes we can make around here. He's right about us being a good team."

Something in her face made him stop. The usual care in her eyes was now mixed with concern.

"Jimmy, I've something to tell you."

"Oh yeah?"

"I gave Mr. Dolan my notice this morning."

Her words came out flat, with no emotion, although her eyes betrayed the anguish she was feeling. She halted, uncertain how to proceed, then pushed on. "I've been working pretty much nonstop for the last four years. I'm taking some time off to go backpacking in Australia. It's something I always wanted to do."

He could tell that it was a prepared speech, much the way perps talked after their first session with a lawyer.

"That's one for the books."

"Yes, I've been thinking about it for some time now. I'm getting to that age where I need to make decisions."

What age was she? He'd never asked. Late twenties, he supposed, a full life still ahead of her. He knew how to answer even if he didn't know exactly what to say—nonchalance and understatement had become second nature.

"Yeah, well we all come to that point in life."

"I'm glad you understand."

"Of course. It will be good for you, a change, like."

"The surfing is much better than Long Beach and now I'll have some time to devote to it."

"Yeah, the waves are big out there, I hear."

He could tell that she had been dreading this talk such was her relief. It didn't matter what he felt anymore, he would make it easy for her.

"Well, I think I'm going to get a drink. Get cleaned up first though. I dozed off on the beach tonight."

"Yes, I was wondering about your shoes."

"Looks like they'll need a good dose of saddle soap."

"Jimmy, there's something else."

"Oh yeah?"

"Conor is coming with me."

"Conor?"

"Conor O'Brien, our barman."

"Oh yeah, Conor. I always think of him as Colin Farrell."

"I know, you told me once."

"I did?"

"Yes."

"Well, good luck."

"Thanks, Jimmy."

She walked toward him and held out her hand. He took it and couldn't help noticing that her silver Claddagh ring was still facing outward. She leaned forward and kissed him tenderly on the cheek. She'd never done that before.

"I spoke to your wife recently on the phone."

"You did?"

"Yes, we talked for a while. She seems very nice."

"She is."

He didn't stop for a drink at the bar, but just before he got to the door, Colin Farrell called out, "Hey Jimmy, thanks for everything."

"You too, man. Watch out for the kangaroos over there."

"I will surely. Take care of yourself, all right?"

"Yeah."

"I'll see you again someday."

"You got it, Conor."

But he knew he never would.

THIRTY-TWO

He'd been engulfed by it for years in the confines of their patrol car, so he instantly recognized the smell, though an important ingredient was missing. It used to be three parts—cigarettes, coffee, and alcohol; now the booze was gone, but he didn't have to be a detective to know Sullivan was in his house. Anyway, his much-worn Yankees 2000 World Series jacket was draped over the hall stand.

Jimmy checked the inside pocket where Sullivan usually parked his Glock. Empty! That meant he was either packing it on his person or on a social visit. The latter was hardly likely given what had gone down between them. Still, the lights were on and if Sullivan wanted a piece of him, there were better places to do it than in the thick of Rockaway.

Jimmy edged silently toward the living room. Had Sullivan heard him enter? He didn't think so. He had slipped in quietly upon noticing the front door was unlocked.

His former partner was lost in thought—studying the framed picture of their graduating Academy class. Well over thirty years ago now, how they'd changed, a host of mostly Irish and Italian kids from all over the city, pumped, primed, and beyond ready to go on the job like their fathers, brothers, uncles, and cousins before them.

Who was Sullivan looking at so intently? He surely had the same picture, though it hadn't been on display in the hovel. Maybe he was just staring at his younger self, wondering where he'd gone wrong. Jimmy had no trouble summoning up the red-haired kid from Inwood; back then Sullivan lived up on the tip of Manhattan with his widowed mother, the high school teacher, who raised and spoiled him, nothing too good for her Richie. Had the drink been his only problem, or did he suffer from the lack of a man around the house? He was definitely bright enough, but there was something missing; he always seemed to shoot himself in the foot, until he finally retreated into his own little Paradise Lost of bars and skells and whores and sordid little West Side deals.

Sullivan turned toward the light, held the picture frame at arm's length, and peered at it. No one would ever have accused him of being handsome—particularly with two fresh slits on his face—but having shed some skin he was once again identifiable as the young man who used to ride the A downtown, full of life and laughter, songs and blarney. He was the soul of the party in a score of bars around the city, and Jimmy basked in his sunshine. They couldn't have been farther apart in miles or attitude: Inwood and Rockaway, opposite ends of the metropolis, the pudgy mamma's boy and the edgy Vietnam vet, yet there was an instant bond. And as Jimmy watched his first partner ogle the picture, he was forced to admit that even with someone as stuck in his ways as Sullivan things could change.

"So," he said quietly and Sullivan almost keeled over from the surprise.

"Sow birdseed," the cop shot back much as he used to in the patrol car before Jimmy got his first promotion and their partnership frayed.

"What are you doing here?"

"When you look at me like that I start to wonder."

Sullivan patted the bulge of his Glock only partially covered by a loose-fitting gray sweatshirt. His frown broke into a slight smile when he nodded toward Jimmy's .38 lying on the table. "It's empty. I remembered where you kept it."

"I'm sorry about your face."

"Doc said it'll fill in." Sullivan shrugged. "Anyway, my boy band days are behind me."

He motioned to a chair. "It's time you and me had a little heart-to-heart."

"You're the one with the secrets." Jimmy remained standing.

"Yeah, I got DeVito on one side ready to dick my pension, and you on the other with over thirty years of what used to be a friendship. The fuck with the both of you!"

"Where's Maggie?"

"Gone to bed. We had our talk."

"What did you tell her?"

"About half what I might tell you, if I think you're still worth it."

Jimmy headed toward the stairs.

"Leave her be, for Christ's sake! She's a lot stronger than you ever gave her credit for. You never knew how lucky you were." Sullivan's voice was quiet but hard. He didn't pull the Glock from his belt, but the threat was implied.

"Now why don't you sit yourself down and let me tell you about your son, and a couple of other things too."

He chose the most comfortable armchair and leaned toward Jimmy in the other. "Brian called me that last Monday night. He was all kinds of upset because you had cursed him out earlier."

"He talked to you about things like that?"

"He always got in touch when there was a problem between the two of you—which was often enough."

"How come you never told me?"

"Because there was no talking to you about that or anything else!"

Sullivan's voice had risen and he looked anxiously at the stairs. When Maggie didn't appear, he lowered it again. "You know, Jimmy, for a smart guy you're an awful fuckin' idiot. Everything the kid did was to impress you. Right until the very end he never shut up bragging about "My Dad is this, my Dad is that.""

"He never said it to me."

"Not in so many words but what was the point? You didn't have the ears to listen!"

Jimmy slumped back in his chair as though he had been slapped in the face; for once Sullivan felt bad for him.

"Anyway, something else had just gone down. The falafel man's daughter came back from Egypt."

"Fatima?"

"Yeah, name never seemed right for a Muslim," Sullivan confided. "You know, Our Lady of Fatima, or whatever the nuns used to call her."

Jimmy acknowledged the observation.

"Brian had left her some pointed messages suggesting they meet but wasn't sure if she'd show. She'd skipped town earlier in the year without giving him the name of some Saudi jerk he had his eye on. Scumbag was mixed up in jihadi shit."

"What kind of jihadi shit?"

"He never told you nothing about what he was up to, did he?" Sullivan crowed. "Didn't trust you, man! You might have blabbed to DeVito, blown the cover off everything."

"What are you talking about?"

"I'm talking about a whole year of investigation that you knew sweet fuck all about. But I knew every last detail because Brian trusted his Uncle Richie."

Sullivan didn't bother hiding the smile of triumph. "He'd come to me when he'd get a tip and needed to bump town in a hurry for Florida or California."

"The hell was he doing in Florida or California?"

"What do you think, Mr. Hotshot Detective? Trying to track down the jihadis who had split Brooklyn and Jersey and find out what they were up to. I used to cover for him with Rosie, say he'd been 'summoned down unexpectedly to DC' or had to go wipe Giuliani's ass, whatever."

"He trusted a drunk like you with his wife's well-being?"

"Who else did he have? You? Sitting out here in your ivory tower?" Sullivan allowed himself another gloating smile. "But it was a lot more than that. If he was out of town and he needed something from Fatima—guess who tracked her down?"

"That can't have been too hard."

"Harder than you think; she didn't answer calls, slept off-campus—thought she was being followed. And I know what she was talking about. Had the same feeling myself, that's why I had the landlord install the security video."

"How about Brian?"

"He was nervous too, especially about Rosie and the kid—felt the walls were closing in, someone on his tail, and time was running out. He was heading to Sarasota as soon as he got the Saudi's name, my gig was to keep an eye on his house until he got back."

He waited for Jimmy to comment but then continued. "I helped him in other ways too, especially when he needed info on certain towelheads in a number of Jersey towns I had access to."

Jimmy did know about Sullivan's Jersey connections and how he got them—hang out around the Lincoln Tunnel on a Saturday night and pull over any Jersey cop driving under the influence. Keep their numbers in his book, apply a little "one hand washes the other" when it was called for.

"He needed tabs kept on some Saudis in Paterson and Jersey City." Sullivan took out his cell phone and flicked it open. "Just took a couple of calls."

"What did he find out?"

"A lot more than DeVito or the other meatheads upstairs, but none of them would listen to him! He wouldn't tell DeVito the full story because the asshole had already blown it, sending know-it-all Louis Esposito in. And Brian might have got those bastards too—the hijackers—I'm telling you. The kid was close, man!"

"How close?"

Sullivan looked back toward the door and the staircase; then dropping the volume he leaned in even further. "Real close. I recognized one of their names when they were identified in the wreckage."

"Why didn't you say something?"

"What did I have? Brian wrote nothing down and I didn't either in case the shit ever hit the fan. Imagine going to DeVito with something like that? He'd have laughed me outta there. And anyway, after what had gone down in the Towers, I didn't trust anyone including DeVito or his lapdog Drew. I could have been walking around with a big target on my back."

He looked at Jimmy for understanding then shrugged his indifference.

"But I had eyes to see, and ears to hear, man. That last night on the Upper East Side Brian was waiting for a call from Fatima—he wanted the name of that Saudi jerk bad. He knew she was out partying in the area, but she hadn't got back to him. Kevin and his probie posse were with us, we must have hit five or six bars looking for her."

"That's what the pub crawl was about?"

"Yeah, he said we had to track her down pronto."

"And he found her, right?"

"Yeah, the very last joint. But she wouldn't give him the Saudi's name. Got up on her high horse, said some Egyptian she told him about had been collared by Immigration and sent home. Of course it was just coincidence—Brian didn't give a fuck about Immigration—but she wouldn't give up on it. So he was working her big-time, giving her the glad eye and pouring drink into her—you know how persuasive he could be. She was crying at the end of the bar that he didn't care about her—was just using her for information. What else was new—wasn't the first time we'd heard one of his "contacts" sing that song.

"The joint was rocking, jukebox blasting, the rest of us all knocking 'em back, then Kevin started passing out and Brian took him outside and packed him off home. When he came back in, Brian asked me for my keys, didn't want to take the young one to a hotel in case she freaked and called security. But he wanted that Saudi's name and nothing was going to stop him—'big piece of the puzzle,' he told me—and figured he'd get it if he could work on her alone."

"He took her back to your place?"

"Hey, it wasn't the Plaza, but no one would lose sleep if a babe was freaking or whatever. I told him what light to use so she couldn't see the state of the place." Sullivan, in his newfound sobriety, blushed at the memory of his filthy hovel.

"She was a mess and it was late, had to be around three in the morning when they split the bar. I hit some other joints, then had some coffee, washed up, changed into my gear. I was filling in downtown and had told him to meet me at eight a.m. in the North Tower with the keys."

Jimmy groaned. "Oh, man." The sheer simplicity of it! He'd been off the job too long, neglected the one element that fueled every investigation—humanity, in all its messed-up craziness.

"Yeah," Sullivan said. "It all ends up down there. He was late, which wasn't like him, and I got worried. Then I seen him entering the building—remember that way he had of walking like he owned the joint? Wasn't like that this time, dragging his ass, something on his mind really bothering him. He tossed me the keys. I raised my eyebrows, you know, had he scored? But he wasn't thinking that way, all businesslike, the golden boy lieutenant on the hunt! So I asked him if he got the Saudi jerk's name. He looked at me for a long time then he nodded and said, 'Yeah, I got it, Richie. He was one of the guys we fingered in Jersey City. Thanks.'"

"Big piece of the puzzle?" I asked.

"'Yeah,' he said real quiet, 'bigger than you can imagine. Last she heard he's in Sarasota. I moved up my reservation, catching a three p.m.'"

"Did he say who it was?" Jimmy asked.

"Are you kidding? By this point Brian didn't trust anyone. I didn't care—I wasn't feeling so good, with the gutful of booze in me, and no sleep, so we just stood there a long time watching the crowd. Finally I asked, more out of something to say than anything else, 'So what are you gonna do?'"

"I wasn't sure he heard me. It was like he had zoned out. I was going to suggest getting some coffee when he said, 'I don't know, man, I don't know where to turn anymore. Sometimes it all makes sense, other times I don't know what to make of it.'

"That sounded odd and I was trying to figure it out, when all of a sudden there was a noise like I never heard before, a god-awful thump like a giant hit the building with a sledgehammer. Those big glass windows come crashing in, everyone ducking, lights going on and off, alarms ringing, people screaming and running into each other. No one knew what was happening. Was like we were all out of our heads with the world shaking around us, and a wind blowing through the walls where the glass used to be. Then someone ran in from outside and yelled, 'A plane just hit the building!'

"'Fucking asshole pilot!' someone else roared and I remember being all pissed off at some yuppie in a Cessna.

"Everyone started to pile toward the door but Brian just stood there saying, 'How could I have been so stupid?'

"Meanwhile I'm trying to pull myself together, put some order on things, when he grabbed me and shouted, 'That's why it didn't make sense! With so many of them in pilot school I thought they'd be hijacking hostages and flying to Libya.'

"I pushed him away. Had no idea what he was talking about. I felt sick to my stomach, especially with the reek of kerosene everywhere and waiting for it to explode, but I knew what I had to do—get people lined up and out the door. Brian was still standing there, totally out of it—I'd never seen him like that before. So I told him to get the hell out of the way if he wasn't going to help. He just said, 'I could have stopped this fucking thing!'

"'What are you talking about?' I screamed, and with that he sprinted off to the stairwell. I yelled after him, 'Where are you going?' But he disappeared into the crush of people coming down, and then the Fire guys all came rushing through in their bunker jackets and ran up the stairs behind him.

"I tell you, Jimmy, you can't believe what it was like—water seeping down out of the ceiling, jet fuel leaking out of the elevator shafts, people jumping from a hundred stories up landing on the plaza outside— the only thing that stood to me was our training. Things come back to you—get people in a line, walk them to the door, some of them were burned bad, man, get them out of there with as little panic as possible.

"Panic? Are you kidding me? Everyone was screaming blue blazes; the noise alone would have driven a man crazy. I was scared shitless. Still, we were moving people along pretty well, but how many were in that dumb building and most of them going nuts to get out. All the time I was keeping one eye on the stairwell, meanwhile the floor was shaking beneath us, the paneling was flying off the walls, girders and electric lines swinging loose, and all these creaking sounds of metal bending like in a horror movie, I still don't know whether it was in my head or for real. Then way later through the dust and smoke I saw Brian coming down the stairwell and I wanted to cry, he'd made it, man, he'd fucking made it, and he was carrying this big redhead in his arms, she was totally hysterical and he was talking all nice to her like they were at a picnic or some shit, and he's got six others holding hands behind him.

"I started screaming and waving at him, I was over the fucking moon, we're going to make it, we're going to get out of there alive, and he was leading them outside and I turned away to do my job, and then there was this big lurch in the building and from out of nowhere he was beside me again. And I said, 'Brian, what the fuck are you doing back in here?'

"And he was still white-faced except now he had all that dust on him too, looked really weird, and he said, 'I should have put it all together, Richie, *hawala* money!'

"'What the fuck are you talking about?'

"'Money transfers from Afghanistan and Saudi Arabia! Flight schools, you name it, all right in front of my face. How could I have been so dumb?'

"All I could think was—hey, man, this ain't no time for *Jeopardy*! I wanted to get out of there so bad. And I thought—this guy's totally lost it, he was all shivering and shit, looked like some kind of ghost. And there was another great big lurch and the floor moved beneath our feet, and I grabbed him by the lapels and yelled, 'Let's get out of here!'

"And he looked at me all crazy and said, 'No way, the Fire guys are all up there with no radio signal. Kevin could be with them.'

"'Are you out of your skull?' I yelled and held on to him. But he caught me off balance, threw me to one side, and ran over to the stairwell just as young Shay Kennedy and another Fire guy from Long Beach came running out. They tried to stop him but he was the star running back all over again, went right through them like they weren't there. I ran after him but they caught me and dragged me out and there was shit falling all around us and in front of us and behind us, and then we were out on the steps of the plaza and taking them three at a time with the whole world tumbling down on top of us."

Sullivan hung his head and stared blankly at the floor. When he looked up he seemed spent and at first he spoke quietly, as if from behind a scrim. But he had held the floor in too many noisy bars and his natural sense of drama soon reasserted itself. "Next thing I remember I was in Kelly's Pub. Place was empty, totally quiet—just me and that Mick bartender stashing the cash, so I went behind the stick and poured out a pint of Jameson's. Oh man, I wanted so bad to get rid of that creaking sound in my ears. I had the pint half-downed when you came out of nowhere and threw me up against the wall, screaming at me, and I was in such shock I could hardly talk to you about the whole thing. I can barely deal with it to this day.

"After you left I must have got a lift out to Rockaway, I don't even remember, except I was in The Circle and everyone was buying me shots, and then I was at your house and all I could see was the hurt on Maggie's face and I didn't want to add to it—just couldn't tell her that Brian ran back in there looking for Kevin when the kid was already safe. Then everyone was pissed at me, and I didn't know what to do except get out of there.

"I was stumbling back toward The Circle when a patrol car picked me up, took me back into Manhattan. DeVito had put out an alert on me. Next thing I know he's yelling at me, calling me a drunk and a disgrace to all my brothers who had just given up their lives. And I was screaming back that he and the other kiss-asses weren't in there helping people get out with the roof caving in, and they didn't see Brian running back up that goddamn stairwell.

"Then he's asking me how much Brian really knew and I told him only what I had to, but I could see he was scared shitless, like he was going to lose his job or something. So he was making all nice, asking me to keep 'our secret'—that he had to talk to the big suits, and not to say anything to you, in particular—he brought up the falafel man's daughter: 'We don't want Rosie or Maggie knowing anything about some college chick, do we?' And all I wanted to do was get the fuck out of there and get a drink, so I agreed to whatever the hell he wanted, I can barely even remember it now.

"And then I was out on the street puking my guts out and I still had that stinking white dust all over me and everywhere I went they were buying me shots and calling me a hero, and I was in and out of bathrooms throwing up and then coming out for more. It was well into the next day before I headed for home.

"Jesus Christ, man, I was scared as shit to go in because Brian had been there more recent than me, and everywhere I looked in that hallway I could see his face and hear his voice and the sound of that fucking building creaking right before it collapsed. In the end I couldn't stand any more so I got down on my hands and knees and crawled up the stairs, but he was still everywhere around me.

"It took me forever to get the keys in the locks and, Mother of Christ, the light was still on—the one I'd told him to use—and I thought maybe he'd come back, but then it hit me that he was gone forever, and he'd forgotten to turn it off when he said good-bye to her that morning.

"And I wanted to fucking die, Jimmy, I swear to God, so I threw myself down on the bed and dug my face into the sheets to make the world and all the faces and the sounds go away. And I was lying there for a real long time hoping to pass out, and then I realized I could smell her perfume on the sheets."

THIRTY-THREE

His faced creased with worry, Fatima's father watched her pass through security. But when she turned for a last glimpse of him he was already heading back through the departure hall, his shoulders hunched against the bustle of the crowd. Then she walked on to her gate stopping only to purchase a copy of *Elle* for her cousin Aisha in Alexandria.

Her father had barely spoken to her while driving to Kennedy along the Belt Parkway. At other times he would have pointed out tankers, liners, and cargo ships entering or leaving through the Narrows, hazarding guesses on the nationality of each vessel. Now he just stared doggedly ahead at the busy highway, his knuckles white on the steering wheel of the Mercedes. He had set the tone by impatiently switching off Hot 97 and inserting a CD of Umm Kulthum the moment they turned out of their garage and onto Shore Road. Fatima had never cared for the revered Egyptian diva but on this particular late September afternoon the woman's voice sounded like a cat in distress.

Fatima slept well the night of Jimmy Murphy's visit. It had been far easier than she imagined to honor her father's wishes, but her decision soon began to grate on her. Hassan was a nice enough guy but hardly "the real deal," as Brian would have put it. The young Egyptian took himself beyond seriously and his sense of humor left a lot to be desired despite his grating high-pitched laugh. Her father had not been pleased when she'd idly mentioned this one morning over breakfast. Her mother had nervously sided with her as always and there they let the matter rest.

The visit from Muhammad Rashid, imam of the mosque, had changed everything. He had always been solicitous and friendly but she could sense his mounting impatience for her to leave their reception room so he could converse privately with her father. Once in the kitchen her mother had chatted loudly about a letter she had received from Leah but Fatima could tell she was doing so to cover the sound of the imam's raised voice. The issue appeared to revolve around Yussef's truthfulness in his previous disclosures to Muhammad.

Soon after their revered visitor had departed without even the courtesy of a good-bye her father summoned her to their reception room.

"I am about to book your flight for this coming Thursday, September thirtieth, to Cairo. One of your cousins will meet you at the airport and drive you to Alexandria."

"I take classes on Thursdays."

"You will have time enough for classes all your life ahead of you."

And so it went, back and forth, with veiled references to perilous times since the invasion of Iraq and her unfortunate relationship with Brian. With her father's anger rising she had agreed as a compromise to take a semester off to visit her relatives and see if indeed she and Hassan would be compatible.

It seemed best to resolve that issue first since her father had declared that he and her mother would also be leaving New York for Alexandria as soon as his business affairs were settled.

How different life might have been had Brian not perished. How different the world since his death! She had no idea if she could fit into the tight fabric of Egyptian society; it was so far removed from the world she had grown to love in New York. But her father was correct—America had changed since the attack. She could feel it in the glances she received whenever she wore her hijab. Besides, it had been totally awkward running into Morgan Bradford at Columbia.

She shook her head in exasperation as she dodged the fatigued but chattering travelers who had just disembarked off the EgyptAir flight from Cairo. She remembered how easily Brian could move through the thickest of crowds the afternoon he had taken her to Times Square. Brian would always be with her in some form or other. She smiled as she hummed one of his favorite songs—he sang it so badly and yet it fit the moment perfectly—"You Can't Put Your Arms Around a Memory." Perhaps not, but somehow or other the song gave her hope and the courage she always associated with Brian.

And as she walked to her gate with a new determination she swore from that moment on she would not allow her life to be decided by men behind closed doors.

THIRTY-FOUR

It was a foggy night, a damp breeze seeping in off the bay, and if Rose concentrated she could hear the distant peal of the chimes from the neighbor's porch. She stretched luxuriously. Liam was down in Rockaway with his grandparents in these last hours of September; it was just the two of them at home. Her body still tingled from Kevin even as she shivered slightly from lying outside the covers.

Was he sleeping or lost in thought as she had just been? His breathing was steady, but it was hard to tell. For over a week after the confrontation with Maggie, he had called the shots the way Brian used to, even got in touch with the architect about adding an extra room for Liam. He was adamant he didn't want to cut and run to Florida, just weather the coming storm. He was sure it would all blow over quickly.

For the first time she had leaned on him, grateful for his newfound purpose. It was as if the boy had become a man overnight. He insisted that Liam spend more time out of his room—they played baseball every day he was off duty, giant confrontations between Mariano and Mikey P with lots of shouting and Yankee-Mets trash-talking.

That first week she watched them from the window, still dazed yet enjoying the new order around her house. But the balance shifted as the full scope of what they would face became clear; and when push came to shove, she began to draw on her reserves of practicality while he retreated more into defiant sullenness.

"Fuck 'em all!" he would explode, and she'd have to shush him then run down to Liam's room to make certain he hadn't heard.

Sure, it wasn't a federal case, they didn't have to tell anyone anything, but Breezy was close-knit and some explanation would be expected. Would they get engaged, married? Kevin was up for both, but it wasn't that simple. Even going down to The Inn would present problems. What would he do the first time he heard a snicker, real or imagined?

And that was just local. What would happen when the papers got wind? "Page Six" would have a field day! But for now no one knew. Jimmy and Maggie would keep their secret. There was still time—but for what?

Her instincts screamed out—go somewhere else, start a new life. She loved the peninsula too and didn't want to leave but Kevin was rooted to it and that worried her. Chances were he'd become bitter with time, withdraw into himself, resenting those who didn't fully accept him, and eventually blame her. Or could she resurrect the smiling young man with the guitar and the endless store of songs who had gone missing one September morning?

They had only each other now. They had to be unified—be as one. But there was the kid too. How would Liam take this? Could they protect him from the rumors and titillation that would sweep like a nor'easter up and down the peninsula?

She squeezed Kevin's fingers and he responded. His life was about to change and defiance would carry him only so far. They would soon get hit by a wave of scandal and vindictiveness. If he broke, all three of them would be lost.

He looked over at her from the shadows. She could make out the shape of his full lips, his tousled hair spilling down on his forehead, his firm cheekbones now absent even a trace of baby fat. He was a beautiful-looking man. She took his fingers and placed them on her breast. He leaned into her until she could see the dark light in his eyes.

They were alike in so many ways. There were no barriers between them. She understood him as she had never understood Brian. And when he took her in his arms she knew all would be well. She would remember this moment—stencil it on her brain. She could feel his excitement grow and then there came an abandonment that she'd never felt from him before as he shed all his insecurities, all his hurts and fears, and it was good to be held by him and to feel all her own doubts melt away. She felt a wonderful clarity that she hadn't since the beginning of the summer.

"Kevin?"

"Yeah?"

"Can you do something for me?"

"Sure."

"I want Liam to wake up next to you tomorrow morning."

"In my mom's house?"

"It would be so great for him. Just think of it! Be nice for your parents too."

In the neighbor's yard a gust of wind rattled a toolshed door and the chimes rang louder than before.

"I guess it's a good idea." He yawned. "Might be a bit scary for him if he wakes up down there in the night and hears a storm."

"Take the Jeep and drop him off at school tomorrow. You know how much he loves it when you bring him—like all the other dads."

She watched him dress, quickly, economically. He always knew where his clothes were, unlike Brian who used to leave his scattered around the floor like a teenager.

When he kissed her good-bye he gazed in her eyes, words were no longer needed between them. She listened to the Jeep start, then its steady purr as he pulled away. When she could hear it no more, she turned to the wall and listened to the pealing of the chimes and then in the distance the first lowing sound of the foghorn.

"At least he got one hit!"

"Huh?" Kevin looked up from his lunch.

"Jeter! Won't be long 'til he gets in the groove again," Jimmy said.

"I don't know. He's not getting any younger."

"You kidding me? He's going to hit for the cycle before the end of the season, I can feel it in my bones." Jimmy defiantly flipped some pages of the news and bent lower over the small print.

"He'd better get a move on, only a couple of days left."

As Maggie was passing by his chair, she squeezed Kevin's shoulder. "It's so nice to have you home again. The boy was thrilled you dropped him off at school this morning."

"It was Rosie's idea. She thought it would be good all around."

When his mother chose not to comment he added, "Anyway, I missed your cooking."

"You could do with a few extra pounds."

"Hey, Kev, know what?" Jimmy said. "We haven't taken the kid to Shea yet."

"There's always next year. Jesus, I'm starting to sound like Brian."

"Yeah, his big line this time of year. Maybe we could go tomorrow?"

"Nah, the architect's dropping by at two o'clock."

"No kidding?"

"Yeah, we're finally going for that extension. It was either that or move to Florida, and I just couldn't see quitting the firehouse."

"Well, that's good news," Maggie chimed in. She ran the hot water and rinsed off some plates before putting them in the dishwasher.

"Put our own stamp on the place, like." Kevin said.

"Couldn't hurt," Jimmy added.

"We were back and forth on it over and over, so one day I just picked up the phone, made the call myself."

"Good man!"

"She'd been dithering about the whole thing. But it all comes down to Liam. You know, whatever she thinks is best for him."

"Well, you and he seem to be getting along well," Maggie said. "I couldn't get a word in edgewise with him rattling on about his Uncle Kevin this morning. And he finished all his pancakes."

"That's good. It's going to be a bit of a change. We're still trying to figure out how to break the news to him."

When neither of them commented, Kevin continued, "In the meantime, I've been working at getting him away from that friggin' computer."

"Any luck?" Jimmy asked.

"For the most part. Other times though he just stares at me. It's spooky. Remember Brian's *What are you doing butting into my world* look?"

"Yeah, hard to forget that one."

"And you and Rose?" Maggie asked. "How is that . . . progressing?"

"Well, like, it's her money, but I'm the one making the phone call to the architect, know what I mean."

"Those things can be sensitive, guy." Jimmy looked up. "Best to take it slow."

"But I had to do something. Whole thing was starting to get to me."

Jimmy returned to the baseball stats as Maggie joined them at the table.

"Rose hasn't been over since we visited."

"Yeah, but there's no hard feelings, Mom."

"There were some harsh things said but I'd like her to know there was no intention of hurting."

"She feels the same, 'sides she's got Liam to consider. Doesn't want anything to come between us all."

"No, of course not. Well, it was quite an evening. I think we all learned some truths, hard though they might have been."

She cast a wary eye at Jimmy, head still bowed over the paper. They'd hardly spoken since he'd told her about his last conversation with Brian. How calm he must seem to the casual eye, but she knew otherwise.

Suddenly Jimmy was on his feet at the sound of a very loud and extravagant ringtone.

"What's that?" Maggie said.

"My new cell. Whole train was laughing at me yesterday. Where the hell is it?"

"Over there by the dishwasher. I can hear it."

"Where? Jesus Christ! You threw the goddamned dishtowel on top of it."

"I didn't see it. It's so small."

"That's the idea," Jimmy said. "Shit. How do you turn this thing on? So different from the old one! Hello? Who? Oh Rosie! How are you? It's a bit hard to hear . . . Oh yeah? Sure, I'll pick him up. I know, school's out at three . . . Yeah, I know your cousin Elaine—got you a free ticket on Jet Blue? Great, but what? . . . The car service is outside? Jesus, it's a bit short notice, isn't it?"

Kevin and Maggie watched him dig the phone into his ear, his face creased with concern.

"Yeah, it'll be good for you, bit of sunshine and look after your mother 'til she gets better. But listen, you better talk to Kev. He's right here."

Kevin stood up awaiting the phone, but Jimmy abruptly turned away.

"It's hard to hear, Rose, signal's bad . . . You're running late, you'll call him from the airport. Okay. Hello, Rose . . . Rosie?"

He held the phone away from his ear then squinted at it before the screen went blank. Kevin didn't even look at him, just stared straight ahead at the kitchen sink.

"That was Rose?" Maggie finally asked.

"Yeah, her cousin Elaine, the Jet Blue girl, just called. A big party canceled last minute, got her a ticket to Lauderdale. She had to take it now or else it wouldn't work. Her mother called earlier, wasn't feeling so good."

He dropped the phone in his pocket and looked across the room at Kevin.

"She said, be sure to keep your cell on. She'll call you from the airport—or Lauderdale."

When Kevin didn't answer, he turned back to Maggie.

"She wants me to pick up Liam after school. He's going to stay with us for a week or thereabouts."

"A week?"

"Yeah, or maybe more. She's going down to look after her mother. Make sure you leave your cell on, okay, guy?"

But Kevin was already on his way to the door. They listened to his resolute footsteps on the stairs.

"What was that all about?" Maggie whispered.

"Ssshhh!" Jimmy pointed upstairs.

"How did she sound?"

He raised his eyebrows.

"It's so sudden," she said.

Jimmy shook his head in disbelief.

"I mean what's he going to do?"

"Better now than two or three years down the line," he whispered.

"Didn't you see the look on his face? Oh God, this is the last thing he needs."

"Looks like your words of wisdom worked."

"How can you say that, Jimmy Murphy? I was coming to terms with things. In fact, I was perfectly content with the way matters were turning out."

"You know something? Someday you should take a shot at rewriting the Bible."

"Well, I admit it was a shock at first but . . ."

"Ssshhh!"

Maggie loaded some cups into the dishwasher and Jimmy bent his head to the paper as Kevin made his way down the stairs and into the kitchen. His guitar case strapped to his back, he was wheeling a small carry-on and lugging a plastic bag stuffed with sneakers.

"I'm heading down The Inn."

"A couple of beers?"

"Yeah, Sweeney and the guys are going fishing for blues. I'll check in on them."

"Will you be home tonight?"

"I don't think so, Mom, I'll be in touch, okay?"

"Oh God, Kevin, it's nothing to do with anything I said that night?"

"It's cool, Mom. Hey, Dad, do me a solid, will you? Drop by the firehouse and square things with the boss. I got some mutuals coming that should cover me for a week or so. Okay?"

"Sure, I'll have a word with Charlie, sort it out."

"I'll write in a couple of days, all right?"

"Write? Where are you going?" Maggie asked.

"Well, after I see the guys off, I'm going to take the train into Times Square. Then I'll either go on a bender or enlist."

"Enlist?"

Kevin took his mother in his arms and hugged her hard, but when she tried to hold on he pulled away abruptly. Jimmy stood up and they shook hands.

"You okay for money?"

"Yeah, I got some bucks and my credit card. Take care, all right?"

He was about to walk past but Jimmy pulled him close and they hugged. For once his son did not tense or turn away. It felt so right after all the years, then just as suddenly it was over and Kevin walked out.

Maggie had just begun to speak when the door opened again. Kevin looked in.

"Hey, Dad, here you go."

He lobbed his cell phone across the room. Jimmy reached out and caught it.

"I won't be needing this for a while. Keep it turned off—save the battery. You can send it on later."

He closed the door again and they listened to him take the steps two at a time then the gate closed behind him.

THIRTY-FIVE

There was no escaping the silence now. It lay heavy on the kitchen, accentuated by every small sound that intruded, the anemic ticking of the clock in the living room, the hoarse chatter of a starling on the porch. They were alone with little but memories binding them together.

She ransacked her brain for something to say, but she felt helpless as a schoolgirl; almost thirty-five years married, she was at a loss for words with a husband who sat there outwardly calm and enigmatic as the Sacred Heart on the wall.

"Oh God, I hope Kevin knows what he's doing," she finally said.

He didn't answer at first, barely looked up from the paper. "He's a man now. Got to do things his way."

"I've always been so hard on him."

"You did your best."

"Did I, Jimmy? Did I really?"

He remained stone-faced, unable or unwilling to answer. She folded the tea towel, placed it neatly on the drain board. Her first instinct was to head upstairs until she remembered her granny's words about vestry widows. For want of something better to do she loaded the rest of the plates into the dishwasher then pressed the start button.

"It's the first time I ever wanted one of my sons to get blind drunk," she said.

"He'll probably do that one way or the other."

"He wouldn't join the army, would he?"

"You'd think he'd know better but there's a lot of craziness out there."

The dishwasher began to rumble; they both looked at it apprehensively.

"At least one good thing—he took his guitar with him," Jimmy added.

"Wouldn't it be great if he started playing again?" She brightened a little. "Dancing too, happy and carefree like he used to be."

"He'll need a new partner."

"I'll dance with him. I could always keep up with him better than . . . well, almost anyone!" She attempted one of Rose's tango swoons but she didn't put enough heart into it and felt ridiculous.

"I worry about Liam in Florida, such pale skin."

He didn't answer and she wondered if he had heard her as the dishwasher rumbled ever louder.

"Florida means two things to me," he finally said. "The Devil Rays and cremation! Maybe you should put on another pot of coffee."

"You'll be late for work. Look at the time."

He stared out the window as the rumbling subsided and the clock could again be heard ticking in the living room.

"I'm not going to work today."

"Dolan's filling in for you?"

"Nah, I had a bit of a chat with him last night. I'm taking a month off."

"Why? Aren't you feeling well?"

"Just need a break. Clear my head, like."

"What will they do without you? What was her name? Marcella?"

The dishwasher suddenly erupted again. She slapped her hand hard on the lid and to her surprise it lurched back to its normal cycle. He didn't seem to notice.

"Marcella is leaving in a month. She handed in her notice," he said quietly.

"Oh?"

"She's going backpacking to Australia, all the Irish kids are doing that nowadays."

"She's leaving in a month, and you're taking off that month? Isn't that a little odd? I mean you were so friendly?"

"I said good-bye the other night, we figured it was for the best."

"For the best?"

"She needs the money for the trip, so she's doing a double, taking my shifts."

She followed his gaze out the window. The errant honeysuckle vine had fallen again and was swaying gently, its flowers long gone, a pruning overdue.

"She'll be coming back after Australia?" she asked.

"No, I imagine she'll go home to Ireland. Her father has a pub there—in Mayo."

"Well, that will be nice for her."

Out in the street a truck laboriously negotiated its way past the lines of unevenly parked cars. After it had rounded the corner he said, "Yeah."

The word lacked any conviction and only succeeded in raising new questions. Swallows were zooming around the garden, flightier than ever now that autumn had arrived. Soon they'd be gathering on the wires ready for their trip south. Maggie wondered if any of them would end up in Fort Lauderdale. Would Rose stare out from her mother's window and recognize their swoops and glides?

Jimmy felt the stress mounting. He stretched his fingers on the table but they were as steady as the day is long. His mind was diamond clear too. No uninvited face hovering before him, only swallows diving and carousing beyond the windowpanes. No jets screaming, no B52s rumbling up above cloud cover, just a regular Rockaway early afternoon.

His life had been punctuated by two conflicts, Nam and 9/11, both of them beyond his control—just as he was finally coming to terms with one, the other had dealt him a grievous blow. He knew he had to let go and put the past behind him. Other people did it routinely and got on with their lives. Why should he be any different? So many things had changed, why hadn't he?

"Life is change, isn't it?" That's what Brian used to say when Jimmy would advise his son not to be in such a hurry, go with the flow. Brian never listened; caution had always been the furthest thing from his mind. But Brian was gone—he'd had his moment, brief though it was, it had been blazing and he'd given it his all. Maybe he had been a wild card and didn't do things by the book, but give the kid credit, he'd figured out something big was coming and did his damnedest to prevent it!

Brian had his failings, moral and otherwise, but he was his own man, and now his secrets and the leads he was following were buried with him. As he was in life, so was he in death, somewhat of a mystery even to those who loved him most.

What other secrets had been buried beneath the rubble? So many lives stalled in full flight. Those spared had to pick up the pieces and carry on. You played with the hand you were dealt—bitching was a waste of time—the card game continued with or without you. Brian would live on through his son and someday the boy would be his own man and come to terms with the memory of his conflicted, heroic father.

Kevin might still have miles to travel, but he was changing too. He'd wake up tomorrow with the hangover of a lifetime, and if finally growing up took enlisting, and learning the hard way in Iraq—then so be it. Hopefully he'd have his father's luck and emerge from that disaster alive. Whatever, it was his life to do with as he saw fit.

And Maggie, she'd lost so much, but had gained something ineffable. He closed his eyes and summoned up the young woman just out of Fordham. Then he watched her staring out at the swallows and caught the full echo of her beauty. That hadn't faded, only become more distinct; it pulsed through the kitchen, and he had a sudden urge to hold her and reclaim the memories. But he couldn't move. He was nailed to the floor by so many things he still didn't understand.

She had changed, she had found her way through the darkness that had almost enveloped her. She would never again be the defiant young woman who had stood up for him in front of her parents the night she announced she was pregnant. When her father had sat there, angry and glowering, she had simply said, "D.W.I.D."

And when the old man snarled, "What's that supposed to mean, young lady?" she had taken Jimmy's hand in hers and said, "Deal with it, Dad!"

That person had slowly wilted beneath convention and was finally swept away one stunning September morning. The world had dealt her the cruelest blow and she was only able to raise herself up by dint of her new faith in God. But so what? Such a belief might make little or no sense to him, but she'd found her way. Now he had to find his, even if he hadn't a clue how to go about it.

She wasn't surprised to see the large shadow deepen over her garden; in fact, she had expected it. Still she had to look through the top pane of the window to see the osprey hovering about twenty feet up. It was as if the bird was displaying itself for her; its brown wings stretched over five feet in length, while its golden calculating eyes surveyed all below.

Such was the implacable nature of its gaze she silently prayed, "Dear God, please don't let the lovely little finch come flitting by."

Then she remembered Jimmy had told her ospreys only hunt fish. But what did Jimmy know. She turned and was about to tell him of the osprey's return but his eyes were closed. Just as well, she'd have been forced to admit her suspicions about the bird's presence. How futile that would be—her husband didn't even believe in the Blessed Virgin let alone her granny's view that the souls of the departed returned to familiar ground in the bodies of birds and animals.

She idly wondered if the osprey could see her. She had grown used to its visits over the last three years. Then with a sudden thud of dismay it struck her that she might never see her friend again; fall was already in the air and it would soon leave for the South. It might never return.

As if in answer the osprey rose into the sky and veered off toward the ocean. It had kept watch over her during the worst of her struggles but she felt stronger now and more hopeful than she had been in a long time. She had mourned Brian for three years and as the shadow of the bird disappeared and the sunshine seeped once more into her garden she knew she could carry on, she would carry on.

When she turned back from the window Jimmy had picked up the newspaper and was reading again. She watched both him and the dishwasher closely. He seemed unaware of its rumbling. How easily he could block things out. Then he began turning pages quickly, scanning columns, his head bent low to the print.

"Hallelujah!" he exclaimed. "We got the keys for Rose's place here, right?"

"You want to go down there so soon? I mean she's barely left."

"As good a time as any!"

He had already slipped into his jacket as she rummaged through the tool drawer.

"I thought maybe you'd help me replant the rest of the *Rosa rugosa*."

"Later for roses, I got more important fish to fry."

"Like what?" She tossed him the keys.

"Like I'm heading down to Breezy to pick up Liam's baseball shirt. Next, I'm picking up that kid after school, dressing him in his Mike Piazza number thirty-one, and driving him to Shea Stadium. And as soon as I get into that nuthouse, I'm going to buy him a hot dog and a

Coke, and I personally am going to drain every last drop of a couple of their overpriced beers. And when I'm finally feeling no pain, I'm going to scream my head off for the fucking Mets!!"

"Please, Jimmy, you know I hate hearing that word in the house."

"You know what? Sometimes that word is a very descriptive and therapeutic adjective and, when applied to the Mets, Yankee fans get a papal dispensation. You should try it."

"I don't need to."

"Remember what I said that night about words?"

"That's totally different."

"Maggie," he said quietly, "how many times have I ever asked you for anything?"

It was true; he'd asked for very little down the years. She'd grown used to him being remote and resolute. Maybe this was a good sign. Much as she found the expression crude, if this was what it took to knock a chink out of Jimmy Murphy's carefully constructed armor, or halt the steady drumbeat of "prideful" in her brain, then so be it. She took a breath and employed an adjective she'd often felt but never voiced about all sports teams: "The fucking Mets."

"I can hardly hear you. Do it for Brian, goddamn it."

"The fucking Mets!"

"That's better. Now, do it for Kevin. Maybe if it's loud enough he'll hear you and won't get on the train."

"The fucking Mets!" She shouted with all her heart and soul.

And with that she buried her head in his shoulder. He had wondered if it might seem strange after so long but her body felt familiar and reassuring, he held on to her and then kissed her through her tears.

"Now let's go to this fucking game," she said sobbing.

"I thought you were fixing the flowers down the church this evening?"

"Oh fuck the flowers! And fuck that dishwasher too—we're getting a new one next week. But I do have to get some sunscreen for Liam," she shouted back as she ran up the stairs.

"Dear God in heaven!" she whispered as she examined her tearstained face in the mirror.

"Hurry up, the *News* says they're giving away Piazza bobbleheads!" he called up to her.

She ransacked her closet and tried on the tailored fuchsia jacket she'd almost thrown out. It was a bit too tight-fitting but so what? At least she still had her figure. Not bad for fifty-seven, might turn a head or two!

She wondered if she should confess her secret about Brian and the fear he'd felt in his last days. No, there'd come a time for that—if things got more settled between them.

"What's keeping you?" he yelled.

"I'm coming. Call Richie Sullivan! And tell him to meet us there!"

"Sullivan? Are you serious?"

She was trying on the vivid lipstick Rose had left behind at the last dinner—some shades too bright but Shea wasn't known for its fashion consciousness—when she heard Jimmy swearing at his new phone; he'd turned on the speaker by accident. Then Sullivan's voice cut off the amplified ringtone and boomed through the horns and din of midtown traffic.

"The fuck do you want now?"

"We're going to Shea, wanna come?"

"I'm on my way to yoga class."

"Yoga? At this time of day?"

"The hell are you laughing at, shoulders drooping down around your ass!"

"Hop the seven. Maggie wants to talk to you."

"Maggie is going to a baseball game?" Sullivan was incredulous.

"Yeah, she got a thing for José Reyes."

"Be an improvement on you! What'll I do with my mat?"

"Ever hear of the seventh-inning stretch?"

Sullivan guffawed for a moment but then sounding a tad apprehensive he said, "There's something else."

"What?"

"I was in the precinct this morning settling a bet with Crazy Joey."

"Oh yeah?"

"Overheard that dumbass detective Drew calling DeVito."

"And?"

"He'd been tracking the young one, Fatima—said she caught a flight out of Kennedy last night—to Egypt."

Jimmy was silent but then said, "I could have called that one."

"Yeah. So I guess that's the end of the story—with her out of the picture no more loose threads, right?"

Maggie could feel her heart pounding as she awaited Jimmy's answer.

"Yeah, I guess, time to move on, Richie. I'll see you at Shea."

Maggie remained frozen to the bedroom floor. If Jimmy was finally coming to terms with Brian's death where did that leave her? The prideful woman so certain of her looks and intellect had long ago vanished down her vanity mirror. She barely recognized the stranger peering back. She could hear her husband waiting impatiently down in the hallway. There was nothing for it—put one foot in front of the other and hope for the best.

Still, she took her time coming down the stairs for she remembered a voice in a thick Galway accent once sternly admonishing her, "Let a man get one full look at you, then carry on about your business—he'll take care of the rest."

Jimmy took in her new look but didn't betray any surprise. She had grown used to that over thirty-five years, after all, he was a cop. So she winked at him for she knew the power of an Irishwoman's wink, and how well it had worked back when they were courting.

As ever he betrayed nothing, but she knew she'd got his attention.

"Better hurry up!" she said. "Mr. Jeter might be hitting for the cycle."

"Jesus Christ, woman, bad enough I'm going to Shea. But Derek Jeter with the Mets?"

She laughed at her own joke and carried on about her business. Jimmy Murphy would take care of the rest.